MILITARY CHIC

MILITARY CHIC

Gigi LaFaux's Fashion Wars

CAROLYN ROHALY

MILITARY CHIC
GIGI LAFAUX'S FASHION WARS

Cover Design by Trevor Stewart

iUniverse books may be ordered through booksellers or by contacting:

iUniverse
1663 Liberty Drive
Bloomington, IN 47403
www.iuniverse.com
1-800-Authors (1-800-288-4677)

This book is a work of fiction. References to real people, events, establishments, organizations, or locales are intended only to provide a sense of authenticity and are used fictitiously. All other characters, and all incidents and dialogue, are drawn from the author's imagination and are not to be construed as real.

ISBN: 978-1-5320-5450-1 (sc)
ISBN: 978-1-5320-5451-8 (e)

Print information available on the last page.

iUniverse rev. date: 10/05/2018

MEASURE.

Number 42 Fracas Avenue.

I checked the address I had scribbled down and looked at the grey rectangular monolith before me. It looked like an East German apartment block. Surely the Collections Week offices couldn't be in there, could they? Headquarters for the country's premiere fashion event in a military bunker? It was intimidating and made me nervous, so I repeated my favourite quote in my head:

> "Whatever you can do, or dream you can, begin it. Boldness has genius, power, and magic in it."

Emboldened, I walked in, and sure enough, the security guard said the Collections Week office was on the third floor. He made me sign in and get a visitor's pass. Who knew fashion was so top secret?

On the elevator up, I admired my pass and smiled to myself. There I was, a girl who'd decided to quit her job as an urban planner in Calgary, a city known for its cowboys, to move to Toronto, a city known for its style, and follow my dream to be a fashion designer. It was my first week in the new city and already I had an interview for a Collections Week position. They must have been impressed with my resumé and all that gratis development work I'd done in South America. Something had touched the Collections Week people to consider my diverse skills. I knew I'd fit right in and have all sorts of intellectual conversations with my stylish coworkers about how clothing transcends design boundaries and how we have to fight against fashion's frivolous image.

I stepped out of the elevator and saw a sea of cubicles. Was I in the right place?

A woman in a grey flannel skirt-suit brushed past me.

"Excuse me," I asked, "but can you tell me where I can find Francine Scrimshank?"

I received a blank look in return.

"Francine? From Collections Week?" I elaborated.

"Oh, Collections Week." Ms. Bureaucrat sniffed. "Over there." She nodded in the general direction of the corner and kept walking. I'd probably cut into her coffee break.

After peeking into three cubicles decorated with photos of predictably boring families, I found the one I needed. The walls were adorned with bad party-Polaroids and pink hearts. Stacks of *People* and *Vogue* magazines littered the floor. A girl was on the phone.

"And then I told him to get a life!" Pause. "Yeah, I know, can you believe it? And then he said, 'Well you got a fat ass!' and I said, 'You know who's got a fat ass? That ho you been sleepin' with. Now that's a fat ass!' And he was just quiet cuz he didn't know I knew."

I made one of those cough-throat-clearing noises a person makes in an awkward situation to announce their arrival.

The phone girl - whom I assumed to be Francine - swivelled in her chair, saw me, and made that "just hold on a second" sign.

I stood five more minutes, waiting for the boyfriend drama to play itsel out. I backed away from the cubicle and looked around, but didn't go too far because I didn't want her to think I wasn't interested. Given the open nature of cubicles, I discovered the girl's boyfriend was cheating on her, but she was also cheating on him, that she'd bought the cutest pair of fleecy pink pyjamas, and had eaten half a McCain's frozen cake, but that was okay, because she'd purged it in the washroom and suspected a colleague may have heard. Then she finished up the conversation with, "Well, I gotta go because some chick is here."

Was I to run in the cubicle or wait for her? If I ran in, she would know I'd listened to her conversation. I didn't want to appear too nosey, so I waited for a bit. When she didn't come out, I poked my head around.

"Francine?" I asked.

"Oh, right. I forgot you were there."

"Hi. I'm Gigi LaFaux. We spoke on the phone."

"Right." She walked past me, out of the cubicle, and around the corner.

Hmmm. It was all very odd, yet amusing somehow.

She returned with a chair and told me to sit down.

"Sorry, we don't have a lot of space. Someone donated this cubicle to us; it's the best we can do for now since we're a non-profit organization. So, you wanna volunteer with Collections Week?"

"Oh, I thought we were interviewing for an employment position."

"Oh no," she giggled. "We only have three paid positions with Collections Week. Most of the budget goes directly to promoting Canadian fashion and producing the shows. There's the director, Veronikkah Hendricks, the Communications Manager, Josh L., and me. Josh L. is hilarious. Nobody knows his real last name and he makes everybody call him 'Josh L.' not 'Josh,' and nothing as silly as 'Mr. L.' You'll love him! You've *got* to meet him! Oh, wait. Do you know him? You look like you'd know him. Anyway, they work from home. I'm the Office Assistant, but I don't like that title. I want to be the Executive Assistant cuz it sounds more important, you know? But I'm the only person with a *real* cubicle, so that's cool. Oh, by the way, you can call me Francie. Everybody does."

Francie had a shoulder-length bob of brown hair with those chunky blonde highlights unfashionable girls sport when they think they're super cool. Plus, when she went to get my chair, I noticed she not only had VPL, but VTL. Visible Thong Line was even trashier than a regular panty line because pants must be two sizes too small for a thong to show through. Francie was probably one of those girls who travel in packs begging bouncers to let them in to the latest hot bar. Usually that bar turns out to be the most boring nightclub around. How was that girl the Executive Assistant to Veronikkah Hendricks? I'd expected someone edgier.

"Okay, Francie, why don't you tell me about your volunteer positions and we can discuss how they match my experience. Did you have a chance to review the resumé I e-mailed two weeks ago?"

"Nah. I've been too busy choosing an outfit to wear to the Toronto Film Festival gala opening. Anyway, you'll be fine because you look cool. I swear it's hard work looking so good. I can't believe it's my job." She paused for a moment, no doubt thinking about the fabulous outfits she'd tried, then continued. "Did you see Johnny Luvv's new video? It's the coolest!"

"No, I haven't. What makes it so cool?" Johnny Luvv was *the* teen heartthrob du jour, but I didn't see the connection between his video and Collections Week. There was nothing I hated more than prefabricated pop crap, but I didn't want to offend Francie since I really wanted to get the gig. I was so thrilled to be talking to somebody involved with the event I didn't mind talking pop culture with her for a while. Strangely enough, even though I don't like mindless entertainment, I can chat about it forever. For some reason, I couldn't remember physics equations, but I never forgot who dated who, song titles, album release dates, or who starred in what shows. Popular culture clicked in my brain.

"Johnny dances all hot and stuff. He's the best dancer ever! Plus he looks like my boyfriend."

"Well, you're a lucky girl," I commented, trying to sound sincere. "How long have you been together?"

"We met when I was eighteen, and now I'm twenty-one, so that makes it…" she counted on her fingers, "three years. I snuck into System Soundbar for a party he was promoting. Anyway, I was so drunk I fell down a set of stairs, and he caught me. He actually caught me! It was so romantic, like that Leonardo DiCaprio movie, *Romeo and Juliet*. I fell right into his arms, and it was like the whole world spun just around us. We stared at each other for a while, but then I had to run to the washroom cuz I was gonna puke. But he followed and took care of me. He held my hair back while I threw up! Can you believe it? He was so kind." She looked over the Polaroids tacked to her cubicle wall and pointed to one. "That's him. Oh, he's so hot, but he makes me so mad sometimes! I do love him though."

To my eye, her man was any other beefy guy in a baseball cap, but one girl's loser was another girl's dreamboat. I was too picky about guys myself, and since I hadn't had a serious boyfriend in two years, I didn't want to make another harsh judgement about Francie. The way she chatted about her boyfriend non-stop for fifteen minutes was kind of endearing, actually. She reminded me about the feelings of first love. My mind flashed to my first love, and I realized I felt the same sort of giddiness when thinking about my new career in fashion.

Francie looked at me and said, "You seem cool. Do you want to be our volunteer coordinator?"

It seemed more a human resources position than a creative job to me, but I wanted to work at Collections Week in any capacity.

"That sounds interesting," I said. "I've managed projects before, so I have the organizational skills to do it."

"What do you do?" she asked.

"I used to be an urban planner, did some international development work, but constant international business travel was hard. Now, rather than design buildings, I want to work on a smaller scale - I want to design clothes. I've always loved fashion."

"Oh, cool."

"Yeah, urban planning was fun, especially when I worked in South American and African villages helping them build schools. It's such a different way of life. People really make time for their families, and there's practically no such thing as time or being late. Conversation is really an art in Southern countries…" I trailed off, noticing Francie's eyes glaze over. I had to rescue the conversation before she changed her mind.

"One thing I loved about travelling was going to markets. It was cool to see fashion all over the world, especially how people from different countries wore North American clothes. In Africa, people would wear these clothes without context or irony. Women wore T-shirts that said #1 Dad and World's Greatest Lover. Men would wear fuzzy pink sweaters. And people would wear cheap tracksuits that said Nuke or Mike instead of Nike. The cultural crossovers were great!" I was excited about it, but Francie looked vacant. I tried a last-ditch recovery attempt so she wouldn't think I was completely mad. "Francie, you should see the shoes in Brazil. You wouldn't believe it. It's worth a trip for the shoes alone!"

Francie's eyes lit up and she asked, "Brazil? Isn't that where Gisele is from?"

"Yeah, everyone loves Brazilian models since they're so comfortable with their bodies. I think it comes from living in such a hot climate. People practically walk around naked. I was embarrassed on the beach with my one-piece swimsuit; I felt like a prude. So it makes sense the country that created the thong would breed perfect models. Brazil is so hot in fashion right now."

"Yeah, is it anywhere near Bolivia? Bolivia's hot right now. We're trying to get Bolivian designers to show at Collections Week," said Francie.

"That's so interesting," I said. "I haven't heard buzz about Bolivian fashion, but you guys are always ahead of the trends. It sounds amazing. If you need any help with that, let me know."

I couldn't contain myself with such a great opportunity. When I left my job, my friends and family didn't understand how I could make such a drastic change from urban planning and development to fashion. The two worlds were so different: one was focused on helping others, the other promoted a self-absorbed, seemingly superficial lifestyle. But the conversation gave me hope of working my previous experience into a new career.

Francie made me happier by saying, "You're perfect for the volunteer coordinator position."

"I'll take it. How and when do I start?"

"You'll figure it out. We've never had a volunteer coordinator before."

RECRUIT.

A week and five phone messages later, I was back at the Soviet Bunker trying to connect with Francie.

"Can you give me lists of your previous volunteers?" I asked her.

"Lists? We didn't keep any lists."

"How many volunteers did you have?"

"Maybe around fifty."

"And you have no records of them?"

"Nah…they were just…kind of…friends of friends. Oh, hey, did you read the fashion section in the paper? They mentioned me!"

"Yeah, I noticed your photo in 'Hip Pics.' Congrats!"

Hip Pics is where people brag about their latest purchases; a fashionista version of Show and Tell. That morning, Francie had paraded a Chanel Rubik's Cube purse past readers. The caption under her photo said:

> *Francie Scrimshank, Collections Week Executive Assistant, adores her new Chanel must-have accessory.*

I was secretly jealous; I wanted to be in "Hip Pics." I wanted a Chanel Rubik's Cube Purse, but it was a month's rent. My bag would have to wait.

"I love your Chanel!" I exclaimed, trying to hide my envy.

"Thanks! Mommy bought it for me in Paris last week. She knows the paper's fashion editor, Chloe Kirkpatrick, who absolutely died when she saw it. Chloe said I simply *had* to be in "*Hip Pics*."

"I agree with the editor," I said. "A bag that beautiful must be shown off. Anyway, back to the volunteers. So I'm starting from scratch?"

"Yup. That's why you're here. You'll interview volunteers in three days."

"How long have you known about that? I'd appreciate it if you communicated your plans in advance so I can get organized. Will three days will be enough notice for people to schedule time for the interviews?"

"If they wanna volunteer with us, they gotta make time. Everyone wants to work for us. Veronikkah even thinks volunteers should pay for their positions," she noticed my disbelieving look and continued, "but I talked her out of it. If anyone wants to volunteer for us, though, they've gotta to drop everything else. Every volunteer must commit to thirty hours."

Thirty hours? How would I convince people to donate that much time? I could do it because I didn't have a job and had saved money to sustain myself. I didn't agree with the Collections Week way of thinking, but I wanted the experience, so I contacted the city's fashion schools and hoped people would show up.

Three days later, I interviewed two hundred potential volunteers. Most were young and inexperienced, but thrilled about a chance to be part of Collections Week. I picked out a few glimmering hopefuls who I called the next day to form a core team, since I required reliable, trustworthy people to oversee volunteers in various sections.

Lola was similar to me: We were both suffering from a quarter-life crisis. She was a graphic designer, but coveted clothing-related work. Lola dressed like me (kind of like a friendly punk); she enjoyed the same indie bands I did, which gave her instant credibilty in my eyes; and she had the hippest haircut ever, and a good friend always needs a cute haircut.

Gregor was from Russia and a bona-fide Fashion Queen. You know the type: he stole glances at his mother's fashion magazines when he was three, created doll-dress collections when he was eight, modified his school uniform when he was twelve, and began his tanning salon and hair bleaching regime when he moved from Russia at fifteen. That was the age at which he began dressing models backstage at fashion shows and discovered the gospel, *Fashion Television*. Now with knowledge of every designer's collection burned in his mind, he could determine the vintage of each piece of an outfit at first sight. He had chubby, fawning girlfriends, whom he loved, but it was easy to see he desperately wanted supermodel girlfriends and boyfriends and only to dress in Gucci and Vuitton. Unfortunately, he was chubby and poor himself, so he could only dream of glam. He sounded like a nightmare, which was true, but he was thoroughly entertaining. Every fashion event needs at least one good Fashion Queen.

Chantelle was a sophisticated and elegant nineteen-year-old. She'd recently started studying fashion design at Ryerson University and carried herself with poise and oozed glamour. She was young, but seemed mature enough to handle more responsibility than changing models into different outfits. She deserved better than that.

Together, I knew the four of us would make an excellent team. We would be able to get our work done and have fun at the same time. Wanting to highlight my team-building skills to Francie and make her feel secure with my decisions, I dropped by her office.

"I have to meet everyone first and make sure they're up to Collections Week standards," she told me. I wondered whose standards those were, as Francie stood in front of me wearing the same turquoise and white striped, one-shoulder, too-tight top from the Gap all the girls were wearing that season.

I wondered how a girl with a Chanel Rubik's Cube purse could commit such fashion blandness and said, "Okay, I'll set up a meeting. What day is good for you?"

Her cell phone rang, so she ignored my question and answered the call. "Hi, Janey! What's up? You won't believe what happened last night. I went out with Brit and Tracey, and who did I see? HIM. Can you believe it? Thank god my boyfriend wasn't there…"

Ten minutes later, Francie was still chatting with Janey, and I had found out she'd broken up with her cheating boyfriend, but then got back together with him, and was still cheating on him with this other guy, who'd had the nerve to run into her on a night out. Her life was a soap opera, and she didn't seem to mind that I heard every word. As tempting as it was to listen, I had to meet a friend for lunch, so when she looked at me, I tapped my watch.

"Oh, Janey, I gotta run. There's this chick here I gotta talk to. We'll chat later." Francie hung up and asked, "What were we talking about?"

Chick? She called me a chick again?

"We were scheduling a meeting so you can meet my team," I responded, trying not to be annoyed by her chick comment.

"Can't do it. Too busy. Get them to me."

"Don't you think it would be better to do it at once so you don't have to schedule three different appointments?"

"I don't work that way. Send them here."

"Francie, they're all really busy. Some are in school and working two jobs, so it will be difficult to get them to your office during the day. Can they meet you in the evening?"

"No, Gigi. I work hard enough as it is, and I'm not gonna devote my spare time to meeting stupid volunteers, okay?"

So my glimmering hopefuls skipped classes and changed work shifts to meet Francie. Each one left five phone messages before she called back. They set up appointments and she was fifteen minutes late every time. After all the craziness, she merely looked them up and down and said, "You're fine."

Assess.

Two weeks before Collections Week, I met the glimmering hopefuls for some social team building before the event. After all my group experience, I knew people worked better after a couple drinks together, so we went to the hottest new lounge in the city, Mirror.

Every Toronto newspaper had raved about the place with mirrored décor and brilliant menu, where models won the coveted serving positions. I was looking for a regular hangout and Mirror sounded perfect.

It turned out it was minimal, not perfect. Patrons had minimal style, servers had minimal brains, tables had minimal chairs, and drinks had minimal alcohol, though they were maximum price. The DJ even played decor-matching music: it was the same bland tripe that dominated the city's radio stations. If that music were a colour, it would be beige.

Distraught that the space didn't match my expectations, I pounded a shot of Goldschläger before anyone arrived. Drinking tiny gold flakes was the only way to cope with the venue-ridicule I'd receive from my new friends. I found a table and worried I'd never find a decent hangout in my new city.

"Did everyone in here get highlights from the same eighties Euroqueen? Hello, Miami Vice!" Gregor hissed into my ear. He wore what I would come to know as his favourite look: Tom of Finland crossed with those sailor-boy Gaultier perfume ads from the nineties. He kind of pulled it off in his own way.

"Oh, Gregor, the hair's just the start. Look, everyone's carrying the same fake Fendi baguette from last season, and they're all drinking Crantinis. Who drinks Crantinis any more?"

"Humph," he snorted. "Can you believe that washed-up DJ? He's so into himself." Sure enough, the DJ massaged his crotch while leering at the nearest fake blonde over his aviator glasses. We both laughed, the DJ looked over and tried to pretend he was busy with his decks. We laughed at him some more.

I thought maybe our judgements were harsh, but brushed the guilt away when Lola arrived and asked, "What's the deal with this place? Everyone's a Barbie or Ken from a Club Monaco assembly line. I don't get it. If you want to look all fake like Barbie, why not glam yourself up and do something interesting?"

"Totally," agreed Gregor.

"I know," I lamented. "When I was eight, my favourite Barbie had a hot pink dress and matching feather boa with silver sparkles. I thought grown-ups always dressed that way, but it turns out drag queens are the only ones who do."

Chantelle joined us. Looking perfect with her hair piled on top of her head in an organized mess, wearing the cutest little black dress, she said, "Nice hot pink dress, Gigi."

"Thank you. I was just explaining why I dress like a drag queen. I blame it on Barbie's childhood influence."

"Oh, me too!" she squealed. "And Audrey Hepburn. My grandmother and I always watch her movies. Grandmother was a chorus member in a few Busby Berkeley movies, and taught me everything I know about glamour."

"Seriously?" we all gasped. That was one cool grandma. No wonder Chantelle was so elegant.

After hearing about Chantelle's grandmother and laughing at our surroundings a little more, we finally discussed Collections Week. Since none of us worked had it before, we didn't know what to expect, but had high hopes.

"Snap that! It'll be nuclear!" exclaimed Gregor, with a fancy arm-swoosh indicating something grand. "Can't wait to see the boys! Toronto's finest, no doubt. Will I be in charge of the male models?"

Lola smiled. "I thought that was my job."

"Actually, it's mine," I proclaimed. "I get first pick and you can have the rest. You're forgetting who recruited you."

"Oh, you poor, delusional girls," said Gregor. "You know most of them won't even be interested in you, just your outfits and makeup tips. Speaking of…Gigi, I love your fuchsia eye shadow! How Björk is that? But back to the model-boys: if any of them do like girls, they're taken. Don't get your hopes up. All the guys are mine."

"Thanks a lot, Gregor. I'll remember the Björk comment, but try to forget the rest," I said, sipping my wine, knowing full well I didn't look anything like Björk, except for my crazy makeup and black hair. "Actually, I think you're wrong. I'll bet any of us girls can get a model-boy at Collections Week before you can."

"You're on, Sugarbee. If you three win one, I'll buy you each a bottle of Dom after the week."

The bet was on.

Gregor changed focus from model-boys to celebrities. "Will there be any stars?" he asked.

"I don't know," I answered. "Francie said some rap and R&B guys attended last year's shows, but I don't know that scene. Plus, I don't understand celebrities who attend fashion shows for the sake of PR. Have you ever watched their interviews? Most of them know nothing of construction or design. When I have a show, any celebrities attending will be there because they know about the clothes, not because the PR rep thinks it's a good place to be seen."

"Agreed," said Lola. "Are you starting a line, Gigi?"

"I'd like to. I want to make clothes so women can look and feel fantastic, regardless of size. Fashion shouldn't be for girls under size six."

"*Mon dieu*!" cried Gregor. "Fashion is about thin, pretty girls and celebrities! You're sacrilegious! It's as if you're burning the bible or telling me Pierre Cardin isn't real."

"OK, Mr. Thin. Why don't I turn the tables and design menswear? Let's put them in hotpants and make man-heels trendy so they know how it feels?"

"Some of us already know how hotpants and heels feel, and we might even like it," giggled Gregor.

"I completely support reverse discrimination," said Lola, raising her glass to mine.

My mind wandered to male model auditions for a possible *Reverse Discrimination* clothing line, but Gregor snapped me out of my thoughts.

"Isn't that all a bit politically incorrect, girls? I don't know you that well, but Gigi, didn't you tell me you were some sort of save-the-earth girl?"

"Yeah," I sighed, preparing to explain my personal dichotomy. "I was an urban planner specializing in low-income housing here and abroad."

That excited Chantelle. "Wow. That's amazing. Why leave such a cool job?"

"It was cool and I enjoyed it at the start of my career because I got to travel: South America, Africa, India. Travelling was great and I loved meeting new people, but I never felt comfortable and apart from building a few schools, I wasn't improving lives. Projects took so long to complete and lost support. They were more about politicians than people. So instead of making the world a better place, I want to make it look better. I finally gave in to my love of fashion. Now I'm here, dreaming about making men wear high heels."

"You've done so much," said Lola. "Was it hard to make that decision?"

"I was twenty nine and thought I should make the change while I didn't have any commitments. I'm not married, don't have kids, don't own a home. It's the perfect time for a quarter-life crisis."

A gorgeous fifty-something woman interrupted our conversation. She looked amazing in a black A-line dress accompanied with strings of chunky black pearls and a few rhinestone necklaces. I looked closer at the sparkle. Those weren't rhinestones; they were diamonds. The lady exuded class.

"Excuse me," the classy lady said, "but I couldn't help overhearing part of your conversation, and you all look so wonderful that I have to ask if you're here with Dylen and Duke Catral."

We would have killed to be with Dylen and Duke, the Canadian twin brothers taking Milan by storm. They always looked so fun in interviews. Unfortunately, the lady was wrong, but it was a privilege to have been mistaken for their crew.

"Sorry," I said. "We don't know Dylen and Duke. We're Collections Week volunteers."

"That's too bad. I heard they were in town, and you would be their type of crowd. I'm Chloe Kirkpatrick, Fashion Editor at the *Globe and Mail*."

"Ohmigod! I always read '*Hip Pics*'!" exclaimed Gregor. We looked at each other, secretly knowing we all wanted to be in "*Hip Pics*'.

She gave us business cards and said, "I'm always looking for new talent. Give me a call whenever you want." Then she dashed out the door.

Gregor swallowed his last sip of wine. "Oh, that was so cool! Could you imagine partying with Dylen and Duke?"

Giddy with fashion excitement, we looked at each other and giggled, daydreaming about hanging out with the fashion elite.

Gregor was the only one to voice our collective thoughts. "Do you think she'll put us in '*Hip Pics*'? We definitely deserve it! Who do you think we'll see at Collections Week and who else is going to recognize our fabulousness?"

"Do you think Jeanne Becker will be there?" asked Chantelle. "She's only *the* greatest fashion journalist ever! I get incredibly star struck. She's done so much for fashion."

I couldn't imagine Chantelle star struck over anybody. She was so calm and poised, it was hard to believe she was nineteen.

"Totally," said Lola. "She intellectualized fashion and placed it beside art, urban planning, design, photography, and literature. I love how she used to be a music reporter; it makes sense for a music journalist to go into fashion. I love watching old clips of Jeanne interviewing musicians for *The New Music*. She interviewed The Police in a bathtub! Iggy Pop asking her to sleep with him until she walked out. Jeanne is a legend." queen

Fashion Television was the TV show that brought haute couture to the masses. Even high-school boys knew the show; they watched it for a glimpse of nipple not usually allowed on TV. For some reason, boobs were acceptable in a fashion context. I was sure the show was responsible for the millennial metrosexual. Those high school boys must have learned grooming and style tips through FT osmosis. For that, we were indebted to Jeanne Becker.

"Ohmigod!" whispered Gregor as he leaned in to the table. "Isn't that Veronikkah Hendricks? She's totally hammered. What's the deal with her eyebrows?"

We looked to the other side of the bar at the same time, which was technically un-hip, but a necessary evil when confronted with a deliciously gossipy situation.

There she was, Ms. Veronikkah Hendricks, the woman in charge of Canadian Collections week, guzzling a Crantini, swaying on her bar stool, nearly passing out. Her surprised eyebrows betrayed her drunkenness, but not her age. It was obvious her best friend was a plastic surgeon.

I couldn't get a good look at her plasticity, though, because she slid off her stool, falling to the floor. Her recovery attempt only succeeded in pushing up her PVC micro-miniskirt, revealing her Brazilian wax to the world. It was part of a work colleague I didn't want to see, and it wasn't the introduction to the Collections Week director I'd expected.

"Have you met her yet, Gigi?" Chantelle asked, looking disgusted.

"No, and I don't think this is the right time for introductions to her Volunteer Team, either. What do you think?"

"There's no way I would meet her now," said Gregor. "I'm not picking up anybody's mess. Everyone has bad days, but really… She's the Collections Week director! You'd think she'd have some dignity."

I agreed with Gregor, but since I was a representative for her and her organization, I thought it best to stay quiet and hide my embarrassment for her tarty outfit. She would have looked much better in a chic black suit. A guy half her age picked her off the floor, so she flopped into his arms and tried to kiss him. He looked to the bartender, imploring for help. Finally the bouncer rescued the poor guy by pulling Veronikkah away, dragging her through the lounge, and stuffing her into a cab.

We sat awkwardly for a minute and focused on our drinks, wondering if we should get involved with an event that had that woman in charge.

I e-mailed a list of volunteer questions to Francie the next day, who replied with a quick message saying she was too busy to write.

Since she couldn't write, I called, hoping for guidance.

"Hi Francie, it's Gigi."

"Ummmm… Hi. How are you?" she responded, unsure of who I was.

"I'm doing well, thanks, but I'm a bit concerned about some volunteer issues."

"Oh, Gigi. It's you. For a moment I didn't know who you were."

I'd met the girl three times in person, talked to her on the phone eight times, and e-mailed her twelve times. How many girls named Gigi could she have known?

I laughed it off and said, "No problem, Francie. Can we talk about the questions I e-mailed?"

"Not now. My boyfriend and I just had this huge fight and I'm telling my friend about it on my cell. I'll call you back." She hung up on me.

I wondered if she behaved that way because I was a volunteer or if she treated everyone with the same disrespect. Perhaps the entire industry operated the same way. After such an introduction to the fashion world, I was having doubts about my career change, but called Francie back the next day.

"Hi, Francie. It's Gigi LaFaux. I'd like to discuss the volunteer issues I e-mailed to you."

"It's not a good time, Gigi. I'm on a deadline and need to finish. I don't have time for this. That's why you're working for us."

"Look, Francie," I whined, "I know I'm just a volunteer and you're busy, but please keep in mind I'm busy too. I'm looking for a job while volunteering full time for you returning phone calls and e-mails from two hundred people who want to help. To do my job properly, I'd like five minutes of your time to clarify some questions so I can move forward."

She paused - I could tell she was annoyed - and then sighed, "What do you want?"

"I want answers to the questions I e-mailed yesterday," I said.

"Is that all?" she asked.

I was stuck in a bizarre Kafkaesque fashion-world bureaucracy.

"Yes." I said.

"Okay, I'll give you five minutes. What are your questions?"

"They're in the e-mail I sent yesterday. Are you at your computer?"

"Yes," she said, "but I printed it out and deleted the message. Then spilled Diet Coke on it by accident. Sorry. Oh, can you hold on a sec? My cell is ringing." She answered her phone and talked about her boyfriend again. I could hear her half of the conversation, waited two minutes, then hung up and called her back.

"Francie, it's Gigi. Five minutes is all I ask. Can you please answer my questions?"

She sighed again and told her cell phone friend she'd call back. "Go," she demanded.

We went through the list and discovered she didn't have any answers.

"You can't be serious, Francie. These are basic planning concerns: signage, the amount of help required in each section, how many greeters you need… You should have known about these months ago."

"Gigi, this is how we work. There are always last-minute changes, so we can't make plans until the week before the event. If you want to know the truth, we just had a disagreement with the venue and designers, so we're changing the venue and the schedule. But don't worry, it's normal."

It was normal to have such a large event change venues and line-up two weeks prior to start date? It didn't seem right to me, but it wasn't my event, so I shut up and reported the news - or lack of news - to my team. During the two weeks leading up to the event, we met a few times to anticipate our roles, but only a fashion boot camp could have prepared us for the battles we would fight.

CALCULATE.

Middle-of-the-night phone calls are either emergencies or booty calls. At one o'clock in the morning, my phone wouldn't stop ringing, and since I didn't know any Toronto guys at the time, terrible thoughts of family members and car crashes jolted me awake. Near hysterics, I answered the phone.

"Gigi, it's Francie."

My family was safe, so I calmed down, but was confused about the late-night Francie call.

"Uh…" I yawned. "Hey Francie, what's up?"

She went yellular on me and screamed, "THIS IS NO TIME TO SLEEP! I NEED TWENTY-FIVE VOLUNTEERS TOMORROW!"

It was a dream in that hazy sleep-wake state. Since I was excited and nervous about Collections Week, I'd dreamt about it since Francie and I had first met. "Twenty-five volunteers?" I asked. "What for?"

"Help in the office!" she snapped.

"Uh, okay," I said, hanging up the phone, falling back asleep.

Morning arrived a second later, greeting me with another ringing phone. Last night's dream flashed into my mind. Could it have been real? Did Francie need twenty five volunteers today? I looked at my clock: eight thirty. I was confused, but fumbled for the phone.

"Hello?" I asked in morning-frog voice.

"Where are the volunteers?"

"Huh?"

"You said you'd get me twenty-five volunteers!"

I was awake, but still confused. "Oh, Francie, I thought I dreamt that. Sorry, I was asleep when you called, and am still groggy. Can you refresh me?"

"You promised me twenty-five volunteers last night," Francie screamed. "Veronikkah is going totally ballistic! She wants volunteers and she wants them now!"

Shit. What was I going to do? Deciding calmness was the best defence, I took a deep breath and said, "Francie, just relax a minute. I apologize for not completing a job you asked of me, but please understand two things. First, I was sleeping when you called, and therefore incoherent. Second, you asked me to find volunteers in the middle of the night for the following day. I'm sorry, but that's a difficult - if not impossible - task."

I was about to add it was rude to call people in the middle of the night to volunteer, but I reconsidered, since I desperately wanted to be at Collections Week.

"I don't care. Veronikkah wants volunteers now!"

"Okay, here's what I can do. I'll phone around to find people for this afternoon. Unfortunately, I have a job interview so I can't help you, but I'm sure I can find some volunteers to help."

"I'll tell Veronikkah, but she won't be happy." She hung up without a thank you or goodbye.

During the next four hours, I called a hundred people asking them to work that afternoon. Amazingly, I found twelve who could do it. It wasn't twenty-five, but it was better than none.

I left Francie a message about her afternoon help, then I dressed and ran out the door, late for my job interview.

Miraculously, my interviewer was also running late, so I hadn't blown my opportunity to work at Swank, a chain of well-respected department stores. I hoped to work in The Lab, a new area specializing in avante-garde design.

But halfway through the meeting, the chipper, blonde HR girl revealed she had no plans for me in The Lab. Instead, she wanted me to supervise an area called Chinabooth, selling overpriced knickknacks for a Focus on China promotional event. How degrading would it be to spend three months in a booth with a racist moniker?

As the interviewer rambled about "buzz" - she really did add air quotes when mentioning it - surrounding the Focus on China event and celebrities who would attend the opening party, I could only think about how I did not want to be the Chinabooth girl. I politely argued the position wouldn't utilize my sales skills and fashion knowledge, but she insisted I was perfect for the position. The last fifteen minutes were excruciating because I wanted to run away screaming, "I will never be your Chinabooth girl!"

In the end, I figured it was best just to be polite and plough through the interview. After leaving Swank, I gave my resume to other stores, knowing I didn't want to work in any of them. How would an urban planner ever find a fashion job?

Chantelle left a message on my answering machine saying, "Gigi, thanks for asking me to help at the Collections Week office today, but it was really strange. Can you call me when you get a chance? Thanks."

I dialled her number.

"Hey Chantelle. It's Gigi. What happened?"

"I know you explained today's work was super important and it was an emergency, but we didn't do anything. When wearrived at noon, nobody was there. Twelve of us waited for half an hour, and Francie finally showed up at twelve thirty. She'd gone to lunch and forgotten we were coming. Then she would start explaining how to put labels on invitations and stuff them in envelopes, but keep stopping to take phone calls. She started telling us what to do about seven times, but never finished. Then, finally, she said we had to meet Veronikkah downstairs and we had to take stuff to her. So all of us went downstairs while only one person carried a box to her car. That was it! We went back upstairs, but by then it was three thirty, and Francie had to leave for a meeting. It was totally weird."

I spent four hours finding people to help that girl and they just sat around? Some volunteers even skipped school and changed work shifts for nothing. I was embarrassed to be involved in the mix-up.

"Thanks for telling me, Chantelle. I'll chat with Francie to figure out what happened."

I called a couple more volunteers, who said the same things as Chantelle, so I dialled Francie and asked if she had enough help.

"Yeah, they were great," she said.

"What did they do?"

"I just got them to move some stuff and mail invitations."

"Well, I spoke with some volunteers who said they didn't do much work. They changed their schedules and rushed to your office for nothing."

"Veronikkah changed her mind about the invitations while I was explaining stuff, so I didn't have much for them to do. Now we're gonna print new ones and send them out next week."

"And you'll probably need volunteers for that?"

"Yeah, how'd ya know? Boy, you're smart."

"I'm here to anticipate your volunteer needs, but it's easier for me to help if I can plan in advance. All you need to do is choose a day in the future for preparing the mail-out, and I'll get people for you."

"But I can't do that because we don't have the invitations yet."

"You can check with the printer for an estimate when they'll be ready. We can schedule the volunteers for the day after, in case printing runs over the estimated time."

"Oh, I never thought of that."

"That's why you have me to help."

Eventually the invitations were sent a week before the event, but I worried about poor attendance and thought invitations should have been sent a month earlier. That would the price for a venue change. It wasn't my event, though, so I tried not to worry. Instead, I focused on adapting to Francie and Veronikkah's work methods.

Days after the volunteer disaster, Francie called with Veronikkah's request for a marketing expert.

"What kind of marketer does she need?" I asked.

"Oh, you know… someone who's good at marketing."

Contrary to what she thought, that didn't help, so I asked, "Are you looking for people to distribute marketing materials or someone to make them?"

"We don't have marketing materials. That's why we need marketing people. Veronikkah also said something about branding, whatever that means."

"Do you actually need someone to come up with a marketing and branding strategy?" I asked incredulously. Two weeks was not enough time to design, plan, and implement those initiatives successfully for an event as large as Collections Week.

"Yeah, that sounds good," said Francie. "Do you know anyone?"

"In fact, I do. My friend Earnest is a marketing genius."

Earnest Jones was a marketing whiz kid I knew from home, recruited by a pharmaceutical company upon university graduation. I knew he was too creative for the job he had at the time, and thought he would like the Collections Week marketing opportunity.

"Great. Send him to meet Veronikkah tomorrow at nine o'clock in the morning."

She hung up and I immediately called Earnest. He didn't care about the unreasonable deadlines and cancelled his next morning's appointments.

"That woman is insane!" Earnest yelled into my phone.

"Who? Veronikkah? I haven't met her yet, but I saw her at Lobby," I replied, restraining my desire to gossip about her alcoholic tendencies.

"She was disoriented and distracted. Our meeting took two hours, yet I still don't know what she wants; her thoughts were contradictory and scattered. But she did give me an information package and invited me to a Board of Directors meeting."

"Wow, Earnest, that's totally cool. The Board of Directors…wow! I'm impressed, and Veronikkah must have liked you, even though she acted strangely."

"The problem is, the information package was amateur promotional copy. It was terrible. I couldn't follow what she wanted and whatever ideas she coherently presented were not marketable or practical. To be honest, I don't think she would be a good person to work with. Maybe I'll go to the meeting, though, to see if it's more organized."

"That's probably best," I said. "When is it?"

"Tonight. Can you believe it? That's not much time to prepare, but I'll try."

"I'm so embarrassed," Earnest wailed into my phone later that night.

"Why? What happened?" I asked.

"Veronikkah completely forgot she invited me to the meeting. I arrived before she did, introduced myself to the Board members, and gave them marketing proposals I prepared all afternoon when I should have been working. They all looked at me as though I was the crazy one and when Veronikkah came in, she asked who I was."

"No way!" I gasped.

"I told her we met in the afternoon and she invited me to the meeting to discuss marketing. Then she snapped at me and said, 'Only Board members are invited to the meetings. I would never invite you here.' It was the weirdest thing, so I apologized and left."

"She should apologize to you, not the other way around," I said.

"I think so too," agreed Earnest. "You know I'd love to help you and work on creative marketing for this, but I cannot work for that woman."

He didn't have to worry about working with her because Francie called me the next day and asked, "Why did you invite your friend to the Board meeting?"

I explained Earnest's version of the story, worried Francie would fire me for the bizarre misunderstanding. No matter how crazy things seemed, I really wanted to work at Collections Week. Luckily, she simply instructed me to never invite people to Board meetings and hung up.

I never heard about Collections Week marketing again.

STRATEGIZE.

The first day of Collections Week finally arrived, and I jumped out of bed, excited to work at Canada's most important fashion event.

Surprisingly, I had tons of energy, considering I completed three non-stop sewing days after finding nothing in my closet fabulous enough for a week's worth of fashion shows. I panicked about catty comments from worldly journalists who would notice I wore four-year-old Dickies pants rather than the latest designer labels. To solve the situation, I made myself an outfit for each day and couldn't wait to show off my designs. I wondered who would be there and if anyone would like my cute black coveralls. Would *Vogue* editors be there? Would they love me instantly and write an editorial on my designs? Would my life become legendary? I could see the story in print:

> Gigi LaFaux's brilliance was discovered at Canadian Collections Week when she was just a volunteer. A Barney's buyer walked past her, couldn't resist ordering fifty outfits on the spot, and the rest is history.

I had a feeling I would succeed as volunteer coordinator and it would lead to good things, so I skipped out of my apartment to embrace the first day of my new life.

Francie wanted my team at the venue by seven thirty to help set up. It was a fifteen-minute walk from my Church Street apartment in the gaybourhood (areas filled with gay boys are always the safest for girls), so I left at seven o'clock because I wanted to be early.

It was a beautiful September morning, the kind where you're convinced summer will hang on forever even though kids are back at school when half the population flaunts new fall clothes while the rest tries holding on to summer by wearing capris and sandals. I was so excited, I wanted to do back flips the whole way. Unfortunately, I could only do cartwheels, and I had so much energy, I actually did a couple. I smiled to myself and hummed "Copacabana," which is what I usually do when I'm in a fantastic mood. Boys in super-short denim cut-offs and white tank tops who were sketched out from partying all night smiled and said, "You go girl!" A sweet transvestite hooker even stopped and asked how I applied my makeup. Wasn't Toronto supposed to be a heartless, cruel metropolis? Obviously everyone sensed I was about to become a huge success.

I arrived at the venue in ten minutes since I practically skipped the whole way. The Carlu was a restored event theatre from the thirties, constructed on the seventh floor as part of an office and retail complex built around Eaton's department store. It was among the first models of a concert hall combined with retail space, and oozed decadent history. Jacques Carlu was the urban planner behind the fabulous Art Moderne jewel that had just been renovated after its closure in the late seventies. Collections Week was to be the highest profile event since the Carlu's restoration and reopening.

Nobody was around, so I took the elevator to the seventh floor. When the doors opened, the space transported me back to the thirties. Since I was the only one there, I took the opportunity to familiarize myself with the space. The first thing I learned as an urban planner was the importance of reconnaissance tours and studying your space, so I applied that knowledge to fashion-event planning.

I ended my private tour at a gorgeous concert hall with a runway already set up. I could practically hear Duke Ellington and Billie Holiday in the room. Unable to resist, I jumped up to the runway, imagining the lights, the music, and what it would be like to come out and bow after revealing my first collection, which would surely be an instantaneous hit. Flashbulbs would pop, people wouldn't be able to control themselves, and everyone would mob the runway, trying to get their hands on the first Gigi LaFaux original. I'd have to be whisked backstage, in demand for coveted *Fashion Television*, *Vogue*, *MTV*, and *Vanity Fair* interviews. I was practicing bows and curtsies when I noticed someone standing in the wings. I stopped curtseying immediately, feeling the hot rush of embarrassment in my cheeks.

"Excuse me," the guy said, "but do you know where the models go?"

I walked over to him. "Nobody's here yet, so I can't give you any directions at the moment."

He stepped out of the shadows, and my heart stopped. The guy was gorgeous! He had a killer jawline and I could see his abs and pecs outlined under his tight black shirt and bad-boy black leather jacket. From under his shaggy, black hair (so black it was almost blue), I saw two amazing ice-blue eyes. I had never seen a guy that striking. He was a hottie with the perfect mix of good-guy/bad-guy style that sent my heart flutter.

Then I noticed his Prada shoes. He was probably gay.

"What are you doing here, if nobody else is around?" he asked.

"I'm in charge of the volunteers, who arrive later in the afternoon, but I'm here to help set up. The organizers should be here in fifteen minutes, and I'm sure they'll know where you go."

He looked at me, but I couldn't tell what he thought. I had to come up with sparkling, witty conversation quickly, or I'd lose him forever. "So, you're a model, hey?"

What a dope. I should have shot myself right then.

"Kind of…yeah…it's embarrassing, though. A model isn't anything more than a living clothes hanger. It's a stupid profession and everyone thinks models are dumb. I only do it for the money. I'm a writer, but at the moment, nobody is interested in my work."

Oh, that was exciting! It appeared the hot model-boy had brains and good looks. How could I keep the conversation going?

"What do you write about?" I asked. It was always good to get a guy to talk about himself.

"It's a mix of fiction and journalism. When I need to pay bills, I freelance for the entertainment weeklies, but I enjoy writing fiction. I'm working on a novel right now."

"Really? What's it about?" I asked.

"Do you know about the Parisian salons of the late eighteenth and early nineteenth centuries?"

"For sure. People got together for intellectual or philosophical discussion. It was the first time men and women could get together as intellectual equals."

He looked impressed. "Cool. You know about them. My novel involves a contemporary approach to modern salons."

"Sounds intriguing. I've been thinking about starting up a salon-type discussion group myself." It sounded like a line, but I meant it.

"Really? What would you talk about? How pink is the new black? What movie star wears the cutest shoes on the red carpet?" He laughed at himself and his unfunny comment.

That was mean. Maybe the guy wasn't as hot as I thought. "No, I want to collect a group of interesting people from different disciplines to discuss everything from the concept of 'being' to Madonna's latest style change. We should be well versed in classic philosophy as well as contemporary popular culture."

"Oh, uh, sorry. I thought fashion people didn't have much to say."

"No problem. It's similar to believing all models are stupid, isn't it?" Even though he made a nasty comment, he was still hot, and I had to convince him I was smart. What was the best way to get his interest?

"But I'm not really a fashion person anyway," I said, deciding to pique his interest with my urban planner background. "I recently made a career change into fashion. There are many intellectual and artistic approaches to fashion; it doesn't have to be about gossip."

He looked at me, and if I wasn't mistaken, he was intrigued.

At that point, Gregor waltzed into the room and yelled, "Good morning, Gigi! Beautiful day for fashion, no?" He looked around, spotted the hot guy and turned his chipper entrance into the cruisiest cruise in the history of cruising. "Who's your new friend?"

I looked at the guy and realized I didn't know his name.

"I'm Dan," he said more to me than to Gregor. Did he wink at me? It was my imagination; no guy that hot would be remotely interested in me.

"Nice to meet you. I'm Gregor. Will you be working with us, stud?"

"Umm..." He was thrown by Gregor's stud comment. "Uhh...I don't know. I'm trying to find out where the models are supposed to go."

"Gigi knows that, don't you Gigi? Gigi knows everything." By that time, Gregor had scrambled up on the stage to get a close look at Dan.

"You know what," I suggested, "Why don't we go out front? It's seven thirty now so the organizers should show up."

We jumped off the stage and went down to the front of the building. Gregor skipped beside me and whispered, "Why Gigi, you're starting early with the model-boys. He's a doll. Mmm...Hot Dan. Don't look too deep into those angel eyes, though, sister. He's gay. Too bad for you."

"Curses!" I whispered. "Your gaydar is better than mine, and I've been trying to figure it out. Why? Why do you think he's gay?"

"The Prada shoes, darling. He's also wearing a BodyBody shirt. No straight guy ever wears BodyBody."

Damn, damn, damn! I knew he was too good to be straight. Maybe he'd let me pat his butt platonically while I stared into his eyes. A girl could dream, couldn't she?

We got to the front and ran into Chantelle and Lola. I introduced them to Dan, and they gave me "That guy's hot!" looks.

We all hung out for a bit, chatting and joking like old friends, except that we all stared at Hot Dan. We could have stayed there forever, but the front entrance was freezing and we couldn't get a warm drink in case Veronikkah and Francie arrived. I looked at my watch and realized we'd been waiting for forty-five minutes. I tried calling Francie's cubicle, but there was no answer, and she hadn't given me her cell phone number. We could only sit and wait.

A few workmen came and asked technical questions about lights and sound. I told the main guy Veronikkah and Francie weren't around yet, and we didn't know the answers. He wasn't happy about waiting, so I suggested they unload their stuff. "We're supposed to have volunteers to help," he said.

"I guess that's us. What do you need us to do?" I asked.

"You can start by loading in all the lighting equipment."

We looked at each other and Gregor whined, "Gigi, you never said anything about loading dusty equipment. I'm wearing a new Hugo Boss blazer!"

"To be honest, Gregor, I wasn't told anything about lifting and loading. If knew, I would have dressed differently myself. Maybe I would have recruited some men," I joked.

"Ha ha," he said, smacking my arm.

I was as happy as he was, but we'd volunteered to help, so what could we do? "Come on, you guys. We can do this. Maybe if we all work together we won't get dirty."

At that point, Hot Dan asked me, "So what do you think I should do?"

What a loser. "Win my heart, and help load the equipment, fool," I thought to myself.

"To be honest, things are looking a little slow right now," I said. "Are you sure you were supposed to be here this early?"

He checked his phone and his face flushed. "Umm, yeah…Maybe I should have checked before I left. I don't have to be here until two o'clock. This is embarrassing."

"Aw, don't worry. If you hadn't gotten here early, we wouldn't have met."

"Good point. Well, I'll see you a bit later."

"You can stay and help out," I suggested, and flashed him my most flirtatious smile. "We could use an extra pair of hands."

"I guess I can do that, since I booked off my whole day."

For the next hour we helped the tech guys, operated the huge service elevators (the grungy kind that are in cool New York lofts), and learned about sound and lighting equipment.

Unfortunately, we weren't dressed to do heavy manual labour. Chantelle's high heels killed her feet, dust covered Lola's aqua skirt, and Gregor was sweating through his Hugo Boss blazer. Luckily, my coveralls were black, so they hid the accident I had with a greasy wheel mechanism, and I thought I looked kind of cute working away. Hot Dan looked even hotter while moving cables and poles. Every so often the rest of us stopped and watched him work.

"So who's in charge of this, anyway?" he asked.

"A woman named Veronikkah Hendricks," I replied. "She used to do PR in England, but she left London to return home and promote Canadian designers. So far she seems to be doing a good job at spreading the word."

"But why isn't she here?" he asked.

"I don't know, but there must be a good reason, otherwise the person in charge would supervise the set up," I reasoned.

The tech supervisor announced completion of the load-out and asked me what he should do next. They were on a tight schedule: they had to be ready to go for afternoon rehearsals and a show time of eight o'clock that night.

"To be honest, I don't know what you should do," I told him. "I wasn't given any technical instructions, but why don't you go into the room where the runway is and start to set it up as you think best? You have more experience with lighting and sound than I do. Didn't you discuss this with Ms. Hendricks?"

"Nah, she was always too busy," he said. "She kept rescheduling our meetings, but now it's the day of the event. Where is she?"

Though I was as agitated as him, there was nothing I could do. Francie hadn't provided any logistical details. As far as I knew, I was only supposed to get people to the venue at a certain time and follow orders. At that point it was nine thirty, the organizers weren't there, and people were showing up with clothes, rolling racks, and display equipment. Media representatives also arrived asking for press passes.

I had no idea where anybody was supposed to go, and they kept asking me questions, so I took charge, made a plan, and allocated tasks. I told the lighting and sound guy to figure out something that would fit all situations and gave him Lola as an assistant; I ordered Gregor to take the display people into a side room to record who they were, where they thought they should be, and what they should do; and I instructed Chantelle to meet the media and ask them to return in the afternoon. I stayed downstairs at the front, introduced myself, and directed people to their makeshift stations.

Hot Dan offered his assistance, so I accepted.

"I'm freezing here at the door," I said. "I hate to ask this of you, but do you think you could find me a tea or a latte?"

"You got it, Princess."

I didn't have time to daydream about Hot Dan calling me Princess because Gregor appeared, begging for help. He explained how a woman had called him an incompetent moron; she couldn't accept we needed Veronikkah and Francie.

When we stepped off the elevator, a woman ran to us, put her face in front of Gregor's and spat, "Well, fool, do you know what to do now?"

I squirmed between them and asked, "Is there something I can help you with?"

"This guy is the stupidest person I ever met. He doesn't know anything!" she screamed.

"I'm sorry, I'm going to have to ask you to calm down and then we'll be able to talk to you." I steered her away from Gregor and we walked through the grand foyer. "I understand you're frustrated. To be honest, I'm frustrated, too. We're volunteers here to help you, and the best that we can do right now is find out what you need. Unfortunately, we weren't provided with instructions on how this set up should proceed, and we won't have any more idea until Ms. Hendricks arrives. So the best we can do is work together to figure out where you're supposed to set up. Yelling at Gregor is not going to help any of us."

She looked at me and realized bitching at Gregor served no purpose. "I'm so sorry!" she cried. "I thought you worked for Veronikkah. I should have known; I've worked with Veronikkah before, and she always does things at the last minute. I'm sorry."

We went back to the room, she apologized to Gregor, and he graciously accepted. He was a trained people-handler from his retail years. He orchestrated everyone in the room to work together, discussing what had been done in previous seasons and what Veronikkah's intensions were, and together they created a floor plan for the displays.

One problem was solved, but what about the other one? Where were Veronikkah and Francie? It was their event, they were late to set up, and left no instructions. Hot Dan even arrived with a latte and helped Gregor. I knew adaptability was vital for a leader, but it was ridiculous for a volunteer to take control of an entire event.

At eleven o'clock, a pink sedan arrived with Collections Week splashed across the hood and doors. Francie stepped out and held the door open. Veronikkah tried to follow Francie, but had problems walking in her outrageously high stilettos. She teetered on her tip-toes, swaying back and forth, turning her head around, paranoid she was being followed by an invisible entity. The woman needed assistance, so I ran outside to help her in.

"Who are you?" she barked.

"I'm Gigi LaFaux, the volunteer coordinator."

"Who? Volunteers? What?"

Francie stepped into the elevator, motioned for me to get in with them and said, "Veronikkah, I told you about Gigi. She's getting people to help us out. She's been great so far."

Wow. Francie noticed my work? How did she do that when she always had a cell phone glued to her ear? I'd never expected that compliment.

"Oh," said Veronikkah, not caring, as she stepped into the grand foyer. "Is everyone here? Is everything ready?"

"There are four of us here now, and Francie told me to have everyone else arrive at two o'clock."

Veronikkah flipped. "What do you mean two o'clock?" she yelled. "This is Canada's most important fashion event! We need everything ready by two o'clock! Did you hear me? Ready by two o'clock! Not start at two o'clock!"

She was one seriously crazy lady, and I deduced that from talking to her for less than five minutes. She still looked over her shoulders wildly at whatever demons pursued her while she yelled at me. I looked to Francie for guidance since I was not used to dealing with nutty fashion ladies, but she was on her phone as usual. I didn't have to worry about Veronikkah for long, though, because something grabbed her attention in the room with the stage, and she tottered off in that direction, muttering something about pink lights.

Francie hung up as Veronikkah left, so it was the perfect moment to brief her on what she'd missed.

"Francie, the lighting and sound guys are here and don't know what to do. So are some designers with displays. And the media are coming in, too. I tried to do the best I could, but I don't know if I gave them the right answers. I thought you would be here at seven thirty. Where were you?"

"Oh, we were getting our hair done. It's very important we look our best."

I looked at her, at Veronikkah, and sure enough their hair had been set. Hilariously, they had the exact same hair cut. Francie had trimmed her hair to mimic Veronikkah's red sixties retro flip-do, though she'd kept her chunky blonde highlights. I can't believe either woman thought that was a good idea. "Um…you guys look great, Francie, but now I need to know a couple things so we can get going."

Her cell phone rang and she said, "Just a sec…Oh hi, Janey! Yeah, you wouldn't believe how great my hair looks…Yeah, my boyfriend's coming tonight. Do you want me to leave tickets for you at the front? If you stop off at my friend Josie's studio I'm sure she can whip up a dress for you…Yeah, it's not a problem; designers do last-minute stuff all the time. Just tell her you're my friend. She'll love it…" She turned her back to me, continuing her conversation as she walked away.

Imploding from frustration, I was tempted to rip the phone from Francie's ear and stomp all over it, but rethought the idea. Probably everyone in the industry worked like this. Remembering *Unzipped* and *Pret a Porter*, I reminded myself the fashion world seemed last-minute, so I indicated to Francie I would wait at the front for her to finish.

Someone walked by my side and a hand fell on the small of my back. I turned to see two ice-blue eyes staring into mine, and I'm sure I blushed.

"Is that Veronikkah Hendricks?" Hot Dan asked.

"Yes," I replied, defeated that such a nutcase was in charge of something so important.

"She's crazy."

"Apparently so, but she's probably got a lot on her mind. After all, she is organizing this huge event."

I wanted to dish about her craziness, but I couldn't be too catty in front of Hot Dan. I didn't want to fuel his impression of fashion people, nor did I want him to think I was evil. Plus, I technically worked for the crazy lady and therefore represented her.

"Is she always that insane?"

"I have no idea. This is only my second time meeting her."

We looked over as she stomped around in a fit near the middle of the long hallway that was part of the grand foyer.

"It's going to be an interesting event," said Hot Dan.

"And it's only just beginning," I said, running off to help Ms. Hendricks. Francie was still by the elevators on her phone.

"Can I help you with anything, Ms. Hendricks?" I asked.

"Where's Francie?" she cried, practically jumping up and down.

"She's on the phone." I put my hand on her shoulder and looked into her eyes. "Ms. Hendricks, I am here to help you. I have three other people right now assisting designers, media, and the technical crew. All you have to do is tell me what you need, and we'll get it done."

She looked at me and I thought she would cry. "I love you dear, you're a doll. This foyer is empty. We need it full."

"Okay…Full of what? Tell me your vision and we'll get it done."

She explained the grand foyer was meant to be a gallery where designers would display clothes, but she kept getting distracted by the room's lights and the sparkly buttons on my coveralls. It took fifteen minutes to determine what she wanted, then I told her about Gregor, how he was with all the designers, and they were ready to go.

She gave me a kiss on the cheek and said, "You are a dream. What's your name again?"

"Gigi LaFaux."

"Well, Gigi, I love you. Quaaludes?"

She actually offered me Quaaludes? That was rather odd, since she was organizing a major event, but it explained her erratic behaviour. I wondered what she was like without drugs, since Quaaludes are supposed to be sedatives, and she certainly wasn't sedate. I didn't know how to respond, so I just laughed, ignored the Quaaludes comment, and took her to Gregor and the designers.

When they ran around trying to accommodate Veronikkah's erratic orders, Hot Dan came up to me and said, "So it's Quaaludes, is it?"

"Guess so. I can't believe she offered some to me. Wait, how did you hear that?"

"She doesn't care about speaking quietly."

Francie interrupted us and said, "Gigi, is this a new volunteer? Why did you hide him from me? Hi, I'm Francie, the executive assistant. I have a job for you." She led him away and he looked back at me with a helpless look.

Damn her! She stole my model-boy! And she had a Chanel Rubik's Cube purse!

I couldn't be jealous of her for long, though, because a man looking very much the dandy in a pinstriped suit walked in. He even had a cane and a red flower on his lapel. He gave Don Cherry the most flamboyantly fashionable man in Canada, not to mention hockey - a run for his money. That was fashion!

PLAN.

Mr. Dandy called. "Veronikkah! Veronikkah! Yoo-hoo! Where are you my dear?"

Veronikkah tripped into the entrance. "Well if it isn't Josh L.!" They did the double-cheek air kiss, creating a marvellously clichéd fashion moment: the drugged-out wacky lady with flamboyant homo. It was too perfect.

"Darling, I'm here to get things ready for the media and our VIPs. It's going to be a smashing night!"

"Oh, talk to that fabulous girl over there," said Veronikkah, nodding in my direction. "She has everything in control."

"Thanks, darling," Josh L. called back to her while walking towards me. "Well, aren't you cute! How retro! Where did you find your adorable little outfit?"

"I made it myself. I'm Gigi LaFaux, the volunteer coordinator."

"Pleased to meet you, Miss Gigi LaFaux. My, what a movie star name! How fabulous! You're precious! Now how can you help me?"

"Let me guess: you need to set up the reception and lounge areas for the media and VIPs. I've got a bunch of volunteers coming in an hour, but let me introduce you to Chantelle. She'll fill you in on everything and you two can work together. Does that work for you?"

"Absolutely smashing, darling!" He air-kissed my cheeks, annointing me a member of Toronto's fashion scene.

I took the stylish Josh L. over to Chantelle who, predictably, he loved her.

"You're so Audrey Hepburn!" he gushed.

She beamed. They were perfect for each other and immediately started working on the reception area.

Lola ran from the concert hall now christened the runway room and said, "I think things are under control in there. Where else can I help?"

Glancing at my watch, I realized it was around one o'clock. One hundred volunteers would arrive shortly, so I told Lola to learn everything she could about backstage. I would send her volunteers to clean up and prepare for the designers' arrival. She ran off and I reflected on my fantastic team. Lola, Gregor, and Chantelle dropped into this situation, and there they were, taking control. They were great, and we were in the midst of some chaotic fun.

Francie burst my bubble. "Where are your shirts?" she barked.

She held her cell phone to her ear, but looked in my direction, so I assumed she was talking to me.

"What shirts?" I asked.

"All the volunteers have Collections Week shirts."

"I didn't know anything about that. You didn't tell me. Where can I find them?"

"They're in our office. I thought you picked them up yesterday."

"No, I didn't. Why would you think that? Are they still there?"

"They must be. Go get them. What are you wearing tonight?"

"Huh? Me? I'm wearing this." I pointed to my cute coveralls.

"No, not you," she said to me, rolling her eyes. "Do you mind, Gigi? I'm talking to my friend."

I evaluated the situation. A hundred volunteers would walk through the door in an hour and I had an hour to get shirts before they arrived. What were my options?

I decided it would be best if I stayed to greet the volunteers, since they'd already met me and I sent Lola to get the shirts. That way, I could begin the volunteer orientation and Lola would return in time for T-shirt distribution by the end of the meeting. I told Francie my brilliant plan.

"No, you can't do that," she barked again. "I only trust you to go into my office. Go! NOW!"

After being momentarily stalled for thought, I had another brain wave. "Francie, can I use the Collections Week car? It'll be faster and cheaper than finding a cab."

"No! That's for Veronikkah's use only. Grab a cab. Go! Go! Go!"

"I'll go in a second; I have to tell my team what's happening. Do we have headsets or anything? All this running around is inefficient and it's going to kill us."

"Oh no. You don't have those?" Francie asked. "Get them too. I'll give you the address." She pulled a pen and paper out of her Chanel Rubik's Cube purse, scribbled something, and gave it to me. "Go!"

I ran to Lola, who was smiling and excited. She introduced me to a guy named Niles, who worked backstage at Paris and Milan Fashion Weeks, and was apparently running backstage for us. He was calm, cool, and well dressed in a gorgeous tailored black suit with a pale lime shirt and pink tie. He was a tiny, adorable man and a welcome relief, because I'd started to think the volunteer team would need to run everything. Though it would have been fun, it would have been a disaster since most of us were new to the fashion industry.

Niles and his production crew had worked a million fashion shows so it put me at ease to know there was someone around who knew how to run an event. Simply being around Niles had a calming effect. He explained how his crew worked. The show producer, Vivian, would always be in the runway room reporting the show start, music, and lighting cues to Niles. He stayed backstage to send models out on time and in the correct order. Lola's job was to ensure volunteers had models dressed and ready to go out on the runway, and she found it a thrilling challenge.

Happy to see that things had worked out, I explained the shirt situation and asked Lola to inform Chantelle and Gregor. Lola would greet, educate, and entertain the volunteers until I returned. I sprinted to the elevator, then to the street, searching for a cab.

After ten minutes standing on the corner of a busy downtown intersection waving my arms at cars going in either direction, I finally found a taxi, got in, and told the driver where to go.

"I don't know that address. This is my first day."

That was no good. I needed something faster than a Star Trek beam whereas that guy would be slower than Oklahoma tourists walking through Times Square.

"I'm in a huge rush so I'll have to find another cab. Sorry. Good luck with your career." I tried to get out, but he'd already started driving.

I heard a clunk; he'd locked the doors!

"I'll get you there, Miss. I promise," he said, peeling away from the curb, screeching the tires.

It became a nightmare cab ride, where every street had something blocking traffic flow: a huge delivery truck, a fender bender complete with road-raging drivers, an elderly lady who took ten minutes to cross the road. By the time the old lady crossed our path, I was tempted to get out of the car and push her across the street. It was three o'clock; the volunteers were probably all waiting, but I couldn't do anything to get to the office faster and it drove me batty. I could only sit in the taxi, willing away my imminent spontaneous combusion due to increased nervousness. Had anyone ever bitten their nails so hard they chewed off a finger? I was about to be the first.

Finally, I got to the Soviet bunker, told the cab to stay, and ran in. Unfortunately, a bored security guard stopped me as I ran for the elevator.

"Where are you going?" he demanded.

"Up to the Collections Week office."

"I'm sorry, Francie gave me strict orders not to let anyone in there this week."

The guard looked mean, but not mean enough to fight against my one ultimate weapon: tears.

I started to pretend-cry and spoke in a high, cracking voice "I'm sorry, officer," (security guards loved being mistaken for police officers), "I just came from the Collections Week venue, and Francie gave me instructions to come here, get some shirts, and take them back to her. I'm just a volunteer, so I don't know what to do."

He broke just as anticipated.

"Oh...okay, Miss, just sign in, leave your I.D., and get what you need."

I practically threw my wallet at him, scrambled to the elevator, and went upstairs.

When I got to Francie's cubicle, I found not one box of shirts, but ten. I picked one up, and it was so heavy, I could barely carry it. I could have cried, but needed to get the job done.

Since I was in such a rush, I carried one box and pushed another with my feet. By the time I'd loaded them into the elevator, I was sweaty and gross, positive my liquid eyeliner was dripping down my face. To make things worse, I had to repeat the shuffling process to get the boxes to the taxi. The security guard wouldn't even help.

By the time I reached the cab, it was three thirty and I still had to make a walkie-talkie pit stop. My idyllic vision of welcoming volunteers and inspiring them to do a great job vanished.

Luckily, the walkie-talkie pickup went all right, though I did have to put a three-hundred-dollar deposit on my credit card, since the store had no account for Collections Week.

Fed up and almost defeated, I was back at the Carlu.

I tried my best to sprint to the front entrance, but gave up and kicked the boxes over to the elevators, cursed my predicament, and told myself everything would be all right.

Arriving on the seventh floor, I noticed everyone in the runway room, so I ran in with one box and yelled, "The shirts are here!" as if it were the biggest achievement in the world. I almost collapsed from exhaustion, desperation, grief, and triumph. I felt as though I'd run a marathon.

When I looked up from the final box I kicked across the floor, I saw a hundred confused, quiet faces.

IMPROVISE.

"Hi! I'm Gigi, the volunteer coordinator. We met at the interviews a few weeks ago. Thanks for volunteering. Here's your first assignment: can I have ten people help out right now? By the elevators, you'll find boxes filled with shirts for you guys to wear."

An excited mix of giggle and chatter rippled through the volunteers. A bunch of girls jumped up immediately and ran to fetch the shirts. While volunteers speculated about the shirt style, I checked in with Lola, Gregor, and Chantelle.

"I'm sorry I took so long. It's a long story I'll tell you later. So how's it going?"

Lola looked panicky. "We've been here since you left, but nobody told us what to do, not even Vivian and Niles. Everyone is just sitting around. So we've just been answering questions."

"Okay. Here's what we're going to do," I directed. "You guys can distribute the shirts and I'll find Francie and Veronikkah. I'll get them in here to talk to the volunteers. Then we'll split into different groups and do whatever we can to get this event going."

Lola, Gregor, and Chantelle nodded in agreement, so I ran to find the organizers.

I rushed out to the grand foyer, but didn't find anyone. I asked a few designers if they saw Veronikkah and Francie, but nobody had. Eventually someone mentioned a private room beside the stage, so I hunted for it. I knocked on three doors before finding them in a luxurious room filled with flowers, wine, chocolates, and dresses. Veronikkah was sprawled on a couch while Francie chatted on the phone and held dresses in front of a mirror.

"All the volunteers are ready to go. Would you like to come down to meet them and discuss tasks?" I asked.

Francie turned her back to me and continued her phone call. Veronikkah looked up from the couch and squinted her eyes.

"Who are you?" she asked.

"I'm Gigi LaFaux, the volunteer coordinator. We met a few hours ago."

"Hmmm...Sweetie, get me a drink…" she slurred to nobody in particular and slumped back down.

Francie looked at Veronikkah, then back to me, and a scared expression crossed her face. "Just go back downstairs and we'll be there! You shouldn't be in here!" she barked, pushing me into the hallway.

"Umm...okay, but we should really start. I ran past backstage on my way here, and the models, hair, and makeup crews are sitting around chatting. Not much time before the show starts!"

"We'll be there!" she yelled.

I stared at the door that just slammed in my face, marvelling over what I'd just experienced. If Francie was Veronikkah's babysitter, it would be hard to pull off a successful night, let alone a whole week.

Worried for the event's future, I ran back to the runway room and found a hundred girls and a few boys stuffed into sausage-like tank tops two sizes too small. "Collections Week, C'est Chic!" was embroidered on the ribbing, pinching and pulling the shirts in unflattering directions. It was the most disastrous group fashion mistake I'd ever seen; the Fashion Police should have shut down Collections Week immediately. Unfortunately,

I had to make the best of it and motivate the horrified volunteers.

"You guys look fab!" I tried to say cheerfully, knowing my smile was a grimace. "Now let's get working and help make this Collections Week the best anyone's ever seen! Here's how it will work. Everyone allocated to work backstage, go with Lola. Media and PR volunteers are with Chantelle. If you're in the designer gallery, you're in Gregor's group. Finally, if you're scheduled for the runway room, you're with me. We'll split into teams now and prepare for tonight's show. Have a great time, and thanks for your help."

I found the box of walkie-talkies and headsets, threw one each to Lola, Chantelle, and Gregor, and said, "Keep in touch guys. Call if you need anything."

As we put on our headsets, Veronikkah wobbled into the runway room.

"Don't you all look delightful?" she tried to purr, but delivered a hiss instead. "You look like a little fashion army! Don't you just love your shirts? I designed them myself."

Did I catch a few snickers from Veronikkah's little fashion army? Admittedly, it was difficult suppressing giggles, but I had to because I worked for that woman.

She surprised me with a cute, inspirational speech about the importance of volunteering and how we all worked together to strengthen the international acceptance of our country's fashion scene. Her eloquence was shocking after her morning's spaciness. She was calm, composed, and impassioned. That was the Veronikkah who made Collections Week what it was.

I hoped she would say something else to her troops, but she glanced to the middle of the room and yelled, "Why aren't there flowers in here?"

It was best to divert people's attention from the increasingly schizophrenic Veronikkah, so I called out, "Thanks, Ms. Hendricks! I'm sure you'll be happy with all our volunteers! Now let's have a great night and fantastic week! Enjoy yourselves! Please split into your groups and your group leaders will give you instructions."

I held a quick huddle with Lola, Gregor, and Chantelle. "Okay, guys. I have to be honest with you. We aren't getting a lot of guidance from Veronikkah and Francie, so we have to use our judgement and do the best we can. If you have questions, call me on the walkie - channel four - and we'll see what happens. Lola, you go backstage and see how you can help Niles. Make sure the models, hair, and makeup people have everything they need."

"Who's Niles?" asked Chantelle.

"He's the backstage part of the production crew. From what I understand, he works with a woman named Vivian. They seem to know what they're doing, so let's follow their lead. Chantelle, you go to the front of the grand foyer and keep working with Josh L.. Gregor, take your team to the designer gallery and make sure all the designers are happy. I'll get my people in here to organize chairs and I'll deal with Veronikkah. How does that sound?"

"I'm a bit nervous, actually," said Chantelle.

I gave her a hug and said, "Don't worry, Josh L. knows what to do. You'll be fine. As I said, just call me with any problems." I hugged Lola and Gregor, wishing them luck. "I'll periodically check in with you guys."

While assembling my team, I sorted through mental notes of what fashion shows looked like on television, assessing requirements.

"Okay, guys. See those chairs?" I pointed to a corner of the room. "We need to arrange them. I know it's not a glamorous task, but someone's got to do it, and it's going to be us. Start by lining them along the runway. Once one row is done, make a new one. Does that make sense?" Everyone nodded. "Good. Okay, you guys can start. I'll check in with Veronikkah and be back." I shooed them off to start working and ran to Veronikkah, who was now muttering about ribbons instead of flowers.

"I don't want flowers anymore!" she said to me. "I see the whole room draped in pink ribbon! Wouldn't that be amazing? *Trés* daring! Then at tonight's opening speech, I can cut a main ribbon, and then they'll all shift places. The entire room will move! A grand, fashionable ribbon-cutting ceremony! It will be fabulous, simply fabulous!"

That was a horrible idea with only a few hours left before the scheduled show start, so I patted her arm and said calmly, "Ms. Hendricks, that's a beautiful idea."

When did I learn to be such a liar? In this case, it was a necessary evil. "But I think it's a bit too late to change your room concepts now. Did you already order the flowers?"

"Yes, a few days ago. Francie was going to do it. Someone should be here to set them up."

"Okay, great. I'll try to find the flower person."

"That's a lovely idea," she said, seemingly already sidetracked from her ribbon epiphany.

I'd learned distraction was my best weapon against Veronikkah Hendricks, and knew it would be a valuable coping mechanism for the rest of the event.

"You stay in the runway room and ensure everything is set up according to your vision. I'll go check on the flowers." I grabbed two walkie-talkies: one each for Francie and me, and ran back to the room where I found her previously.

She answered the door in a horrible grape-purple satin dress covered in beads and sequins, with frayed seams in an attempt to look "edgy". She was a kindergarten project.

"Do you like my dress?" she asked. "My friend Josie made it."

Not wanting to answer the question since I didn't want to offend Francie or her friend, I asked, "Do you know anything about flowers? Veronikkah said you ordered them for the runway room, but there aren't any there. Oh, and wear this headset so I don't have to keep running around to find you." I shoved the walkie-talkie and headset into her hand.

"The flowers! Um, yeah, they're on their way," she said and closed the door in my face again. I could tell she was lying, so I couldn't wait to see what would happen.

As I walked away from the room, my walkie-talkie buzzed to life. <<Gigi, are you there?>>

<<Yes, go ahead.>> I was so excited to deliver my first walkie-talkie communication and speak into a headset. I felt like a pop star.

<<Gigi, it's Chantelle. I've got a bunch of models at the front entrance, but I don't know who they are or where they go. What should I do?>>

<<It's probably best to send them backstage.>>

<<Niles to Gigi. Yes, send models backstage. They should come up through the freight elevators.>>

<<Great, Niles. Thanks.>> Wow. That was fun. What did I do without walkie-talkies all my life? I decided all my friends should have such handy little gadgets. They'd be great in a club.

<<Gigi, it's Chantelle again. Some guy is bringing in flowers and needs a signature. Should I sign for them?>>

<<No, just direct him to the runway room and get him started. Veronikkah is probably in there, so get her to sign for them.>>

<<Okay, thanks.>>

<<Niles to Gigi.>> The walkie-talkie action was hilarious. It reminded me of when I was little and we used to play *Dukes of Hazzard* on my street, pretending we all had CB radios. I felt like a walkie-talkie natural.

<<Go for Gigi.>>

<<Gigi, what's your twenty?>>

What was he talking about? <<What's my what?>>

<<What's your twenty? Is this your first time on a walkie-talkie?>>

<<Yes.>> Damn. I thought I was a pro, but I guess my newness was detectable.

<<When someone says that, they're asking your location.>>

<<Oh, okay, I'm on my way to the grand foyer.>>

<<Can you come backstage? I'd like you to hear the logistical rundown.>>

<<Sure. I'll be right there.>> I ran backstage and saw Niles surrounded by tall, skinny girls and handsome boys. I tried to find Hot Dan, but Niles found me first and explained backstage logistics: makeup, hair, and dressing. He divided the group into equal parts and allocated everyone to stations.

After the talk, he approached me and said, "I wanted you to hear how everything works. I also wondered if you have a model list."

"No, sorry Niles. All I know is that I needed volunteers here at two o'clock. Now they're here and we have to do what we're told, but nobody gives us instructions. You're the first."

"Who do you think would have a model list?" he asked.

"Probably Veronikkah or Francie," I said. "Let me check."

I turned on my walkie-talkie. <<Gigi to Francie.>> No answer.

I tried twice more, never hearing from her. That meant I had to find her and call Niles with any information.

I ran through the runway room to check on volunteers. Josh L. was tutoring them on VIP seating, so I checked with him to make sure everything was okay.

"Your volunteers are fantastic!" he exclaimed. "I *love* little volunteers." He patted two of their heads and winked.

It was nice he was enthusiastic, but his condescending tone implied, "I love having people around to do all the menial tasks. I'm going to take advantage of them as much as I can."

"Great!" I said, trying to stop my bad habit of reading too much into people's words. "I'm just hunting for a model list for backstage." I eyed his clipboard and noticed a huge list of names. "You wouldn't by chance have it, would you?"

"This is the seating list, sweetie. Try Veronikkah, won't you?"

"Thanks," I said, seeing her in the middle of the runway room educating a group of volunteers on floral displays. Every flower needed a ribbon exclaiming, "Collections Week, C'est Chic!" She was also instructing them to tie ribbons around their necks because she thought it would be cute. Everyone was working so well together so I didn't want to spoil the moment, but I had to ask about the model list. Veronikkah paused from her flower and ribbon display and told me icily, "Francie deals with lists, darling, not me."

I kept trying Francie on the walkie-talkie, but she never replied, so I continued to the designer gallery in the grand foyer, hoping I'd run into her. To do that, I had to walk through the front entrance, taking the opportunity to check in with Chantelle.

She'd organized the registration tables brilliantly. They faced the elevators to greet guests at the same time as forming a barrier in front of the runway room doors.

"How is everything?" I asked.

"Great!" she beamed. "Josh L. gave me a media list, so now we're organizing passes and the reception area. I've also got a girl downstairs directing people."

"Wonderful! Keep up the good work."

"Oh, do you think it would be a good idea to give the downstairs girl a walkie-talkie?" she asked.

"Yeah, I do, but I don't think we have any extras. I'll check with Francie and let you know."

Walking further through the grand foyer, I arrived in the designer gallery, which was beautiful. There were mannequins everywhere, along with creative displays separated by pink and white chiffon. It was a fashion dream, and I ran up to Gregor, who was helping hang a sign.

"Gregor, everything looks great!" I exclaimed, giving him a hug and kiss.

"It does, doesn't it? The designers are wonderful, and the volunteers really know what they're doing. Most are in retail management and display; they're fantastic."

"That's because I'm the volunteer coordinator," I joked with a wink.

I tried Francie again on the walkie-talkie, but she still didn't answer. When I finally got to her office, she was dishevelled and seemed embarrassed. Further inspection revealed the source of embarrassment: there was a man in the room. She introduced him as Darryl, the party promoter for the opening gala. At first I thought they were making out, but wondered about her boyfriend. Darryl wasn't the guy in the photos she'd showed me at my interview. Maybe they were on a break. Even so, Francie wouldn't be so irresponsible when she had an event starting, would she? I put it out of my mind and asked about the model list.

"Oh, I thought I gave that to you," she said. "Here's an extra copy. Oh, and don't let mothers, boyfriends, or any friends of models backstage. There's only a small amount of room and we need to make the best of the space."

"Sure thing," I said. "Do you think we can get any extra walkie-talkies? We need one for the volunteers greeting people downstairs."

"It's unnecessary and not in our budget," she said.

"Maybe then, if you're not using yours, could we use it?"

"ARE YOU CRAZY?" Francie yelled. "I NEED TO BE ACCESSIBLE AT ALL TIMES!"

I left the Collections Week office dejected, but she called after me.

"Speaking of walkie-talkies, your team is using too many. Can I get some back?"

I pretended not to hear her as I rounded the corner and ran away.

<<Gigi for Niles. Are you there?>>

<<Go for Niles.>>

<<It's Gigi. I'm coming with the model lists.>>

<<You're a peach.>>

I delivered the list to Niles backstage, and happened to walk into a swarm of male models trying on white suits. Most were in their underwear, so I didn't look at their faces, but from the neck down the eight men were beautiful. One guy in a corner, who had a smooth back in the shape of a perfect V. He was thin and muscular, but neither too much of one nor the other. I admired his cute butt. When he turned around, the front wasn't too bad, either. When I got past his amazing pecs, I realized it was Hot Dan. Our eyes met, he cocked one eyebrow and smiled. I was so embarrassed, I shuffled away because I knew my face had tuned scarlet. But as I turned around, I caught myself looking back at him, and may have even given him a little wink. Then I seriously had to run away because I'm shy when it comes to guys. Sure, I'm a confident girl and can flirt, but usually with guys who don't matter. When I'm really attracted to a guy, I get super-embarrassed. In this case, I could only run away.

En route from backstage to the runway room, I reflected on my day so far. Despite the confusion, I enjoyed running around, making sure everyone was okay, and relaying messages back and forth. I felt organized and in control of my job. But most of all, I was excited for the night to start and to experience the fashion industry in full swing. I checked my watch.

<<Gigi to the team. It's almost time for guests to arrive. Are we ready to begin?>>

ENGAGE.

<<Chantelle to Gigi. The guests are here! What do I do with them?>>

I thought about it for a moment.

<<Do I let them into the runway room?>>

<<NO! The runway room is NOT ready! Do not send in guests!>>

<<Okay, but who was that?>> I asked.

<<It's Vivian. The show producer.>>

<<Thanks, Vivian,>> I said, adding, <<that's a big ten-four,>> thinking it would make me sound like I knew what I was doing. Instead, I sounded like a hick.

<<Where should I tell them to go?>> asked a distressed Chantelle.

<<Send them in the desiger gallery to look around while they wait,>> I said.

<<Good idea.>>

<<Gigi to Gregor.>>

<<This is Gregor.>>

<<Did you get that?>>

<<Yes. Send in the guests! We're all ready in the designer gallery. Are there any cute boys in the crowd?>>

While early guests sauntered into the designer gallery, I wanted to check on the runway room volunteers and introduce myself to Vivian. Rehearsal was in full effect: music blared, lights flashed, and models walked down the runway. It was the closest I'd ever been to a real fashion show and it was fabulous. I was part of Collections Week, and I could see all this stuff first-hand!

As I ventured further into the runway room, I saw all the volunteers with the "Collections Week, C'est Chic!" ribbons around their necks. Unfortunately, the effect wasn't as cute as Veronikkah envisioned. The way the font was arranged on the ribbon, some of the volunteers looked as though they had been beheaded and patched back up again, à la Frankenstein. Some ribbons left such long ends they looked like dog leashes. It was ridiculous, but I was learning that whatever Veronikkah wants, Veronikkah gets.

Josh L. stood at the end of the runway, barking orders at the volunteers, so I asked if everything was okay.

"Oh, Miss Gigi, so glad to see you. We need all your volunteers to stuff gift bags."

"Can you use the ones who are helping you out here? All the other volunteers are busy in their sections."

"Sweetie, we have five hundred bags needing to be filled and placed on chairs. The show is about to start and this needs to be done! We only have ten volunteers here and they're working on seating plans. I need more help!"

Five hundred gift bags? How were we going to do that?

<<This is Gigi. Attention all units!>> Did I really just say that? Mental head-slap. I was panicking. <<Can I have everyone's attention?>>

<<Lola here.>>

<<Chantelle here.>>

<<It's Gregor. What can we serve you, mistress?>>

<<Volunteer emergency in the runway room. We need five hundred gift bags stuffed STAT! Does anyone have volunteers to spare?>>

<<I have two.>> From Gregor.

<<Chantelle here. I can only spare one. Guests are coming and it's getting crazy.>>

<<This is Lola.I can send most of my volunteers as long as you return them before the show. Everyone is familiar with the outfits and their models.>>

<<Great. Thanks, guys. Send them to the runway room now and tell them to report to me!>>

Five minutes late, we had an assembly line of fifteen new volunteers dropping cosmetics, CDs, perfume samples, and magazines into little pink bags embossed with "Collections Week, C'est Chic!" I wondered how Veronikkah, Francie, and Josh L. were clever enough to have commissioned the bags, but not organized enough to have informed me of them before now.

Halfway through bag production, Josh L. yelled, "We've run out of perfume samples! L'éclair is one of our biggest sponsors! What are we going to do?" He stomped all over the place, his face turned red, and sweat poured down his face. It wasn't fashionable, and certainly not dandy.

He freaked out over perfume samples? It wasn't as though the world was ending, but in his world it was apocalyptic.

I suggested, "Why don't we put all the bags with everything in the front rows? We'll make it appear as though only the VIPs were meant to get the perfume samples."

He smiled as he wiped sweat off his forehead with his ascot and said, "You're brilliant, Dear."

I didn't think I was that brilliant, but at least it calmed him down.

<<Chantelle to Gigi. There are tons of people here now. When can we let them in?>>

<<Chantelle, it won't be for a while. The runway room isn't ready. Send them to the designer gallery.>>

<<But the media want to go in and set up and they're being really pushy.>>

<<Let me check.>>

I asked Josh L. if there was a publicist to deal with media, but he said it was our responsibility and nobody could enter the runway room until everything was perfect; the media could not see the area in disarray. I relayed the message to Chantelle.

<<Thanks,>> said Chantelle, <<But now I have people who say Darryl put them on the guest list. Who is Darryl? Am I supposed to have a guest list?>>

I remembered Francie's embarrassed grin and messed hair.

<<Darryl is the party promoter. I met him an hour or so ago. He must have a list for you, but I don't know anything about it. I'll try to find him or Francie and get it for you. In the meantime, tell Darryl's guests to wait in the designer gallery and check back with you in fifteen minutes.>>

<<Gigi to Francie.>>

<<Gigi to Francie.>>

No reply. Why bother with walkie-talkies if the organizers never used them?

<<Gigi, it's Lola. Francie's backstage.>>

<<Thanks, Lola.>>

I sprinted backstage to find Francie and Veronikkah surrounded by makeup artists. I may not have known much about the fashion industry, but I did know about project management. Applying makeup should not be a priority for someone in charge of a major event. I was mad about Veronikkah and Francie's lack of professionalism, so I squeezed myself between makeup artists.

"Francie, I have a question for you."

"I can't talk now. Can't you see we're getting our makeup done?"

"I need help with the guest registration. Some guests say Darryl has them on the guest list, but Chantelle knows nothing about it."

"You gotta talk to him about it."

"Okay. Do you know where he is?"

"Yeah, he went out for a bit. He should be back in half an hour."

"Half an hour? The show will have started by then!"

"Oh, no. Fashion shows are always late. You guys will be fine. When Darryl comes back, I'll tell him to go to the front with his guest list."

I couldn't believe Francie's attitude. Even if she didn't care that her guests would wait for more than half an hour, I did. Collections Week was becoming my event.

"Can you call Darryl and see what he says?" I pleaded.

"Gigi, I told you I'm getting my makeup done. It's super-important Veronikkah and I look good for the press, so I don't have time to answer all your silly little questions. Just go and do it."

CONFRONT.

What was I supposed to do? Everything? I needed more guidance, but my walkie-talkie buzzed again.

<<Gigi, it's Lola. Are you slacking and getting your makeup done while we do all the work?>>

I looked around the backstage area, saw Lola through a mass of models and racks of clothes, and laughed.

<<Gigi, we need water! The models are dying, and volunteers have been here for almost seven hours and haven't had a drink.>>

<<Mine too,>> agreed Gregor.

<<Ditto,>> said Chantelle.

Water sounded logical to me, so I turned back to Francie, who wasn't caring about logistics at all. She was in her makeup chair reading *People* magazine.

"Francie, do models and volunteers get any water?"

"Yes, didn't you get the bottles? They're all in our office. Here's the key. Go get them."

"Uh, thanks," I said, taking the keys from her.

I recruited people from the runway room to help with water duty and reminded Josh L. about media reps trying to get into the runway room.

"Admit the media with cameras," he said. "They should have come in earlier because they need to set up."

"Uhh...thanks," I said, wondering why he didn't say so earlier. I relayed the message to Chantelle, along with the news that Darryl wouldn't be back to help her.

<<What doI do?>> she asked, losing her cool veneer.

<<I'll be there in a minute, after I deal with our water crisis. In the meantime, tell Darryl's guests to wait. Let the media crews with cameras into the runway room for set up.>> I amazed myself with my multi-tasking proficiency. I thought I sounded like a fashion pro, not an urban planner who'd landed in a new profession.

The volunteers and I ran to the Collections Week office, where we cleared out the bottled water boxes and put most of them into an empty room we passed in the backstage hallway. I figured we could claim it as our own, since nobody else used it. As we moved the boxes out of the office, Gregor radioed.

<<Gigi, do we have water yet? It's so hot over here, I'm afraid my volunteers will pass out.>>

<<It's in the empty room on the second floor. Send a volunteer to get some for your crew.>>

<<What about food? They're getting hungry.>>

<<Francie promised me meal tickets redeemable at the designer gallery café, but I haven't seen them yet. I'll check into it and get back to you, but they won't be able to take a break until the show starts. We need everyone available to help as much as possible.>>

<<Roger. That's a big 10-4, good buddy,>> said Gregor in his best trucker-voice, which passed as a big, gay trucker.

Francie was still in the makeup chair when I returned her keys. "Francie, you promised meal tickets for the volunteers. They've been here for hours without a break, and they're only getting water now. Can I have the tickets?"

"I don't have time to deal with this now, Gigi. The tickets are in the office and must be monitored very carefully. Can't you see I'm in the middle of makeup? You'll get them later."

"I thought it would be best to have them eat during the show and then they can help with crowd control afterwards."

"We'll see. Later."

"Okay," I said, walking away, jostled by models, hair stylists, and makeup artists. For a moment I was temporarily stunned. What was this world? I had no time to think about it because Chantelle called my walkie-talkie again.

<<Chantelle to Gigi. I don't know how much longer I can keep media from going into the runway room! They're really mad!>>

Crap! With everything happening, I'd forgotten to tell Chantelle to let them in.

<<Let them in now. I'll be right there to help.>>

As I ran towards the runway room to check on progress on my way to the front entrance, Niles stopped me.

"Gigi, do you know that girl over there sitting with Francie?"

I hadn't noticed her when I'd spoken with Francie earlier, but she was easy to miss. She had mousy-brown hair, and dressed as any other girl in her late teens might be. She was short, a bit chubby, and had brown eyes that looked black. Her face had a rabbit-like quality, but not in a cute, fuzzy-bunny way. No, she reminded me of the mean rabbits from *Watership Down*. I could tell I wouldn't like her, but concealed it from Niles in case she was someone special.

"No, I don't know who she is," I said.

"She came backstage a while ago and said she was the volunteer in charge of backstage. She bossed everyone around and totally changed the hair and makeup order I established with the models. She slowed down the show by half an hour and I don't even know who she is."

"Couldn't you stop her?" I asked.

"No, because she came in with Francie and Veronikkah."

"Didn't you discuss this with Francie before you started? I thought you had tons of backstage experience. That girl looks nineteen."

"That's why I'm confused. I thought Veronikkah hired me to run backstage, but that girl screwed up everything."

"Niles, I'd love to help you, but I've got to check on the runway room. Can you and Lola try to sort this out?"

"Okay, yeah. I wondered if you knew her since she's a volunteer."

"Don't look at me, I've never seen her before."

<<Gigi, I need your help!>> begged Chantelle.

"Gotta run, Niles!" I yelled, starting my sprint to the runway room to get to Chantelle.

Most of the gift bags were on the chairs and Josh L. looked happy. I asked him about Chantelle's guest problems, but he said she would be fine; it was more important for him to be in the runway room. I thanked him and ran towards the front entrance to rescue Chantelle.

I fought my way against the flow of journalists and found myself stuck among hundreds of people trying to push into the runway room. It was a fashion madhouse. To compound the mayhem, my walkie-talkie buzzed.

<<Gigi, it's Gregor.>>

<<Go ahead Gregor, but I can't hear very well because I'm in the middle of all the guests at reception.>>

<<One of my volunteers is crying and I don't know what to do.>>

It turned out Veronikkah had terrorized a volunteer, called her a sloppy mess unfit for Collections Week, and instructed her to go home.

<<That's terrible,>> I said, <<but I can't do anything about it right now since I'm needed here. Why don't you tell her to sit down somewhere and take a break? Send her home if she wants to go, but if she really wants to stay, get her to do something where she's not seen and keep her away from Veronikkah.>>

<<Thanks.>>

<<Oh, and give her a hug and apologize for us all. I feel really bad about this, but I just can't get to you.>>

<<No problemo, chiquitita.>>

Focused on squeezing my way through the front entrance crowd, I found a frazzled Chantelle at the reception desk with four equally stressed volunteers. People swarmed them, yelling, "Darryl said I was on the guest list!" Others claimed to be Francie's friends, on the verge of getting aggressive. No wonder Chantelle had been struggling. She saw me and I could tell she was on the verge of breaking down, so I addressed the crowd.

Without an audio system in the front entrance, I stood on Chantelle's reception desk and yelled, "Attention ladies and gentlemen! Welcome, and thank you for attending Collection Week's opening night gala!"

It wasn't the most professional way to communicate, but it worked. The Collections Week opening night crowd softened so I continued.

"I have a few announcements about this evening's event. If you are a member of the media requiring audio-visual equipment set up, you can go into the runway room now. You should have signed in at this front desk and received a pass. Have the pass ready to show to volunteers at the door. Other registered media members will be admitted next. Sponsors will be seated after that, followed by Francie and Darryl's guests. We will announce each group's entrance time. At the moment, we ask everyone to relax in the designer gallery so media representatives can get to the doors." The crowd shifted a bit, with quite a few people going into the designer gallery. Gradually media members reached the door.

I got off the desk, amazed the crowd of hundreds had actually listened to one person, and Chantelle gave me a huge hug. "Thank you so much! I almost lost it," she said.

"No problem. I'm just here to help. Now let's see what's happening with the guest lists."

We looked in every pile of paper for missing lists, but couldn't find any. Since the guests had been told to show up, the organizers probably wanted them there, so we made the executive decision to let everyone in, trying to record as many people's details as possible.

Veronikkah teetered into the front entrance, Francie following behind. She stopped a volunteer door greeter, pulling the ribbon from her neck. "Who told you to wear this?" she demanded. "We only have a bit of this ribbon available and it's for VIPs only."

The volunteer - a shy fashion design student - shrunk away from Veronikkah, looked at the floor, and muttered, "Someone from the runway room gave it to me and told me we were all supposed to wear them."

"Take it off now! Find me who told you that!"

I ran to intervene. "Excuse me, Veronikkah. When you were in the runway room this afternoon looking after flowers, you told the volunteers to wear ribbons."

Not knowing how to respond, she decided to blame me for the mishap.

"Are you lying to me? I wouldn't have done such a thing! This is special ribbon! I want all the ribbon off NOW!" she yelled, forgetting the press members surrounding her. Or maybe she did remember and thought it was a good way to exhibit her power. Whatever the case, it wasn't my place to argue, even though I thought it was misguided to worry about ribbons when guests were confused and unhappy.

<<Attention everyone! This is a code red alert!>> I said into my walkie-talkie, trying to make fun of this absurd situation. <<Veronikkah wants ribbons off all volunteers! Repeat: no volunteers should wear ribbon!>>

Lola chimed in. <<What are you talking about?>>

<<Veronikkah just got mad that volunteers were wearing ribbon and wants it off everybody now.>>

<<Wasn't she the one that wanted it in the first place?>>

<<Ummm...Yes.>>

<<Sorry, I don't have time to worry about that now. We're dressing models.>>

<<Just do your best. And so you know, there are still a couple hundred people waiting to get in. The show probably won't start for a while.>>

<<Really? I'll tell that to Niles, because he thinks the show is going to start in five minutes.>>

<<Five minutes? No! It can't! We've got to get guests in! I'll go check if the runway room is ready!>>

I told Chantelle I had to leave, but she had everything under control by then. Then I announced media and VIPs could enter together. I knew it contradicted what I said earlier, but I didn't want anyone important to miss the show. As I went into the runway room with the group, I looked to my left and saw legendary fashion journalist (and my personal idol) Jeanne Becker beside me. I couldn't believe I was that close to her. Unfortunately, I ended up stepping on her foot because, in a dash for the best seat, a drag queen on my right pushed me. Luckily Jeanne smiled, told me it was okay, and joked about pushy fashion crowds. Before I knew it, we were separated as she found her seat and I ripped ribbons from volunteers' necks on my way to Josh L..

When I got close to him, I noticed his fear. He ran around, tapping his clipboard, trying to seat guests. Volunteers delivered guests to him and he provided approximate seating locations. It was a tedious and inefficient process, surrounding him with an angry mob. There was no way I could ask him about show start, so I looked to the tech booth, hoping to see Vivian. There was only a guy, so I approached him and asked about the show's timing.

"I don't know when it will begin. I only start it when Vivian tells me."

I called Niles and Lola on my walkie-talkie. <<We'll need at least thirty more minutes to seat people. The runway room is insane!>>

Niles replied, <<That's going to make the show over half an hour late! I don't run late shows!>>

<<Niles, here's your choice: you have no audience or you start the show late. What will it be?>>

<<It will have to be late. Just keep telling me when guests arrive. By the way, have you seen Veronikkah and Francie? They're supposed to be backstage to prepare for Veronikkah's speech.>>

<<I last saw them in the front entrance, but that was ten minutes ago.>>

<<Okay, thanks sweetie. Keep me posted.>>

As Niles said those words, I saw a woman in a day-glow orange faux fur fox wrap throw a glass of red wine into the face of a woman wearing a silver sequined tank top. It was a fashion fight, so I jumped to the front row to intervene, worried I would end up the recipient of a miscalculated bitch-slap.

As I got closer, Orange Fox lady said, "You've taken my seat for the last time, you trash-writing hack!"

Silver Sequins retorted with, "I don't see your name on it!"

"That's because you tore it off!" screamed Orange Fox. "You wouldn't have to fight over seats if you had a magazine anyone read. Nobody cares about *Sparkle*. It's dated, old, and needs a Botox injection, just like its editor!"

Silver Sequins was ChiChi Chihuahua, editor of *Sparkle* magazine, and from my years of pop culture studies, I realized Orange Fox was Lucinda McRuvy, entertainment reporter for Canada's daily gossip show. It took me a few minutes to recognize Lucinda because she looked ancient in real life. The camera hid her wrinkles well; she was the one who needed Botox, but I wasn't going to say it. Instead, I had to concoct a way to stop the catfight.

Grabbing a volunteer, I explained the situation, directing her to take ChiChi away from Lucinda and find her a seat. If she couldn't locate something, she should take ChiChi to Josh L.

We ran over and I said, "Ms. Chihuahua, I think I saw your seat over there," pointing to another area of the runway room. This volunteer will help you find it.

Both women looked at me sceptically, but Chichi collected herself and followed the volunteer, scowling back at Lucinda.

"Thanks, darling," purred Lucinda. "I hate that woman."

"No problem. Please enjoy your evening, Miss McRuvy."

She gave me her card and said, "Call me if you need anything. By the way, your outfit is adorable."

"Thanks. I made it." I twirled around and gave her a quick pose.

"It's cute. Well done."

I had never had a more exciting night. I couldn't wait to call all my friends back home in Calgary to relay everything.

I looked around, wondering what to do next, when I saw Francie and Darryl intertwined, armed with wine, speaking to a guy I recognized as a local DJ. I asked Darryl about his guest list.

He looked at me with a buttery smile and said, "Hey, no worries, baby. I'm taking care of it."

"So you've already been to the front and talked with Chantelle?"

"Huh? Uh, oh yeah, baby. Don't you worry about the guest list. Everything is fine."

Not trusting him entirely, I looked to Francie for guidance, but she was too busy chatting up the DJ. They dissected the previous night's party. Francie complained about how she'd wanted to stay later, but left at four o'clock to get up early for her haircut. I wasn't going to get any help from her, so I thanked Darryl for his time and was about to call Chantelle on my walkie-talkie when I felt his hand on my butt. I glared at him, but he dove back into conversation with Francie and the DJ, thereby ignoring me. I would never be able to trust that guy.

I walked away from the trio and radioed Chantelle. <<Gigi for Chantelle. I just saw Darryl. He said he took care of the list. Are you okay up there?>>

<<Yeah, Gigi. Things are fine now, but I never saw Darryl. We're signing in people as you and I discussed.>>

<<Okay, keep doing that. How many people are out front?>>

<<There are probably about a hundred more.>>

That was when the lights flickered; the music became unbearably loud, then softened. A man announced, "Ladies and gentlemen! Welcome to the Collections Week opening gala. Please take your seats; the show will begin in two minutes."

Two minutes? With a hundred guests in front and more than half the inside guests unable to find seats, it didn't make sense.

<<Gigi to Niles and Vivian. Are you there?>>

<<Gigi, it's Lola. Niles is on a different channel, but he's beside me. What can I tell him?>>

<<We can't start the show in two minutes! The guests are still coming in, and half don't have seats!>>

<<I'll tell him.>>

There was a pause, then Niles came on the walkie-talkie. <<Gigi, we've got to get things moving, is there anything you can do?>>

<<I'll just tell Chantelle to let everyone in, and I'll help seat guests in the runway room. Hopefully it will work.>>

<<Okay. We'll start in two minutes.>>

<<This is Chantelle. I heard all that. Should I just let everyone in?>>

<<We have no choice. Let them all in, but try to keep them calm.>>

<<Gigi to Gregor.>>

<<Gregor here.>>

<<How are things in there? Do you still have guests in the designer gallery?>>

<<Most are gone, but there are still about fifty people.>>

<<Get them out of there and into the runway room!>>

I ran to the runway and tried to help people find seats, especially those in the first row. It was bedlam, with people crowded around Josh L., complaininq. It was a hopeless situation once the announcemer urged everyone to sit anywhere.

That's when Francie ran up to me and yelled, "What's going on? I thought all the seating was under control! What are the volunteers doing?"

"They're helping people find seats," I told her.

"Why is that guy telling people to just sit anywhere? Josh L. worked for hours on the seating."

"Francie, only Josh L. has the seating list. That's why it's taking so long. I don't know why he isn't sharing it with the volunteers, but he isn't, and we're doing the best we can. As far as I know, Vivian and Niles want to get the show moving because it's already over half an hour late."

"Don't they know fashion shows are always late? They shouldn't make those decisions. They work for ME and should tell ME these things."

Francie turned from clueless Jekyll to Ms. Fashion-Hyde before my eyes. I'd originally slated her as slightly incompetent, immature, and a bit naïve, but had given her the benefit of the doubt for the sake of a career change. Working with her was a learning experience, an exercise in how not to behave.

Yelling back at Francie would have compounded her anger, so I tried to provide a calm explanation. "Francie, if you wore a headset, we could communicate and get your advice for this type of situation. Since you aren't wearing one, we can only do what we feel is best because we need immediate answers and it usually takes fifteen minutes to find you."

"I have no time to discuss this with you now because I have to find Veronikkah. She has a speech and I have to be sure she's ready. And for your information, I cannot wear a headset because it will ruin my hair and I must look good for the press. Veronikkah told me that."

She turned away, walking straight into a mass of people competing for the best seats. They pushed each other, yelled, and tore at clothes. A string of pearls fell and rolled over the floor, causing two people to slip. It wasn't the sophisticated fashion audience I'd expected at Collections Week; instead, the crowd resembled English football hooligans, though slightly better dressed. There was no way I wanted to be in the middle, fighting for my life, so I found a safe space by the passage between backstage and runway room and let the mob fight for seats.

<<Attention all volunteers! This is Gigi. I'm in the runway room and I can't get out. I can't hear walkie-talkies anymore because it's so loud. The show is about to start, so keep doing your best and we'll reconnect after. By the way, Francie is looking for Veronikkah to give a speech, so if you see her, send her backstage. Good luck.>>

People were still entering as the lights dimmed while obnoxious, migraine-inducing house music pounded over the speakers. It was dated techno with a large bass voice informing us, "Collections Week, C'est Chic!" Was that song made specifically for Collections Week? It was a sad statement when a supposedly cutting-edge event had a soundtrack that sounded like 2 Unlimited's "Get Ready for This." It could have been interpreted as an avant-garde retro nod, but from what I saw from their personal styles and work ethics, Francie and Veronikkah didn't have the skills to be ironically cool.

The lights changed from pink to purple and whirled around in sync with the song. The effect transported me back to rave days when ecstasy was called "X," making it hard not to laugh at the outdated spectacle. Even seasoned veterans ChiChi and Lucinda stifled giggles in their front row seats on opposite sides of the runway.

Mr. Announcer boomed overhead, "ARE YOU READY FOR COLLECTIONS WEEK?"

He was obviously trained by carnies from the fair ride where they yell, "DO YOU WANT TO GO FASTER!" He received no guest response. No self-respecting fashion crowd would show the remotest sense of excitement for that particular exercise.

The announcer wasn't the only one floundering. Veronikkah was in the wings preparing to take the stage. Francie stood behind, supporting her boss. I envisioned the forthcoming disaster: Veronikkah would trip onto the runway and pass out during her speech. How had Collections Week managed to get this far under her misguidance? It was only my first show and already I knew a million ways to improve the event.

Mr. Announcer yelled, "Please put your hands together for Ms. Veronikkah Hendricks, the Collections Week director."

Half the crowd clapped sloppily, as people do when they have a drink in one hand and programme in another. There was near silence as Lola pushed Veronikkah up the stairs to the runway. Luckily the momentum of the push propelled Veronikkah to the podium, giving her something stable to hold on to as she prepared to speak.

She smiled and looked around, as a queen might address her court. It hit me that perhaps this was a real-life case of "The Emperor's New Clothes". The Emperor was a fashion show coordinator, and the new clothes were an event. Nobody had the courage to tell that woman her event was a disaster and she dragged it down with her own disorganization.

Veronikkah kept smiling a moment too long, making her seem spaced out, but she managed to deliver an elegant and inspiring speech about promoting fashion as an intellectual and commercial pursuit. She spoke well, and at the end of her two-minute talk, some people actually cheered. I also stood up taller and felt a sense of pride at being involved in the event. Maybe she wasn't as bad as I thought.

As Veronikkah left the stage, volunteers took the podium away and I saw Veronikkah lose her balance. About to fall down the stairs, she grabbed for the wall. Unfortunately it wasn't a wall. It was a scrim that was thin enough to topple. Luckily Francie anticipated the potential disaster and jumped to her aid. She helped her down the stairs and they disappeared backstage.

The lights dimmed, accompanied by a rare remix of the dance song *du jour*. Everyone was excited until the runway lit up with ultra-white light. An audible gasp came from the first row, and the immediate reaction was to shield one's eyes from the sun. I adjusted to the light after a few seconds and realized the runway had to be bright for good photos, but because of the shock, most of us missed the first model's entrance. Eventually everyone's eyes adapted after the model was halfway up the catwalk. It wasn't until the model reached the end and stopped for her second pose that Mr. Announcer yelled, "Ladies and gentlemen, we present to you the latest collection by Mr. Antoine Mistou, called Rise."

The opening night gala publicity had announced a top-secret designer. Collections Week wanted to keep everyone guessing, but I'd found out from Francie a few days before the event they had not confirmed anybody. I was so busy running around all day, I didn't have a chance to check who finally confirmed. Antoine Mistou was the perfect start to the week.

He was a fashion bad-boy, and though it's a label overused in the industry, he classified an *enfant terrible*. It was only his third season with his own line, Rise, but everyone loved him. He was a media and socialite darling, though he was always rude in interviews, acting as though he was in a higher realm than the interviewer. Nevertheless, his garments were gorgeously tailored, creative, and despite his young age of 23, he already had a signature style.

His previous season's collection had been inspired by death, Satan, and heaviness. The palate was a series of blacks, reds, and wines with some rich blood-berry tones. The collection was lauded in all the major magazines and earned him a *Fashion Television* featurette. The collection he was unveiling at Collections Week was opposite, however, showing lightness, rebirth, and spirituality. The clothes were white and transluscent. They were gorgeous: each model emitting an angelic radiance.

The girls floated down the runway in layers of light fabrics. With extra-long sleeves and asymmetrical skirts flirting between micro-mini and matronly, Mistou's models were other-worldly. Their faces had a dewy, just-woke-up glow, highlighted with sparkly appliqués. The models had individually styled crystal webs in their hair, making each one an elf-fairy-angel princess. They embodied power, confidence, and calmness, emitting a soothing effect on the crowd. Everyone was quiet, mesmerized by the collection. It was an unbelievable experience, yet unnerving to witness how the combined spectacle of clothing, beautiful women, music, and lighting could affect a crowd. Each girl who walked the runway seemed to get more beautiful and graceful as she walked.

Just I thought it couldn't get any better, it did. The menswear scene began with Mistou's first male angel. He looked assured, protective, and forgiving, and as he walked past me, I realized it was Hot Dan. He moved confidently, not arrogantly, but with slight vulnerability. He played the angel-muse well. And his outfit was amazing: he wore an elegantly deconstructed suit jacket, which flowed down the back, echoing wings, without looking like a cheesy raver kid. His trousers were cut and sewn in such a way they were capri pants one minute, and then looked like trousers with another leg movement. Without a doubt, Mistou was a magician, an artist. Not only did he understand garment construction, but he knew how to create a show, from accessories to models. I knew everyone in the room wanted to be able to study each piece individually. The clothes demanded to be touched, not looked at. The collection was unbelievable, and I could tell from faces in the audience I was not the only person who felt the importance of his work.

As Mistou's world swept me away, the runway went black, and a recorded voice recited some Bible verse about damnation. The way I interpreted it, we were all going to Hell. That didn't seem such a good way to end a show. I didn't think it wise to scare or threaten people when you relied on them to buy your clothes.

I looked around the audience, finally noticing who was there. From what I could tell, the only fabulous people were journalists like Chloe Kirkpatrick. Everyone else looked conspicuously like Francie and Darryl, dressed in mall clothes. The rest of the crowd wore fashion-safe Banana Republic black suits. It was obvious they'd gone to the show directly from bank jobs. I didn't see any well-known socialites, let alone publicity-hungry stars. As much as I hated the idea of seeing ignorant celebrities chat about fashion without garment construction knowledge, I thought a few famous, sparkly people in the audience would have made an exciting night.

What's more, the entire show was only twelve minutes long. All of today's hard work was for twelve minutes? We made people stand around for an extra forty-five minutes for twelve minutes? From the clips I saw on television, I believed fashion shows were huge spectacles complete with sets, entertainment, hors d'oeuvres, and fabulous people. Nevertheless, I thought back to those beautiful, intelligent clothes and realized the day's craziness was worth the reward.

EVALUATE.

As people began to leave the runway room, I ran backstage to find a quiet spot to contact everyone via walkie-talkie. Instead, I found the *Watership Down* rabbit-girl ordering people around and yelling at Niles. He saw me and made a "What can I do?" face.

I was about to intervene when I bumped into Francie. "Remind Eva to bring the programs to the press conference tomorrow morning," she said.

"What programs? Who's Eva?"

"She's in charge of backstage, and our most valuable volunteer. She's over there talking to Niles." So the rabbit-girl's name was Eva.

"If she's a volunteer, why haven't I met her yet?"

"She's working with me. She's my right-hand girl and my best friend."

"I'm confused. I thought Niles was in charge of backstage."

"Well, he and Vivian think so, but I don't trust them. Eva's volunteered with us since Collections Week started. On the record, she's in charge of hair and makeup, but technically, she's in charge of backstage."

"Isn't that confusing? Won't there be some communication mix-ups?" Since they were friends, I didn't tell her Eva had already contributed to the show's late start.

"It'll be okay. Just remind her to get the programs. Here's her cell number." Francie pressed a piece of paper into my hand.

Since we were only a few steps away from Eva, I asked, "Why can't you remind her?"

"Because Veronikkah and I are going to the after-party. We must be present at every event all week. Good night." She walked out, leaving me exasperated and confused.

Guests were still milling around. Didn't she and Veronikkah have to preside over the event until all the guests left? My walkie-talkie buzzed me out of confusion, so I moved to a quieter backstage corner.

<<Gregor to Gigi. What's happening?>>

<<To be honest, Gregor, I don't know. I assume most people will leave because the show's over.>>

<<Well, the bar in the designer gallery is open and tons of people are coming in. It's like they all got out of rehab; they're heading straight for the bar.>>

<<I guess we should let them continue to drink and have a good time. Francie and Veronikkah didn't provide instructions on what to do next. They're leaving to do business offsite, putting us in charge. What do you think? Can your volunteers monitor the designer gallery?>>

<<Yeah, no problem. But some are taking breaks.>>

<<Okay, when people are finished in other sections, I'll send them to you.>>

<<Sounds good.>>

<<Gigi to Chantelle.>>

<<Chantelle here.>>

<<How are things up front?>>

<<We cleaned everything up during the show. I think we're finished.>>

<<Great. Why don't you send your volunteers to Gregor while you check in with Josh L.? Make sure you keep the guest records from tonight.>>

<<Will do.>>

<<Did you get that, Gregor?>>

<<Yes. I'll get Chantelle's volunteers. Thanks, sweetness.>>

<<Excellent. I'll check on the runway room to see if I can get any more people for you.>>

I was about to go back to the runway room when I remembered Niles and Eva the evil rabbit-girl. They were arguing and Niles was exhausted.

Stepping between them, I put on my brightest smile, extended my hand and said, "Excuse me, I'm sorry to interrupt, but my name is Gigi. I'm the volunteer coordinator. Francie told me you're looking after hair and makeup."

She stared through me and after a moment she snarled. It could have been a, "Hi," but I couldn't tell.

Slightly scared of her bark, I continued. "Francie gave me a message to make sure you get the programs to the press conference tomorrow. Do you know what she was talking about?"

"Yes."

"Okay, well, she gave me your cell phone number. Should I call you later to remind you?"

"No."

Could she speak more than a syllable? She wasn't the warmest person I'd ever met. I had no idea what had happened, but there was a tense atmosphere around them. I looked at Niles, who was calm on the outside, but I noticed his hands were clenched into fists so tight his knuckles had turned white.

I had to intervene and save Niles. "I hope you don't mind, but we need to talk for a moment," I said, pulling Niles away from Eva before she had time to respond. If we lived in a cartoon world, Eva would have turned red with smoke exploding from her ears.

"Thanks, Gigi," sighed Niles.

"You're welcome. I didn't know whether I should get involved, but I thought things weren't looking good."

"I have no idea who that girl is. She says she's in charge of backstage and now you just said she's in charge of hair and makeup. I'm confused, and it's no good because we have to pack everything up and get all the clothes out of here in good order, or the designer is going to kill us. I have a system of checklists I use, but that girl is just sending everyone out without checking."

"To be honest, I just met her, as you saw. Prior to that, Francie told me she is 'officially' in charge of hair and makeup, but 'unofficially' in charge of backstage. I don't really know what that means, so take that information and act on it how you will."

"What am I supposed to do with that? Is she paid? If any of the designer's clothes or accessories walk out on a model, I'm to blame. I'm getting paid."

"She's not paid, so you have to stand your ground. I don't know who has authority over this. If you're a paid staff member, I think it should be you. But since I'm the volunteer coordinator and she's a volunteer, it's my problem. Then again, she's Francie's friend, so I don't know what to do. If it's unbearable, maybe we should both approach Francie. Keep me updated, and if I have to step in, I will, but now I've got to check on the runway room and make sure it's getting cleaned up."

"Okay, thanks Gigi. I'll let you know how it goes."

"Good luck. Oh, and when you're finished here, tell Lola to call me. She can't dismiss her volunteers until I know that we have enough to deal with the leftover guests. We need as many people as possible in the designer gallery."

"Will do," said Niles as he approached Eva the evil rabbit-girl. They both tensed as they neared each other - as cats do - so I suspected things wouldn't work out easily. Nevertheless, I had to check on the runway room.

When I got there, volunteers were clearing discarded gift bag remnants. I told the volunteers to take any leftovers since they worked so hard. They were so impressed, and many were positively giddy from the experience, even though a couple of them said the guests had pushed them out of the way when they were directed to seats. A volunteer even told me Philipo Snively, a well-known stylist from New York, took a swing at her when she told him to wait. Apparently he stuck his hand in her face and yelled, "Back off, bitch!" When she tried to make him wait, he almost hit her, but she ducked. Though she took her volunteer position seriously, she didn't want to get injured, so she let him do what he wanted.

I was appalled. Wasn't fashion about sophistication and elegance? The crowd demonstrated neither quality, and I worried about the volunteers. What would happen the next nights? I told them to report any similar incidents to me in the future, and encouraged them to take more gift bag leftovers, hoping it would make them feel better.

It didn't take long for volunteers to clean up the mess. Most guests had left the runway room, so the technical crew packed up and went home. We straightened all the chairs for the next day so I figured the runway room crew was finished for the night. I approached Josh L. to get final approval on team dismissal before reassigning volunteers to the designer gallery.

"Oh, no. They can't leave. They have to stay until every guest is gone," he told me.

"Isn't there security or paid staff to check on that through the evening?" I asked.

"No, that's a volunteer duty. Hey, do they have *gift bags*?" He delivered the words snobbishly.

"Yeah, there were a lot of perfume samples on the floor, so I told them they could keep whatever was left over."

"Oh, no no no. They can't do that. What if I need them later?"

"That's the least we can do for these volunteers. They have been here for over eight hours without barely a break. We practically had to fight to get them water. They've been on their feet the whole time, and haven't complained once. A guest almost assaulted one girl. If you want to go and tell them they can't have a few of the tiny perfume samples the guests discarded, then go ahead. But I'm not going to be the one to tell them."

He looked at me with a look of unexpected shock and compassion. "Someone hit a volunteer?"

"Philipo Snively almost did, but she ducked out of the way."

"Okay, you're right. They can keep the samples. It's just that all leftovers are supposed to go to Veronikkah and Francie."

"They left for a party. Pardon me if I speak out of line, but if they cared that much about perfume samples, they would be here to monitor the event. Since they aren't here, I'm sure it's fine." I looked at the exhausted volunteers, sitting down for the first time that day, about to pass out. "Look at them. They've done a great job and that job is now finished in the runway room. Plus, I need people in the designer gallery because that's where most of the guests are, and we can't have stolen items. Can I just keep two here and send the other ten to the gallery?"

He looked at the girls and understood what I said. "Okay, that sounds fine."

"Thanks."

I went back to the girls and told them the plan, apologizing about the long day. Surprisingly, they all smiled and said they'd had a blast, making me extremely happy...amazed, but happy. Even though I thought the organization was a disaster, other people still thought things were okay. Maybe I was too hard on Francie and Veronikkah because I'd managed huge projects before. Maybe I simply had to adjust to a new industry.

Ten girls went to the designer gallery with me, while two others stayed back. I couldn't believe the crowd when I went to the front entrance and into the Gallery. There were tons of people and by that time, half were drunk and it felt like a club. Unfortunately, it wasn't a club I wanted to go to. It was more of a meat (or is that meet) market than a post-fashion show party. I was happy to see Chantelle had cleaned up Reception and helped Gregor. But I was unhappy to see drunken guests running into mannequins. At least the volunteers were quick enough to either protect the clothes or grab the drinks out of people's hands in time, but I didn't know how long the luck would last. Even though we were volunteers, we were liable for the merchandise. A red wine stain on a garment meant death for us; I didn't want to deal with Veronikkah's wrath.

I delivered the ten volunteers to Gregor and asked him where the designers were.

"They left during the fashion show. Veronikkah told them nobody would be in this room after ten o'clock."

"Then why are people here?"

"I don't know. They just came in. Veronikkah wanted the bar open; it doesn't make sense. So now they're drinking and dancing. How long do you think they'll stay, and more important, when are they supposed to leave?"

"I have no clue. I'm sure Francie and Veronikkah have that answer, but they're gone. I don't know what we're supposed to do. Maybe I'll ask Niles and Vivian."

<<Gigi to Niles.>>

<<Go for Niles.>>

<<Do you or Vivian know anything about an after after party?>>

<<No. We're only hired for the shows. I don't know who deals with the after party. Where is it?>>

<<Well, one seems to have taken hold in the designer gallery. Everyone is here and we don't know how long they're supposed to stay. We're worried about all the garments because guests are getting drunk. I'm so scared someone will ruin an evening gown on display. I don't know what to do.>>

<<Why don't you check with venue staff?>>

<<Excellent suggestion. Thank you.>>

<<No problem. Also, we're almost finished cleaning up here. The designer went home with all his clothes and accessories, so that's all taken care of. The models, hairstylists, and makeup artists all left, but you and I should talk about Eva.>>

<<Okay, but we can't do that now. How about a meeting when things calm down?>>

<<Perfect.>>

Gregor and Chantelle heard everything, so they took their new volunteers while I asked the bartender about the night.

"I'm supposed to be here until two in the morning," he said.

"Two o'clock?" I gasped. We'd been there since seven in the morning and had to stay until two o'clock? We had to be back at nine the next morning. None of us would sleep for the entire week.

For the first time that day, I actually stopped to take a breath, and noticed a Corbusier-inspired sofa calling me. The chrome forms suggested an obvious knockoff, but at that point I wasn't picky about what sofa I would sit on. It still looked good, and was a decent reproduction. Would it really hurt anybody if I sat for a minute? I'd been on my feet all day; I deserved a rest. Without contemplating it further, I sank into the sofa and realized it was a mistake. There was no way I would be able to stand up ever again.

"Sitting down on the job, I see," breathed a husky voice, flirtingly close to my ear. A glass of white wine magically appeared.

I turned around to see Hot Dan holding the wine.

"You need this drink. Take it."

"Thanks, but I'm working. I don't think I should drink on the job."

"Why not? The person in charge obviously does. Besides, I saw Veronikkah and Francie leave a long time ago. It's fashion. Nobody will care."

He was right. I deserved a drink. I took the glass from him and said, "The least you can do is keep a lady company while she snatches a secret drink." At least I composed myself enough to flirt.

"If you insist," he said, sitting beside me. Words could not describe the man's beauty, and I impressed myself with my ability to actually talk to him normally, though I reminded myself to stay cool.

"You're an angel for bringing me a drink," I giggled.

He blushed. I couldn't believe I'd made him blush!

He laughed, looked at the floor, and said, "Don't give me grief about that angel crap. You should have seen the designer before the show. He was running around, flapping his arms, and singing, 'You're an angel; you're heavenly! You'll inspire your audience!' It was so cheesy."

Maybe from his point of view the show was cheesy, but it was magical to me. "To be honest, it wasn't cheesy at all. You guys were fantastic. The show was truly inspirational."

"Seriously?" he asked.

"For sure. The clothes were gorgeous, and the models were amazing. Before you guys came out, the audience was out of control. Everyone was pushy and rude. It was horrible. But when the first model came out, she calmed everyone down."

It was clear he didn't believe me, so I stopped. I wasn't about to tell him how hot he was, because then I'd slip into stalker territory.

"Well, you weren't too bad, either. I saw you running around all day solving problems. I also heard people talking about what a great organizer you are."

"Really? I thought I was just running around without a direction. I've never felt more disorganized in my life."

I heard a buzzing in my ear.

It was Gregor. <<It appears our coordinator is neglecting her duties. She's too concerned with a model to be helping the volunteers.>>

Hot Dan was saying something to me, but I couldn't hear him because Chantelle chimed in.

<<She just wants to make sure she wins the bet. Are you enjoying the wine, Gigi?>>

I looked around and saw the two of them grinning at me from the other end of the room.

Lola joined in harassing me. <<Is that the same hot guy from this morning? I dressed him tonight and got to see him in his underwear.>>

Then Gregor said, <<I'll bet Gigi will be seeing it soon!>>

I couldn't stand it anymore. Knowing Hot Dan couldn't hear any part of the conversation, I said, <<Maybe I've already seen it!>> Then it was my turn to blush and giggle. I looked at Chantelle and Gregor, who hugged each other, laughed, and waved. Hot Dan looked at me as if I had Tourette's.

"It's hard to have a conversation when you have a walkie-talkie buzzing in your ear," I explained.

"Is it your first time using a walkie-talkie?"

"Yeah. Oh my god. Could you tell I was a walkie-virgin? It's weird. I've been having a million conversations all at the same time today."

"No, you're a complete professional." He said this as Lola and Niles entered the gallery with their volunteers.

As they passed, Niles said into the walkie, <<Way to go, Gigi. That guy was my favourite model from today. Judging from how he looked in his underwear, I'd say he has a huge cock.>>

"Ack!" was my only reaction, apart from choking on my wine, nearly spitting a mouthful out on Hot Dan. That would not have been the best way to get him. I looked away and noticed everyone on a walkie was crying from laughter. The situation was ridiculous and although I wanted nothing else than to talk with Hot Dan all night and gaze into his eyes, I ended the teasing. Otherwise I was sure I'd mix up my walkie conversation with my Hot Dan conversation and say something completely embarrassing. Plus most of the guests were either leaving or hovering near the bar by that point. They weren't a threat to the displays any more.

"Listen, Dan. Thank you so much for the wine and the chat. It was a wonderful way to end this crazy day. But right now I've got to try to clear people out of here and meet with my team."

"No problem. I just wanted you to know you did an amazing job." He leaned over, brushed my hair away from my eyes and kissed my forehead.

Oh my god. He kissed my forehead! HE KISSED MY FOREHEAD! Why, oh why didn't we make out? He was sure to be an amazing kisser. I contemplated grabbing his jacket lapels and dragging him closer to me, but he stood up. "It was nice meeting you. See you tomorrow."

Snapping myself out of my kissing fantasy, I asked, "Oh, are you working tomorrow?"

"Yeah, I'm working at practically all the menswear shows."

"Then I guess we'll be seeing a lot of each other."

"I guess so. Bye sweetie." He winked, turned, and walked away. Damn! No straight guy ever calls a girl sweetie the first day he meets her. But my heart still fluttered as he walked across the room, looking like a British rock star. Damn again! Did he just cruise another model-boy?

He wasn't even out the door before Gregor, Chantelle, Lola, and Niles pounced on me.

"Ooooooh, girl!" said Niles with a jaunty finger-snap.

I smacked his shoulder. "How could you say that about him as you walked by? I nearly choked."

"The Heimlich manoeuvre would have been a good excuse to get his arms around you," laughed Gregor.

"You've got a dreamy look in your eyes, there, kiddo," said Niles. "Be careful. I heard he has a boyfriend."

A boyfriend? How could he? Sure he was the hottest guy I'd seen in real life, and hot usually equals gay, but he'd acted quite straight a few moments before. My heart sank because although I was ga-ga over the guy, Niles knew his gay guys better than I did. I resolved to be a better sleuth when it came to Hot Dan, and by the end of the week, I'd know for sure. Until then, I had to guard my heart. Although I loved hanging out with my boys, I did also enjoy sleeping with them once in a while. It didn't matter how hot Dan was; I didn't want another gay boyfriend. I wanted a real one.

Wait, what was I thinking? I didn't want a boyfriend. I valued my independence. I liked doing whatever I wanted after work. I enjoyed hosting cocktail and manicure parties for my girlfriends. I always laughed at furniture shopping couples with the bored guy and the girl dragging him around to different sofas and chairs, chatting about different colour combinations. Why didn't girls ever notice that guys were ready to poke their eyes out after too much armoire talk? I never wanted to be part of that. My life was practically a guyatus (a hiatus from guys), unless I needed them for some reason or other, with that reason usually being sex or needing some carpentry done. I was a sophisticated, urban single girl all the way. But something about Hot Dan made me forget my self-imposed rules.

I snapped out of my thoughts and pleaded, "Leave me alone! You guys are all awful! But since you're here, why don't we debrief the day? Let's clear guests away from the displays and send the volunteers home. We can sit here, talk, and keep an eye on things at the same time."

Everyone agreed, so we dismissed the volunteers and contained the drunken guests closer to the bar. At one in the morning, most drunk people are either obnoxious or compliant. Luckily for us, these ones were compliant, so we started our meeting.

We gathered around the group of Corbusier replicas.

"First things first," I said. "Thanks for helping today. I don't know what I would have done without you; you were truly amazing. Thank you. For your hard work, I'll treat you to a drink while we debrief. Get yourselves to the bar!"

When we settled, Niles spoke first. "I want to thank you, Gigi. Without you, I don't know how we would have done anything. Veronikkah and Francie didn't help at all. Even though they were the organizers, they didn't do anything other than schmooze and get made up. I've worked this event for the past three seasons and this was the smoothest, which is thanks to your team."

We all looked at each other and smiled, giddy from the compliment.

"Seriously?" I asked. "Because I had no guidance either. We only did what we thought best."

"Well, you're smart people because your best was amazing. You make a stellar team. You were organized, worked with an effective chain of command with Gigi solving logistical problems. I'd say you were a strong, disciplined team, but disciplined in a fun way. I look forward to working the rest of the week with you."

I was proud to hear I'd succeeded at my first fashion event and had arranged an excellent team. What's more, it was encouraging to hear someone else realize Veronikkah and Francie's incompetence. I worried that was how the entire industry operated, but it was nice to hear other people felt the same way I did.

We shared stories of highs and lows from the day, but overall, everyone was on a high, chatting for an hour until the guests left. It was two o'clock in the morning, but we weren't tired; we were rejuvenated from the day's excitement and happy to be there. Eventually we left, looking forward to regrouping the next day for the morning press conference.

ORGANIZE.

Models scurried in various states of undress, electronic music thundered overhead, and corsets flew everywhere. Jean-Paul Gauthier flitted about, freaking, muttering French obscenities. Nobody understood him while he screamed, cried, and tore at clothes. Finally I looked at a model, realized she had no shoes, put some red stilettos on her, and shoved her onto the runway. Jean-Paul threw his arms around me, handed me a glass of champagne, then kept me in tow through his post-show interviews, claiming I was the goddess who saved his show. I shone in the magical glory of camera lights, smiling and giddy. Everyone buzzed around, music blasted louder, ringing in my ears, making me dizzy.

That wasn't ringing the song; it was my phone. Jean-Paul's praise was a mere dream. He left me back in my apartment at six twenty-five in the morning. My alarm was set for six-thirty.

I picked up the phone and mumbled, "Hello?" in early-morning groggy voice.

"Gigi, it's Francie. Where are you?"

"I'm at home. You're calling on my landline." I'd just woken up after three and a half hours sleep and was still smarter than her.

"Why aren't you at the venue?"

"I thought the press conference was at ten o'clock. Lola, Gregor, Chantelle, and I will be there at eight, and the rest of the volunteers arrive at nine. We discussed this last week."

"You should be there now!" She was freaking out.

"Why? What's going on?"

"You should just be there!"

"Francie, I'm sure everything will be fine. We stayed until close last night and cleaned up the Carlu. Two hours should be enough preparation time, shouldn't it?"

"I want you there."

"Okay, I just woke up, so I'll get there as soon as I can, which will probably be seven-thirty." Though she frustrated me, I felt honoured she relied on me to do a good job, that I was doing something so important for fashion in my first industry experience. So I hopped out of bed, cranked some feel-good music on my stereo and prepared for the second day at Collections Week.

The phone rang again. "Hello?" I asked.

"It's Francie. Did you get those programs?"

"Programs? Oh, right. Eva got them."

"No, she told me you would get them."

"No, both of you told me she would take care of them. I know nothing about them, except that I reminded her about them last night."

"That's not what she told me, and she's been working with me for so long."

"I'm sorry, Francie, I don't have the programs, and I told you what I know."

She hung up.

I continued with my makeup, although the second phone conversation had sapped some of my excitement. The feel-good music pissed me off.

Then the phone rang. Again, it was Francie.

"Something happened and I need you to get the programs." She was worried, her tone serious.

"What happened?"

"Ummm..." she paused. She tried to think of something to tell me.

"Francie, just say it. It's best to be honest with your colleague and let me know what's going on."

"Okay. But don't tell anyone. We lost the sponsor car with most of the programs." A luxury car company provided all the Collections Week vehicles. The company probably never thought someone could lose a car.

"What? Why did you ask me about the programs if you knew Eva had them in the car?"

"Well…we kind of hoped you had extras."

"Was the car stolen?"

"No."

"How do you lose a car?"

"Ummm..." again, she tried to think of something to say. Lying is not a great personality trait, but sometimes it is necessary. Francie was a terrible liar.

"Since Eva had the programs, did she lose the car?" I asked.

"Well, not exactly. We were just out last night, and, ummm...I can't give you the details."

I was only a volunteer, but Francie and Eva tried to make me a scapegoat. Since I wanted to do a good job, though, I had to offer to help them. I also felt sorry for them for being so stupid.

"Here's the thing," Francie said. "You can go to my office and pick up some extra programs and take them to the venue."

"I can do that, Francie, but didn't you tell me you live five minutes away from your office? I live a forty-five minute walk from your office. Couldn't you just pick them up on your way in?"

"Guess so," she grumbled and hung up.

What had I done wrong? I thought I was only being smart by saving time, but I guess logic didn't make sense to Francie. The phone rang again.

"Can you just take a cab?" Francie asked. "I'll reimburse you today."

"Yes, I can take a cab, but doesn't it make more logistical sense for you to get them?"

"Well, I'm not exactly at home…"

"Where are you? At the venue already?"

"No, I didn't stay at home last night," she said with that mix of guilt and pride a girl has after a raunchy night out.

I wasn't thrilled at doing Francie's work while she recuperated from a night of good sex, even if it was with slimy Darryl, but I had to be nice to the girl. After all, this was my foot into the door of the fashion industry. Against my gut instinct to tell her to do it herself, I agreed to get the programs and explained it would make me late.

"That's fine," she said, hanging up on me.

After retrieving the programs from Francie's office and still arriving first at the venue again, I relived yesterday's craziness. After a day, I felt experienced with fashion shows; yesterday's set up was a thousand years ago. No doubt I'd found my natural habitat, even if it was infested with schizophrenic coordinators.

Looking around, I tried to visualize the press conference location since neither Francie nor Veronikkah had told me where it was. The runway room was the logical choice since it had the AV system and chairs, so that was where I took all the programs. Everything was as clean and immaculate as we'd left it, so I walked into the designer gallery to check on the displays and ran into a short, blonde woman.

"Good morning, can I help you?" I asked.

"No, I'm good," she said.

For all I knew, she planned to steal all the display items, so I needed to know who she was. "I'm Gigi, the volunteer coordinator."

She fell for my ploy and introduced herself. "I'm Patsy, the event planner."

Event planner? I didn't know there was a separate event planner. I thought Veronikkah and Francie did that. If she was the event planner, where had she been the day before, and why didn't anyone tell me about her? Thinking back to day one, I realized how many people popped up without Francie mentioning who worked where.

"I didn't know there was an event planner," I said.

"Dear, do you think this thing could be run without an event planner?" she laughed with a condescending giggle.

I didn't like her tone. I could tell she would treat me like a five-year-old during all our interactions. Her clothes were offensive, too. With jeans so tight, Camel Toe was a compliment.

I stood taller to make her feel less superior and said, "Oh, the event started yesterday. I didn't see you around, so I assumed Veronikkah and Francie were the event planners."

Ms. Camel Toe gave her condescending giggle again and said, "Oh, I'm sooooo busy these days. Yesterday I had to organize a luncheon and premiere party for Natasha Slovonovich. It was very important." She stressed the "very" with a faux-English accent.

"I love Natasha Slovonovich! She's so cool," I said, trying not to be star struck by association. "I love that she can act, write, sing, and make music. She's so talented. What was she like? Was she nice?"

"Unfortunately, she couldn't attend," Ms. Camel Toe replied, implying she'd planned it that way.

How could she organize an event for someone who didn't even attend? And why did that take her away from Collections Week? I suspected it was a sore point for the woman, so I didn't pursue it, but instead asked, "Well, should we set up the press conference."

She looked at me as though I'd extinguished a cigarette in her hand. "I <u>don't</u> set up." She said, stressing the "don't" with the same faux accent as earlier. "I am the person who thinks up the ideas. I'm the idea-person. I bring in the concepts."

I got it the first time. She didn't have to repeat herself. Then again, maybe she did. Judging from her Natasha experience, she probably had to reiterate her ideas a million times to get important people to attend her events. I got the hint she wasn't going to be helpful, but I had to ask if she knew where the press conference would be.

"It's Veronikkah's job to determine that. I come up with the concepts. I'm the one with the ideas," she said again.

The woman had some sort of issue with her career, but I didn't have time to debate the merits of being an ideas-person, so I asked, "Should we call her then? I don't have her phone number, so could you call her to find out? It's almost eight o'clock, which means we only have two hours to set up."

"Oh, I can't do that. I have strict orders never to call Ms. Hendricks before nine o'clock." She was a trained sycophantic puppy dog.

"Isn't this an emergency? We should really get started. She'll probably be up anyway."

Ms. Camel Toe looked at me with another odd expression. This time it was as though I'd killed a baby. "I can't do that. One must always do as Ms. Hendricks says. I have strict orders."

Given the disorganization and incompetence I'd experienced since starting with Collections Week, I was not feeling as tolerant as usual. The woman was clearly a waste of skin and I figured she wouldn't help anyone. Not only did she miss the first day of a week-long event she'd supposedly planned, but she had no clue what was supposed to happen and was scared to ask. Why were people so scared of Veronikkah Hendricks? Sure, she was mean and crass, but she forgot everything she said or was said to her. Unfortunately, though, I didn't have her phone number. I finally had Francie's cell phone number, but her phone went to voice mail automatically. Once again I had to make important planning decisions on my own for an event I didn't know much about. Luckily, my team arrived.

"Good morning, cupcake!"

"Hey Gregor," I replied with a hug, introducing him to Ms. Camel Toe. She gave us a half-smile and went to tour the venue.

"What's with those jeans?" whispered Gregor. "I thought this was a fashion event."

"Shhh...Gregor, watch what you say. You never know who's around, and you don't want to offend anyone," I said, then added to myself, "even if the outfit is horrible."

"I don't understand," whined Gregor. "I expected the most stylish people in the country to be here. Last night, I only saw four interesting outfits. We're the best dressed people here, and we're wearing these trashy tank tops."

I agreed. The fashion police would have had a full detention centre with the previous night's crowd.

"You know, Gregor, I visited a museum in a small German town once. It was the Museum of Crime and Punishment, and my favourite things were the fashion crimes."

"They seriously had fashion crimes?" Gregor asked.

"Totally. If you can believe it, people were punished if they wore collars too long or too short. If they were caught, they had to wear wooden collars for at least a day."

Gregor smiled and clapped his hands. "We should bring that back. Who would we start with?"

"How would it look for the Collections Week director to be charged with a fashion crime and be stuck with a wooden collar during the event?"

Gregor and I laughed so hard we didn't notice Chantelle and Lola arrive, but when we did, Gregor filled them in. They both thought Francie should wear the wooden collar first. After giggling a bit longer, we arranged programs on all the runway room chairs.

Eventually Ms. Camel Toe walked in and demanded to know what we were doing. While she wasn't looking, Gregor mouthed, "Camel Toe" and mimed a wooden collar behind her back. It was hard not to laugh, and even harder to explain logistics to Ms. Camel Toe when she had no idea what we were talking about. She didn't even realize the press conference was that morning; she thought it was in the afternoon.

I heard a light, whimsical voice sing, "Good morning, little volunteers!" Josh L. made his grand entrance twirling a cane. "Are we all ready for the press conference? Where is my little Audrey Hepburn?"

"Here I am!" said Chantelle in an equally sing-songy tone.

"What are you all doing in here?" asked Josh L.

"We're getting ready for the press conference by placing programs on the seats," I explained.

Josh L. looked around and asked, "Here? Oh no! *Quelle horreur!* We're having the press conference in the designer gallery. And what are these program things?"

I explained the program fiasco and why we were setting up in the runway room.

Josh L. sighed, "I swear I love that Veronikkah Hendricks, but sometimes she's a bit...uhhh, foggy. She must get some better help. Three days ago, I told Francie these programs were no good. Spelling mistakes. And look… they're lavender. Lavender was so last season."

"We can't do much now," I said. "We'll have to use them."

Josh L. lamented about lavender while we moved a few hundred chairs and programs into the designer gallery. Ms. Camel Toe watched.

We arranged the last few chairs and programs, making the designer gallery look fantastic. It was a grand, wide hallway, elegant and calm. It was the perfect place to make a large event seem intimate. The designer displays made a beautiful backdrop for a press conference about clothing designers. At least Veronikkah and Francie were right about something.

As we congratulated ourselves on good work, the remaining volunteers arrived, so we allocated duties. It was quarter after nine and everyone was in place in the front entrance and designer gallery when Veronikkah walked in.

"What is this?" she shrieked.

Josh L. ran up to her and explained we were ready for the press conference.

"No!" she screamed, waving her hand in his face. "It's supposed to be in the runway room! Change it now! Where's Francie? She's in charge of the press conference!"

Josh L. tried to calm her down while her face turned a strange purple colour. He explained how everything was ready to go and looked fantastic in the designer gallery. We'd even tested the P.A. system.

"No!" she screamed again. "It's not right! It must be in the runway room!"

"But Veronikkah, sweetie. The press will arrive in fifteen minutes. Can't we just do it here?"

"No! No! No!"

I had to admit the woman had a strong vision. It was an admirable trait until it destroyed one's rational capacity. Clearly Veronikkah's vision went beyond reason.

<<Gigi here. Everyone listen carefully. You aren't going to believe this, but Veronikkah wants everything back in the runway room. I repeat: the press conference will be in the runway room. Send all your volunteers to move chairs and programs from the designer gallery to the runway room. We'll do it fast so everything will be in place before the media arrives.>>

<<Are you serious?>> Lola groaned.

In fifteen minutes of running back and forth between rooms, we rearranged the venue and moved the chairs and rearranged them in the runway room. We were an amazing team. I thanked all the volunteers and sent them back to their stations.

I took a quick break and sat down on one of the chairs I'd started to despise. It was only nine-thirty in the morning and I was exhausted. Veronikkah walked in. I was sure she would yell at me, but instead, she sat down beside me.

"You. What's your name again?" she asked.

I must have told her my name three times yesterday, but told her once more.

"And you're a volunteer?"

I humoured her and explained who I was.

"What do you think of the event so far?" she asked.

"I think it's great." I lied. I was a horrible liar, knowing Veronikkah could detect my deceit.

"But if you were to improve anything, what would you do?"

Did Veronikkah Hendricks really ask me that? It was flattering - but slightly disturbing - she cared.

"To be honest, Ms. Hendricks, I would improve communication and pre-planning. There were a few mix-ups we could have avoided."

"What were those?"

It was surprising to talk to her one-on-one. She was rational, so calm. Nine-thirty was probably too early for her to start drinking. Due to her sincerity, I told her about Ms. Camel Toe's absence, the mix-up between Eva and Niles, how nobody had introduced the Collections

Week team members to one another, and that there had been no explanation of the press conference.

She paused and said, "You were right. The press conference should be in the designer gallery. It was better in there."

I couldn't believe she said that. "We can't move it now!" I whined. I had to whine; the thought of another set up made me tired, so I pleaded my case. "The media should arrive any minute. It would look awful to allow them to see us move chairs in a panic."

"I appreciate your honesty. We'll leave things as they are. Now where's Francie? I can never find that girl when I need her."

I said I hadn't seen her assistant yet, but I did mention the missing car.

"What?" She yelled. "What happened to the car?" Her face turned purple again.

Uh-oh. I thought Francie had told her since it was such a huge deal, but Francie seemed to keep secrets from her boss. I was going to get her in trouble, but I'd started, so I had to finish the story.

Veronikkah was livid. She didn't say anything else to me, stood up and walked out the room.

<<Lola for Gigi.>>

<<Go for Gigi.>>

<<Models, stylists, and makeup artists are here for the two o'clock show and there's a guy here who wants a modelling job. He's backstage, but not on any lists.>>

<<Well, then, he's probably not a model. Tell him he needs to be on a list. He can come back when he is.>>

<<Thanks.>>

It was time to get on my feet again, so I ensured all volunteers were ready to greet guests. As I suspected, media members schmoozed, and to my surprise, they sipped Champagne and ate breakfast pastries. I wondered who'd arranged that because it was a nice touch. It must have been Veronikkah's idea.

Veronikkah was doing her job, but where was Francie? Fifteen minutes before the press conference, she was nowhere to be found. Shouldn't she have been around to talk to members of the media with Veronikkah? Then again, I was new to this industry. What did I know? From what I could tell, nothing was planned in the fashion business; it was all last minute. Maybe I needed to adjust my expectations. Somehow, though, that didn't seem right. Why would I lower my expectations and quality of my work output just because that was the industry standard? Wouldn't it be better to raise the standard instead?

I hung around the front entrance, ensuring the sign-in process went smoothly, but Josh L. and Chantelle had everything in control. I decided to stay in the vicinity to keep an eye on things and learn about press conferences. I had never been to one before, and was excited to be near people whose work I read or saw while pursuing my fashion obsession.

While I snuck a cream puff, I overheard a conversation between two women.

"Do you know why Collections Week changed venues?" asked one woman with spiky red hair. I guessed she was a newspaper columnist from a smaller city. She just didn't have the right air about her to be a cosmopolitan fashion journalist. She was well-dressed, of course, and her hair was cute, but her Prada shoes were three seasons ago. No fashion journalist in this city would be caught dead with anything more than two seasons old. "I didn't like the other venue last season; it was so far away from downtown."

"Yeah. I heard Veronikkah got in this huge fight with the owner and he said she couldn't take Collections Week back there. Apparently she didn't pay him for the last two years!"

The woman was a fashion-spy, so I tried to hear more by pretending to fix a floral arrangement beside them.

"You know what else I heard?" she continued. "The modelling agencies haven't been paid from last season. Not only that, the big rumour is she never paid people when she owned her company, and that's why she came back home. She got such a bad reputation in London that nobody would work with her. She's good at covering up her past."

"Wow!" exclaimed Spiky. "Oh, and I have to tell you, I saw Veronikkah's assistant, Francie at Hot Stuff yesterday, asking the owners to donate clothes for her and Veronikkah to wear at the Collections Week opening gala."

Hot Stuff was a chic boutique selling clothes so hip, nobody knew the designers. The Hot Stuff buyers found the coolest things before everyone else. Shirts in the store started at a hundred dollars and went up from there. I never bought hundred dollar t-shirts, but the fashion people did. Apparently Francie and Veronikkah wouldn't, though.

Spiky continued, "They wouldn't give her anything, so she threw a tantrum. When she left the store, the owners said they would rather go broke than have those two wear their clothes. How could two people so unstylish be in charge of a fashion event?"

At least I wasn't the only one unimpressed with Francie and Veronikkah's clothing choices.

<<Lola to Gigi.>>

Damn! I would have to miss the good gossip. Not that I like gossip, but a girl never resists a juicy story.

<<Go for Gigi.>>

<<You won't believe this. Remember that model guy I asked you about ten minutes ago? Well, he's now walking around with Veronikkah and she's begging Niles to include him in the shows!>>

<<Really? I thought all model decisions were made weeks ago.>>

<<That's what Niles told me too. I don't know what to do.>>

"I don't know what to do" had quickly became the Collections Week mantra, so I said, <<Just do what Veronikkah wants. No matter how crazy it seems, it is her event and we have to follow her lead. I'm sure you and Niles will figure out how to deal with this. I'll go back there in a minute to give you a hand.>>

<<Thanks, Gigi.>>

I started for backstage and ran into Francie.

"I'm so tired," she moaned. "This is such a hard job."

She thought her job was hard? I had trouble figuring out when she actually did any work, but just said, "Oh, Francie. Veronikkah is looking for you. She's backstage."

Fear crossed her face. She was terrified of her boss.

I continued, "The press conference is ready to go in the runway room. It should probably be starting soon. Anyway, you might want to go find Veronikkah because she's worried about the car."

Francie's eyes bulged. "You told her about the car?"

"I thought she knew. If it happened to me, I'd tell my boss first. Isn't she in charge of the event? Shouldn't she know what's going on?"

"NEVER tell her anything bad! Only report the good things, otherwise she'll freak out. Now what am I going to do?"

"Just go talk to her. I'm sure it will be okay."

"Not when I've lost a fifty-thousand dollar car!"

Francie seemed about to cry or throw herself down the elevator shaft; I couldn't tell which she'd prefer. She had a point and I knew she had a lot on her mind, but I had to ask about food for volunteers.

"I can't think of that now!" she cried. "Besides, Patsy deals with that. I've got to go." She didn't care if I knew who Patsy wasor not; she just left.

If Patsy was in charge of volunteer food, it explained why we hadn't got any the day before. It also meant I had to find Camel Toe. I almost radioed for her whereabouts when I came face to face with Chloe Kirkpatrick.

"I remember you from Mirror," she said. "I'm Chloe."

"I'm Gigi. Nice to meet you again."

"How long have you worked with Collections Week?" she asked.

"I'm just volunteering," I replied. "I recently moved here and decided to change careers. I thought it would be an interesting experience and a good introduction to the city's fashion industry."

"Indeed," said Ms. Kirkpatrick. "You will have quite an experience working with Veronikkah."

"Oh? Have you worked with her?" I asked.

"We were acquaintances in London a few years ago."

Hmmm. Given what I'd just overheard, I suspected Chloe was someone Veronikkah hadn't paid, so I pried a little further. "And what do you think about her work with Collections Week?"

"Let's just say it's good someone is trying to raise Canadian fashion awareness on the public barometer."

That wasn't a promising comment, so I steered our conversation away from Collections Week to the fabulousness of Ms. Kirkpatrick's fashion section. We discussed local designers and I felt bold enough to tell her how I would improve the fashion reader's experience. I couldn't talk long with her, however, as Lola buzzed in my headset.

<<Where are you? That model guy is driving us crazy!>>

<<I'll be right there.>>

<<Gigi, before you go, you need to come help me. Now! It's Chantelle. Hurry!>>

I ran to the registration desk, where four large, tanned men in suits and dark glasses surrounded Chantelle. They were living *Reservoir Dogs* characters.

"Hey Chantelle, what can I do for you?"

She tried to be nice, but the group intimidated her. She said, "These men tell me they are the Bolivian designers. They say Ms. Hendricks expects them, but I don't see them on any lists, and Josh L. went into the runway room. Can you help them?"

Designers? They looked more like criminals, but who was I to judge?

I looked at them, smiled, and said, "Good morning gentlemen. I'm sorry we don't have your names on a list, but we'll get it sorted out right away. Ms. Hendricks is backstage at the moment, preparing for the press conference, but we'll try to bring her to you as soon as possible. In the meantime, feel free to have a pastry and mimosa while we contact Ms. Hendricks."

I seriously offered mimosas to four frightening Bolivian men? I was an idiot. The men stared at me and stayed at the registration table.

<<Gigi to Lola. Is Veronikkah back there with you?>>

<<Yeah, she's getting made up. Niles and Vivian say the press conference will start in five minutes.>>

<<Okay, I'll make an announcement and get everyone into the runway room. In the meantime, can you do me a favour? Can you tell Veronikkah the Bolivian designers are here? We don't know what to do with them. Oh, and how is that wanna-be model situation going?>>

<<Oh, that's fine. Niles figured Veronikkah would forget about him, so we said we couldn't use him and he

left. He didn't look like a model…too short. Anyway, I'll talk to Veronikkah.>>

<<Thanks. Do it as quickly as you can and get back to me.>>

I turned to the Bolivians slowly with a smile that tried to emit, "I'm not scared of you at all," but it likely read as, "I'm sure each of you has a gun and could snap at any moment."

"Listen, gentlemen," I said. I didn't know what I would say to appease them, but the walkie-talkie saved me.

<<Gigi, it's Lola. Veronikkah is coming right out to greet the Bolivians.>>

<<Great. Thanks.>>

"Sorry about that, gentlemen. It's hard to have two conversations at once," I laughed, pointing to my headset. My audience was not amused. "Anyway, Ms. Hendricks will come out to meet you. If you could kindly wait over to the side, we can register the remaining guests."

Luckily they did what they were told, but none of them took a mimosa or pastry.

"Thanks, Gigi," whispered Chantelle as she registered the waiting reporters.

I announced the impending press conference and ushered people into the runway room. When most people were inside, I realized the Bolivians were still in the front entrance.

<<Lola, it's Gigi. Where's Veronikkah?>>

<<She's on her way.>>

Veronikkah waltzed into the front entrance. She greeted the Bolivians in a businesslike manner, with hand-shakes rather than the double-air kiss customary to most fashionistas. It wasn't how I envisioned a group of visiting designers to be welcomed. Once again, though, I reminded myself I was in a whole new world. Perhaps fashion business etiquette was different from other industries. I made another loud announcement about the press conference, and Veronikkah escorted the Bolivians into the runway room.

Once everyone was inside the runway room, Chantelle asked, "Were those scary guys really designers?"

"They must be, since the Bolivian designer showcase is tomorrow night," I replied.

The press conference went well if you wanted to hear Veronikkah talk about her greatness and Collections Week's importance to the international fashion scene. At least that was what it first sounded like, but as I moved closer, I realized the woman was a passionate, motivated speaker who knew what to say; she was a dynamite saleswoman. She was on the runway selling her ideas about branding, unifying, and promoting Canadian fashion. She even had a guest speaker from *Wannabe a Rock Star* - the reality television series of the moment - who discussed the need to integrate fashion and television, how both could be cross-promoted.

Veronikkah then introduced the Bolivian Reservoir Dogs as representatives who would help to bring northern and southern countries together. To my surprise, she used all the right international buzzwords such as "building bridges" and "knowledge exchange." She emphasized fashion as a world associated with sweatshops - the farthest thing from *haute couture* - in developing countries and it was up to us to change it. She knew what she was talking about and truly inspiring. I never thought my previous life and my new direction would meld together.

Engrossed in the speeches, I was perturbed when two women whispered in front of me. I was going to shush them when I overheard the gossip.

"...she was so wasted, I'm surprised she can even stand up this morning," said one woman who wore a fabulous grey felt cloche hat with pink feathers attached to one side.

"No kidding," said her colleague. "I walked in on her, Francie, and Darryl doing lines in the VIP section at the after-party. Veronikkah was still going strong at two o'clock, but I saw Darryl, Francie, and that girl who's always around Francie - do you know her? The bossy one - they left in one of those horrid pink cars around that time."

"Yeah, they're always so messy."

"Well, get this...A friend of a friend called this morning and said Darryl disappeared sometime between last night and this morning. Francie called her friend, who is a friend of Darryl's. She was frantically looking for Darryl because he left with the Collections Week car!"

"Seriously?" gasped Cloche Hat. She was desperate for more gossip, as was I. Though technically it couldn't be considered gossip if it affected one's work situation, could it? If I worked with them, even in a volunteer capacity, I should have known what they were doing, right?

"Don't tell anybody," whispered the colleague, "but Darryl's done this before. When he does too much coke, he disappears for two or three days. Francie must be crying in the bathroom."

Everyone knew fashion, parties, and drugs are part of a whole package, much like sex, drugs, and rock 'n' roll, but these people were in charge of an event. Couldn't they save their partying to celebrate a successful week? Unfortunately I couldn't eavesdrop anymore because I heard buzzing in my ear.

<<Gigi, it's Gregor.>>

<<Go for Gigi,>> I whispered, walking away from the press conference so I wouldn't disturb anyone.

<<My volunteers are bored. Can they go on breaks or get some food?>>

Right. The food. How could I keep forgetting the food?

<<Sure, you can let them go on breaks, just as long as there are enough people to monitor displays when the press conference is finished. There will be a bit of a break between eleven and one anyway, since the first show starts at two. I have to get meal tickets from Camel...uhhh...Patsy, the event planner. I see her in the press conference, but I can't interrupt her now. Keep reminding me, though. Oh, and make sure the designer gallery is spotless. I don't want Veronikkah to worry about anything in there.>>

<<Okay. Done.>>

<<Thanks, Gregor.>>

The press conference wrapped up, so I waited around to discuss meal tickets with Camel Toe. She tried to get Veronikkah's attention, but she was busy with television crews, so I approached.

"Hi Patsy. I have a quick question. Francie told me you might have meal tickets for volunteers. They didn't eat yesterday and some worked for more than twelve hours."

"Sorry, dear. I don't look after that. Francie misunderstood."

"Thanks."

That meant I'd have to go back to Francie. With each directional contradiction and mismanagement, my spirit broke. It was only the second morning of the event and I was emotionally drained. Wasn't it supposed to be fun? I was learning a lot, but felt like I was running the show and making Veronikkah's decisions.

<<Gigi here. Has anyone seen Francie?>>

Gregor answered, <<She just walked into the designer gallery.>>

<<Thanks. Can you tell her to stay there? We need to talk.>>

<<Sure.>>

I ran into the designer gallery and saw Francie sitting in the café with eight girls. Each had a plate of food and as I approached, I heard one girl say, "Thanks for breakfast, Francie. You're a great friend. Thanks for inviting us to Collections Week."

"No problem. I look after my friends. Besides, I have hundreds of these meal tickets." As Francie said that, she exhibited a small stack of paper.

She was feeding all her friends with food meant for volunteers. I popped up beside her to restore justice.

"Francie, can I ask you a quick question?" She rolled her eyes, trying to demonstrate superiority.

"Can't you see I'm eating? I never get a chance to rest."

"Francie, I haven't eaten this morning, either."

"Oh, well then eat. Here's a meal ticket." She pulled one ticket out of the stack.

I thought of all my starving volunteers and made my move.

"Oh, yes, we'd all like to eat, thank you. That was exactly what I wanted to discuss with you. I need about two hundred meal tickets for today's volunteers: one hundred for lunch and one hundred for dinner. But you're already on top of it. It seems as though you have enough right there."

She tried to hide the tickets and made excuses about how she needed them, but I grabbed three-quarters of her pile.

"That's great, thank you. If I need more over the next few days, I'll let you know." I walked away as quickly as possible, before she had time to object. She wouldn't make a big deal out of it in front of her friends. I felt a bit bad about being devious, but I felt worse for people who volunteered days and nights to make Collections Week successful. I didn't want to be the person responsible for denying people food and water. Slave to fashion I may have been, but slave-driver I was not.

MOBILIZE.

<<Gigi to everyone. I have meal tickets. I'll deliver them shortly and then you can give them to your crews.>>

<<Yay!>> said Lola.

"Finally!" said Gregor, as I snuck up to him.

"Take these," I said, stuffing a few into his hands, feeling like a fashionable version of Robin Hood. "I've got to make it quick because I kind of stole them from Francie, so I want to get away from her as soon as possible."

"Understood, Cap'n."

I ran to Chantelle, did the same thing, and made my way backstage. I felt like a spy, looking over my shoulder to ensure Francie didn't intercept meal ticket deliveries. As I slipped into a back hallway in an under-utilized backstage area, I turned around a corner and ran into a pair of gorgeous blue eyes. Hot Dan looked as sneaky as I did.

"Aaaah!" I jumped back. "You scared me!"

"Uh, sorry," he smiled.

Could he hear my heart beat? The man set me on fire. Then I saw his clothes: he wore a cowboy shirt. I hated western wear. Not only was it a cowboy shirt, but it was a stylish, vintage cowboy shirt; too stylish, in fact. It was Grand Ol' Opry stylish, back in its fifties glory days. Did I detect a hint of metallic in the shirt? He looked mighty fine, but also mighty gay. Why did all my crushes have to be gay?

"What are you doing here? The first menswear show isn't until four o'clock."

His eyes darted around. "Uhhh...they told me to be here by noon for makeup, hair, and fittings. I went to the bathroom and somehow got lost. How do I get back?"

"Follow me." I grabbed his big, gay hand because it was too hard to resist touching him, and led him backstage. "There you go, safe and sound."

"Thanks, sweetie. Guess I'll go over to makeup." He turned to walk away.

"Maybe you should get fitted first to get rid of that shirt," I mumbled.

"What?" he asked, turning back.

Did I say that out loud? I was such a loser sometimes. How could I recover?

"Don't you get fitted first? To test the clothes in case of last-minute alterations?" Good one, Gigi.

He pretended to accept my recovery. "No, it's hair and makeup first."

"Okay, well, have fun."

<<Gigi's at it again. Will she stop flirting and do her job?>> It was Lola, laughing from the other side of the room.

"Ha-ha. Very funny," I said as I got to her. "Unfortunately, he's got to be gay. Look at the shirt. Listen; here are meal tickets for your volunteers. You might want to let them break while hair and makeup people are busy, before the shows start at two."

Niles found us and asked, "Have you seen Francie's good friend Eva?"

"No, not yet," I answered.

"Well, we worked out an agreement where she would be in charge of hair and makeup, but I haven't seen her yet today. Everyone's ready to go, but awaiting her orders."

"Can't you do it? Aren't you paid to be in charge of backstage?"

"Technically yes, but Veronikkah talked with me this morning. Eva told her I took her job. It's outrageous, but Veronikkah gave me strict orders to leave Eva with hair and makeup."

"Well, if she isn't here, you've got to start, right?"

"Yes, otherwise we'll have late shows, and I hate late shows. I don't do late shows."

"Then do what you have to do. If it makes any difference, I'll vouch for your decision."

"Thanks, Gigi. You're a doll." He hugged me and kissed me on the cheek. It felt nice to be loved.

<<Chantelle to Gigi.>>

<<Go for Gigi.>>

<<There's someone here who says he's a volunteer.>>

<<Really? Volunteers were supposed to come in at nine and then the next shift starts at five. Who would come at noon?>>

<<His name is Jerry.>>

<<Jerry? I don't recognize a volunteer named Jerry, though he could be a last-minute volunteer from Ryerson University. A professor said she might send some students. I'll be right there.>>

I ran to the front entrance and saw Chantelle talking to a short, scruffy guy with dreadlocks. White guys with dreadlocks were the biggest losers on the planet. I didn't remember that guy from the interviews, but then again, I'd met hundreds of people over the past few weeks. Still, I probably would have remembered his gross dreads. He didn't look like a fashion student, either. You can spot them in a crowd, wearing normal clothes punched up with twists. No, Jerry-Dreadlock wanted to be a skater, but had never tried riding a skateboard in his entire life. A fashion student would have at least accessorized with a skateboard. I walked over to them.

"Hi, I'm Gigi, the volunteer coordinator," I said.

"Hi, I'm Jerry."

"And you're here to volunteer?" He nodded. "I don't remember meeting you. Are you from Ryerson?" He nodded. "Okay, then. Let's see where we can use you."

He was too scruffy to have contact with guests, so I called Lola. <<Lola, it's Gigi. Do you need an extra volunteer?>>

<<Yeah, sure. We could use another person on backstage security.>>

<<Okay, I'll send a guy over to you. His name is Jerry and he has dreadlocks.>>

<<Wait a second, is he short and scruffy-looking?>>

<<Yeah. Why?>>

<<I think it's the guy who wanted to be a model!>>

<<You're kidding! Do you still want him backstage if it's the same guy?>>

<<Well, if he's willing to help out, it wouldn't hurt.>>

Jerry-Dreadlock went to meet Lola backstage.

Fifteen minutes later, when I checked on Gregor's team in the designer gallery, Lola called.

<<Gigi, guess what? It was the same guy! Now he's backstage showing his portfolio to stylists and makeup artists. He's being a pain and distracting them from their work.>>

<<Sorry, I thought he'd be okay. Give him a warning that he's there now to volunteer, not to solicit work. Tell him if he harasses anyone again, he can't volunteer anymore.>>

<<Will do.>>

<<Chantelle to Gigi.>>

<<Go for Gigi.>>

<<I have someone here who says she is the reigning winner from the 'Miss SuperPageant' Contest. Apparently she's delivering the Collections Week opening speech.>>

Why was a beauty pageant winner there? Fashion and beauty contests were completely different; one was art and commerce, and the other was just plain cheesy.

<<I don't know anything about that, but I'll try to get an answer.>>

Luckily, Veronikkah walked into the designer gallery, flanked by the Bolivians. I saw her face change to a reddish colour after she passed a display. I recognized an imminent freak-out, so I ran to her aid.

"What's wrong with this display?" she demanded.

I looked at it, and it seemed to be a fine metal and glass display with a flower on top. I didn't see anything wrong, so couldn't answer.

Luckily she didn't wait for me to talk and screamed, "There are no sponsor magazines here! Get some magazines!"

"Where are they?" I asked.

She glared at me. "In the Collections Week room, of course."

"Okay, we'll get them out."

"Thanks, Lulu."

Lulu? Who was Lulu? Her inability to remember my name was ridiculous. Nevertheless, I had to do my job and help the woman, which meant getting those magazines out on display. I had just grabbed two volunteers to help when I remembered Miss SuperPageant.

"Oh, Ms. Hendricks, Miss SuperPageant is out front, claiming she is opening Collections Week. I don't know anything about it. Do you?

Veronikkah frowned, trying to remember anything she could about Miss SuperPageant.

"Oh yes," she said. "Francie called her in as a guest speaker. Have her go to hair and makeup."

While I found volunteers to help me with the magazines, I called Chantelle and told her to get a volunteer to escort the beauty queen backstage and asked her to explain things to Niles and Lola.

Halfway to the Collections Week office, I remembered I didn't have a key, so I radioed the crew to see if anyone could see Francie. Nobody did, so I figured she was in the office. When we got there, I heard voices inside and eventually Francie answered my knocks. At least I didn't have to run around to find the key, and Francie showed us where to get the magazines.

The room was an absolute mess. They hadn't been there two full days, but it looked as though four bands had been through, complete with groupies, booze, and drugs. Champagne bottles and dirty glasses littered every surface, along with opened makeup samples, magazines, and clothes. I looked at the glass coffee table and saw some powder residue, along with a credit card and curled up twenty-dollar bill.

The toilet flushed and as the person opened the door, she said, "Francie, I can't do any more. I swear I'm gonna puke."

It was Eva. She looked at me, I looked at Francie, and Francie looked at her. They were snorting coke, but tried to come up with some lame food-poisoning excuse. It was just after noon and they had work to do. Was it right to confront them about their unprofessional behaviour? Or was it professional to be a cokehead in the fashion world? Was I the only sober person at Collections Week?

I chose to avoid the whole situation by shoving the volunteers away from the room as quickly as possible, hoping they wouldn't see the coffee table and ask questions. I didn't say anything else to Francie or Eva, but sent the volunteers back to the designer gallery with instructions for Gregor. I had to talk to Niles to discuss my discovery.

<<Is Niles on the walkies?>> I asked.

<<Go for Niles.>>

<<It's Gigi. I need to talk to you. Are you backstage?>>

<<Yeah, sure. What is it?>>

<<I'll tell you in person,>> I said, running there as fast as possible.

When I got to him, I dragged him to a corner and said, "I don't know who to talk to about this, but you're the most logical and trustworthy person I've met here."

"Gigi, you can totally trust me. You look worried. What is it?"

"Well, as you know, I'm new to this industry, so I'm still trying to figure out what constitutes professional behaviour. I didn't think common sense would be lost when entering the fashion world, but nobody operates normally."

Niles held my shoulders and told me to take a deep breath. Then he said, "Veronikkah and Francie are not normal for this industry. I think they're rude and unprofessional. So anything you've got to say is safe with me."

That made me feel better, because I didn't want to make enemies in the business I loved, even if it was filled with crazy people.

"Thanks, Niles. Okay, I was just in the Collections Week office, and totally saw evidence of cocaine use. I knew fashion and blow went together, but I didn't think the organizers would actually be high while working on the event. I don't have a problem with people partying on their own time, but they have responsibilities, and now I know why everything is so disorganized!"

"Did you see anyone doing it?" Niles asked.

"No, I just saw residue, credit cards, and curled up bills. I didn't see anyone doing it, but it was pretty obvious."

"Hmmm...It is a well-documented fact Veronikkah used to be a coke addict and small-time dealer. She was the subject of a *Toronto Today* article a few years ago. She claims to be clean, though, and nobody ever thought she would be high again while doing her job."

"What? She was a dealer?"

"Yes. She was in jail for a while, too."

"Seriously? How did she get such an important job?"

"You heard her talk. She's convincing. Plus, she has good connections and a rich father."

"Really?" I asked. "At her age she had to rely on her father?"

"Unfortunately, yes. And a return to coke would explain her increasingly erratic behaviour over the last few weeks."

"You mean she's not normally like that?"

"No. Usually she's focused and passionate; that's why Vivian and I are here. In past seasons, she's been less flaky, so it's a shame she's using again. Not everyone in fashion behaves that way, you know. Most people are dedicated to their work. While fashion shows are parties for a lot of people, organizers usually separate work from partying."

"Thanks," I said, still trying to process everything. "I'm sorry I blurted everything out to you, but I wondered what was happening and how Collections Week actually operated before my team came along. Not to be conceited, but I feel we're doing everything."

"You are, and you guys are amazing. Apart from Veronikkah and Francie's sloppy work, this has been the most organized Collections Week ever."

"Thanks, Niles. By the way, I don't know if it is actually Veronikkah who is doing the drugs. I suspect it might be Francie and Eva, if not more people. They were the ones in the office when I saw all the stuff."

Niles frowned. "I guess that's why I haven't seen Eva today… Oh well. It's not much of a loss because she wasn't much help anyway. But I imagine she'll be a crabby nightmare when she does show up backstage."

He stopped and looked me directly in the eyes. "Listen," he said, "tell me if you see anything else. It's important for us to know this kind of stuff."

"Sure, but what do we do about it?"

Lola interrupted to inform Niles that Adriana Stewart, the day's first designer, still hadn't shown up with the clothes and it was an hour before show start.

He said to me, "I've got to go," and shrugged his shoulders. "If nobody witnessed anything, there's nothing we can do about it. Let's keep each other informed." Then he and Lola ran in search of Adriana.

I breathed deeply and tried to process the morning's events. Then I felt someone beside me. I turned to see Hot Dan's hot eyes. He was gorgeous, but slightly creepy with his tendency to appear out of nowhere.

"Hey." I couldn't think of anything interesting to say, and was too distracted by my new knowledge to flirt.

"How are things going?" he asked.

"Oh, you know, the usual," I lied. The usual? How was the experience usual? I desperately wanted to spill everything about Francie's incompetence, drug use, Veronikkah's lack of leadership, and the general craziness of the event, but I didn't know the guy. I reminded myself that I worked for Veronikkah and Francie; gossiping about them was unprofessional no matter how ridiculous they were.

Hot Dan put his hand on my shoulder and said, "If you ask me, everything looks far from usual. I know we just met yesterday, but if you need to let off some steam, you can come to me."

Yeah, I knew how I could let off some steam...I imagined our meeting earlier that morning ending with him pushing me up against the deserted hallway wall, looking into my eyes...wait...that guy was so distracting. It was as if he had a superpower. He was able to erase women's minds with a quick glance… He could undress girls with a single look...He was Super Distraction Man!

"...and then we all said '*Olé*' and drank the tequila!"

He must have told me some story, but I'd completely zoned out. Luckily, the walkie-talkie saved me.

<<Chantelle to Gigi.>>

I motioned to Hot Dan I was about to have a conversation with a headset.

<<Go for Gigi.>>

<<Veronikkah's here, and she's going ballistic. She's making volunteers cry.>>

<<What?>>

<<She's screaming, telling volunteers they're incompetent. One girl wore a sweater because it's freezing in here, but Veronikkah told her she looked like a homeless person and should leave. Those scary men are with her, making everything worse.>>

<<I'll be right there.>>

I looked at Hot Dan and said, "Veronikkah's scaring volunteers in the front entrance. I've gotta go."

APPROACH.

I saw Veronikkah scolding the volunteers, the Bolivians behind her. All the girls cowered from her, trying to hide tears.

"None of you should cry," she lectured. "That's completely unprofessional. If you can't take criticism, you're in the wrong industry. This entrance is a disaster. You CANNOT wear sweaters in here; I don't care how cold it is. You have a Collections Week uniform, and you should show it off proudly."

Nothing about those cheap, ribbed tank tops constituted a uniform instilling pride. Where did Veronikkah learn to manage and motivate people? She wasn't going to build a strong, intelligent team by scaring people. The volunteers didn't deserve that kind of treatment, especially when they'd donated their free time.

She left the volunteers quaking in fear and walked to the registration desk - followed by her pack of Reservoir Dogs - to examine the papers Chantelle and her crew had arranged neatly. In a grand, dramatic gesture, she swiped them off the table. "Who is in charge of these papers?"

"I...I am," Chantelle stammered, stepping forward meekly.

"Did you pull them out of a dump? They're horrible. We're registering fashion's most important people here!"

I couldn't watch any more volunteer-slaughter and had to intervene.

"Ms. Hendricks, is there a problem here?" I asked. "What can I do to help?"

I gestured to Chantelle to back away from Veronikkah and assist her dishevelled group. I figured I could distract Veronikkah and fix the situation.

"These papers!" she fumed. "Look at these papers!"

They were blank white pieces of paper for computer printers and photocopiers.

"What's wrong with them?" I asked.

"We need sign-in sheets. Are these people buyers, media, sponsors, or designers? We're building a database so we can improve guest numbers in future seasons and make it more worthwhile for designers to show with us. How are we going to know all this with blank pieces of paper? Where's Francie? She knows all this. I need Francie!"

It appeared we had another miscommunication on our hands. Or, more accurately, Francie had forgotten to communicate again.

"Ms. Hendricks, I assure you we didn't know you needed this information. I don't know where Francie is right now, but next time I see her, we'll discuss it. In the meantime, a show will start in forty-five minutes. Guests will arrive soon, so there's nothing we can do about it now. Let's get the volunteers to make the best forms they can and we'll try to have some professional ones later today or tomorrow. It's the best we can do."

Her body relaxed a little and her face contorted to a confused state. "You mean Francie never told you about this?"

"No, I'm sorry. She didn't. But we'll try to fix it now, okay?"

"Yes, that sounds good, Lulu. I'm going to find Francie." She and the Bolivians walked away.

Lulu? Why did she keep calling me Lulu? Should I have corrected her or was it better not to complicate things?

It pissed me off, but I was more concerned with my new superpower: Super Problem Solving Girl. Hot Dan wasn't the only super hero around. I could find a solution to any conundrum within minutes! I was a miracle worker! I was marvellous! I was daydreaming.

Chantelle stood beside me, so I told her everything and helped prepare for her guests. Then I remembered Lola and Niles backstage.

<<Gigi to backstage. Gigi to backstage! Did Adriana arrive?>>

<<Yes, everything's fine now.>> It was Lola. <<Adriana was lost in another part of the building, but we found her and everything fits. Niles says the show will start on time.>>

<<Excellent. Good job. Did everyone hear that? The first show of the day will start on time. Get ready, guests will arrive any minute.>>

I felt great, ready for the shows - and possibly battles - ahead.

COMPARE.

Gregor, Lola, and Chantelle mobilized their teams as socialites and journalists assembled in the front entrance, so I inspected the runway room.

I left Josh L. with a crew and appointed a brilliant girl from the previous night to be his special helper. She should have had a headset, but we didn't have extras and I didn't want to bother Francie with another request for fear of meal tickets retribution. Everything was running smoothly in the runway room.

The Runway volunteers seated the guests, an easier task after the night before. Josh L. was still the only one with a seating list, but overall, traffic flow was improved for a perfect start to the day's shows.

At precisely two o'clock, the lights dimmed and the cheesy "Collections Week, C'est Chic!" house anthem returned, proving fashion shows *could* begin on time. The lights danced and Veronikkah appeared on the runway in the middle of a bright spotlight. It was so bright, it caught her off guard, making her a fashionista-in-headlights.

Looking surprised, she tried to act cool. "Woo! Everybody! Welcome to Collections Week! Yeah! Put your hands together! Woo!"

Silence. Nobody responded to Veronikkah's failed attempt to be a VJ.

"All right...Uhhh...Thanks for coming to Collections Week...and...uhhh...supporting great clothes everywhere." She gazed into space.

If I hadn't seen her previous two speeches, I wouldn't have believed she could speak.

"Now...uhhh...I'd like to introduce you to a special guest who will open Collections Week…" She stared for a moment, then announced, "Here she is...Miss SuperPageant!" She regained some energy and clapped her hands as the beauty queen walked toward her.

Unfortunately, Miss SuperPageant tripped and fell into Veronikkah as they leaned in for the mandatory double-cheek kiss. The crowd gasped and giggled, and I saw ChiChi Chihuahua stifle laughter in the front row. ChiChi looked fantastic in giant Chanel sunglasses and vintage tuxedo shirt, complete with ruffles.

The honoured guest began talking. "Good afternoon, ladies and gentlemen. It is an honour to be here at this event, uh…"

"Collections Week, you moron!" I wanted to scream. Luckily I do have some inner censorship capabilities.

Apparently Miss SuperPageant wasn't so blessed with the ability to refrain from blurting out her thoughts. "Ooops! I forgot where I am. Just a minute. I'll be right back. I left my speech backstage."

She walked off, abandoning Veronikkah on the runway.

Miss SuperPageant returned, unfolded a crumpled ball of paper, and continued exactly where she'd left off. "Collections Week," she said with a proud smile.

It was almost too painful to watch, but it was so bad it had to get good.

The beauty queen continued, "It was so nice of Miss Veronique Henderson to invite me to open your shows." Veronikkah's face turned red, but Miss SuperPageant continued, oblivious to her mistake. "I just want to take a few minutes to talk about how important fashion is. I love fashion, and without clothes, we'd...ummm...

well, we'd all be naked!" She flashed a huge, beauty-contestant smile. You could practically see the Vaseline blobs on her teeth.

Everyone in the front row tried not to giggle, but it was contagious and impossible to control. When Veronikkah took over and said, "We're blessed Miss SuperPageant offered to demonstrate the walk she'll take to the Queen of the World Pageant in Istanbul this summer," giggles radiated through the audience.

The lights danced again as we heard RuPaul demand, "You'd better work!" The first beats to "*Supermodel*" inspired Miss SuperPageant to strut her stuff, crisscrossing the runway, stopping every now and then for a *Zoolander*-inspired pose. The sad thing was she took her walk seriously, which ended the audience civility. The unbearably hilarious combination of outdated song and serious posing brought the front row of fashion heavyweights to insane laughter. The more Miss SuperPageant posed, the funnier she became. I felt sorry for her, but even the feelings of embarrassment couldn't overcome the absurdity. More than half the audience laughed until they cried, but Miss SuperPageant was too focused to notice. In fact, she looked quite happy prancing down the runway.

As Miss SuperPageant finished her walk, the laughter died down just in time to hear her say, "Good luck with your event. Thanks for having me," as she blew kisses and walked off the stage. Veronikkah didn't know what to do, so she disappeared and we heard the "Collections Week, C'est Chic!" song again, followed by an introduction to the first designer of the day.

Despite the unfortunate prelude, Adriana produced a smooth show. Compared to the previous night, guests registered easily and the crowd remained manageable. They were ladies-who-lunch, buyers-who-buy, and journalists-who-love-a-free-gift-bag. The audience reflected Adriana's collection of classy, well-tailored business attire. I found the aesthetic too conservative, but she knew her target market, that her clothes would sell well in upscale boutiques. It was only her fourth season running her own label, (she previously worked for Demure, the most conventional clothing label in the country), but she knew the fashion business, and her tried-and-true approach would sell.

Before I switched careers, I'd noticed a division in fashion: those who design to sell and those who design for design's sake. I wondered how the ultimate artistic designers supported themselves. Not many people can afford to wear artistic triumphs, nor do many have the courage to wear them. Must fashion always oppose business and art? To me, successful designers were ones who melded the two, but that was rare. Why was it so difficult to design and make delightful, wearable clothes? Did ego drive designers to think, "Create and they shall wear?" What about "Create what they want to wear?" Was it that difficult to mix business with creativity? In Adriana's case, she was aiming for business rather than creativity.

The show after Adriana, however, was a different story. It was a recent design-school graduate who called himself Xia, though his real name was Sherman Hung. I helped Niles and Lola backstage because Xia was a known diva. His outfit indicated he would be hard to handle: he wore a Vegas-showgirl red-feather headdress with a ripped, punky T-shirt, black hotpants with sequined flames, cowboy boots, and hot-pink tube socks pulled to his knees. Backstage, he alternately yelled at Niles and Lola or cried that he would fail. He was probably correct about his impending failure because nobody succeeds by treating people poorly, especially when starting out. He also made terrible clothes. They were elaborate productions of sequins, feathers, mirrors, reflective tape, and tubing. He tried to be a cyberpunk club kid, but the result was a mishmashed statement screaming, "Look at me! I'm trying to be creative! I'm a fashion grad!" To make things worse, Xia stitched garments on models five minutes before the show.

Niles stood next to me and groaned, "This show will be a disaster."

"Why do you say that?" I asked.

"I've seen these shows before. Kids try to say everything their first show. They don't know how to refine their ideas and end up overwhelmed. Oh well. We'll try our best. I want you to stay backstage. We'll need your help."

"Okay, sure." I was thrilled to be part of the backstage excitement since I'd spent most my Collections Week time at the front of house.

The action didn't stop backstage: Niles double-checked models and outfits; Lola briefed volunteers on how to quickly change clothes; volunteers scrutinized outfits, discerning how certain pieces of tubing fit together; and everyone searched for one missing earring.

"I MUST have that earring!" whined Xia. "It's the centrepiece to my entire collection! I can't show my work without that earring!" He sat down in a corner and whimpered.

I intended to soothe him when a model intercepted me.

"How is my walk?" she asked.

I looked over at Xia's corner, saw Lola consoling him, and figured he would survive. The model walked past me and struck a pose.

"Your walk looks all right to me. Great pose." I didn't know anything about model walk etiquette, but her pose was actually quite good; I could see the front and side of the outfit all at once, which, to me, was a good clothing display.

"You think so?" she asked.

"For sure. You're gonna be great."

I looked at Lola and Xia, who seemed fine. In fact, he preened his showgirl feathers, ready to tackle the show.

"Five minutes, everybody!" yelled Niles. He lined up models and marked notes on his clipboard.

"Five minutes!" screamed Xia, who stopped preening. "I'm not ready! The wedding dress isn't here!"

Niles flipped through his clipboard papers, searching for the outfit list. "Wedding dress? You didn't include a wedding dress in your outfit and model order."

"That's because I decided to add it last night. My boyfriend's sister will bring it and model it too."

"I'm sorry, we can't include it," said Niles.

"Why not?" Xia demanded.

"First, as I explained, it wasn't on your list. Second, if neither is here, neither can be in the show. We can't wait because there are six more shows after you today. If yours is late, all others will be late as well. Third, your model needs to see hair and makeup.

It can't be done in five minutes. Don't forget your choreography matches the music. Do you have enough end music to include the last model?"

"Of course I do!" huffed the designer, his feathers waving wildly. "She WILL be in the show!"

Suddenly Veronikkah appeared out of nowhere. "What's the problem, boys? Did I hear something about a wedding dress?"

Xia beamed. "Oh, yes, Veronikkah, sweetie. I made the most fabulous wedding dress last night, but this guy says I can't include it."

Veronikkah turned to Niles and said, "That's not true, is it Niles? We must foster this creative talent. If Xia wants it, he's got it."

Xia stuck his tongue out at Niles when Veronikkah looked away.

Niles frowned. "It could screw up the choreography."

"Tut-tut, none of that. It will be fine. I don't hire you to make judgements. I hire you to do your job."

"But my job is to make judgements."

Veronikkah didn't hear Niles because she'd turned to celebrate Xia. "I came to wish you luck, dear."

"Thank you, Veronikkah. It's an honour to show at Collections Week."

"Good," she smiled. "Do you have your cheque for me? You do need to pay before you show."

"Right. It's in the mail."

"Good boy. Have a good show. I'll be in the front row making sure it's up to Collections Week standards. Here's your goody bag! One for each designer!" She gave him a tiny package and walked away.

Xia sneered at Niles, so Niles whispered, "Fine. If your model and dress arrive, it will be your choice, but we start now." Niles turned to everyone backstage and yelled, "Okay, people! We're starting! Models, come with me!"

Niles arranged the girls at the stage entrance. "Xia! Are you going to stay here and approve the looks or do you have a stylist?"

"It's all me, baby!" squawked Xia.

"Well, then, come stand by me and get them ready."

Xia went to the runway entrance, no doubt experiencing a mix of pride, enthusiasm, and apprehension about his first show. He bounced around like a flamboyant mid-nineties club kid, but it was easy to see his fear.

The models lined up; the volunteers stood by the clothing racks, outfits in hands, ready to change models. I heard the "Collections Week, C'est Chic!" song again. What was with that annoying? I knew I'd hate it by the end of the week.

Niles asked Xia, "Is there anything you want to say to your models and crew before we start?"

Xia nodded. "Ladies, you're sexy! You're strong! You're Runway Queens!" He spun a little pirouette as he said the last bit. I knew one person who was a Runway Queen.

The lights dimmed backstage, making it difficult to see the clothes, but it was workable. The models transformed from giddy girls testing their walks to tall, focused Amazons. Niles stood at the entrance, listened to his headset, and held back the first model. Lola made sure they stayed in line. A makeup artist with a gigantic powder brush travelled up and down the line, dabbing glitter on the models, and a hairstylist sprayed a cloud of hairspray around each one. There was so much mist, a product-induced aura swirled around the line-up. Finally Niles let his arm free, allowing the first girl to walk onto the Runway.

Silence coated backstage as we gauged audience reaction. We exhaled a group breath after hearing some applause. Clapping was good. Xia smiled, completed last-minute touch-ups to his second model - namely hair-fluffing and accessory placement - and Niles let her pass.

The next four models went out and the first change worked well. I helped the second model's dresser undo shoes, since the dresser was focused on taking off the corset. Unfortunately, one hook wouldn't unhook. The shoes got off all right, but I looked at the hook, where metal was entangled in the fabric. The dresser and I tried everything, but couldn't find a way to undo it without tearing the corset. Fashion-panic set in.

Niles yelled, "Where's Cynthia? She's up in three! We're missing Cynthia!" Cynthia was our corset girl.

There was no way we would have her ready before the next two models.

"What's wrong?" asked Niles.

"The hook's broken! We have to rip the corset!" I called back.

"No! Not the corset!" screamed Xia. "Not the corset! Bring her here!"

I made one last attempt at the hook when I heard a woman say, "Yoo-hoo! I'm here! Am I too late?"

I looked to see who'd yoo-hooed, when I miraculously freed the hook from the corset. The model would make it!

"She's free!" I yelled to Niles, who raced over as I turned to see who the new voice belonged to. A girl held a big, puffy mess of metallic cloth, mirrors, and plastic tubing.

"The wedding dress!" Xia beamed. "You!" he pointed at me. "You! Get her in the dress and do her hair and makeup!"

I looked at Niles and Lola for guidance, but they were doing too many things at once. Niles reported model timing updates into his headset microphone, dragged the half-dressed corset model into line, held back other models, and made sure none walked away (they had a nasty habit of leaving the line-up to practice walking and posing). Lola ferried between the line-up and changing area, tried to help the dressers with miscellaneous accessories, and kept the flow of models running smoothly. Neither noticed the bride, so I took her to hair and makeup.

At the hair and makeup section, I called to Eva, but she ignored me, chatting to the stylists instead. She tried getting their attention by showing off her pony skin boots, the most hideous shoes I'd ever seen.

"Eva!" I huffed (yes, I huffed, which was something I never did). "This model needs hair and makeup in five minutes. Xia added her at the last minute. Can it be done?"

Some stylists grabbed their equipment, but Eva said, "No way. We finished all Xia's models. We don't do last-minute additions. Five minutes is impossible!" She turned to the stylists, trying to revive the pony skin boot discussion.

I agreed with her that five minutes was impossible, considering they'd averaged twenty to thirty minutes for each prior model. Unfortunately, I had to get the girl to Xia and think of a tactic to do so.

I'd noticed Eva was an ass-kisser, so I said, "Before the show, Veronikkah promised Xia he could have this last-minute addition."

Eva's eyes widened. "Veronikkah promised that?" She was suddenly a puppy dog, eager to please her master, so she barked to the stylists, "What are you waiting for? Get to work!"

"Thanks, guys," I said.

Two makeup artists stood in front of her and three hairstylists brushed out her hair.

"We have two minutes, guys," I announced. "Let's get this done!" Then I whispered to the model, "Do you mind if we get you into the dress while you're getting all this done?"

"No! Just do it!" she screamed. "Get me ready! I want to walk down that catwalk!" She stuck out her arms, and I pulled off her clothes.

I didn't know who was more embarrassed or what was more degrading: the undresser or the undressee. Either way, backstage dressing was odd and it was best to get it over with quickly. That case was especially strange with the crowd of stylists and bizarre wedding dress creation. It had a million straps and openings and by the time I'd figured it out, I realized I might have put it on backwards, since straps and metallic frills exploded everywhere off her body.

"That's it! Time's up! I'm taking her!" I yelled, thanking the stylists, dragging the dishevelled model-bride away from her pit crew.

When I delivered her to Xia, I noticed her eye makeup was uneven: one makeup artist had applied it more heavily than the other. When I explained the situation to Xia, he said, "No problem. It's avant-guard. I don't care. She's my bride. She MUST be in my show!"

I left Xia with his bride and assessed the chaotic backstage scene. Half-dressed models, confused dressers due to Xia's complex creations, the hairstylist followed models with a can of hairspray, the makeup girl spilled glitter everywhere, Lola tried to help the dressers, and Niles waited at the door, stomping nervously. "We have a dead Runway! Nobody's out there! We need someone NOW!" he cried.

I looked around and found the girl closest to being dressed, so I grabbed her and led her to Niles.

"Does order matter?" I asked.

"No, we just need someone!"

"Here! Get her out there!" I pushed the girl to him, and he shoved her out to the Runway. It didn't matter she didn't have shoes.

There were three outfits to go before the bride, but nobody was ready, so I made an announcement. "Dressers! Get your girls over to Niles and Xia. Take the clothes! Take the accessories! Just get them over to the Runway entrance! They need to go out now!"

As the dressers gathered their models, clothes, and accessories over to Niles, I passed Lola and asked, "Are you okay?"

"Just doing my best," she replied, somewhat deflated, thanks to the chaotic show.

"Don't worry; the clothes are hard to figure out."

"No doubt. This skirt's even ripped. I swear, we didn't do that; it came to us like that."

"Does Xia know?" I asked.

"Yeah, he said it was ripped before. Who would show a ripped skirt?"

"Beats me," I said.

"Anyway, thanks for helping. This show is crazy! The others haven't been like this."

That's when Niles announced, "Okay people, three more until the finale. Get ready for the finale!"

"No, there are four more," said Xia. "My bride is here." He pushed her out from behind the line and shock crossed Niles's face as he saw the hideous, lopsided bride. Looking as though made of decayed and stripped metal; she was Arnold Schwarzenegger's cyborg at the end of *The Terminator,* minus the red eyes. Cyberpunk, she was. Bride, I wasn't so sure.

Niles looked at Xia and said, "We can't put her on. She's not ready. Her makeup isn't done and the dress is falling apart. Besides, we only have thirty seconds of music left, which we need for the finale."

"Veronikkah said I could do it," he whined.

Niles sighed as he let the second-last model pass. "Okay, go ahead, but I'm only trying to help you. I don't think it will do you any good to send out this outfit. People will remember her dishevelled look rather than the dress."

Xia scoffed. "It's my show. I want to send her out!"

"Okay fine," Niles said to Xia. Then he yelled to everyone, "Okay, people! Get ready for the finale! Make sure all the girls are in their last outfits and get them all in line!" Niles let the last girl go before the bride.

The second-last model came back and Niles said, "Okay, bride, get ready, and...go!"

The bride tried to walk out, but tripped over Niles. He picked her back up and pushed her forward. "Just get out there!" he cried.

We all stood, dumbfounded after the last few moments, but we didn't have time to reflect on anything; we had to organize the finale. The models lined up and everyone buzzed around them, picking off lint, fixing stray hairs, and adjusting accessories. The bride came backstage and tripped again. I ran over and dragged her to the end of the model line. Halfway there, I noticed her tears.

"What's wrong?" I asked.

"I fell three times!" she sobbed. "I can't believe it! I ruined everything!"

We had no time to discuss her destruction of Xia's show because less than half the models were out for the finale when everything went silent.

"What happened?" screamed Xia, running over to Niles, grabbing his jacket lapels, shaking him senseless.

"Just a minute, I'm trying to find out," retorted Niles, pushing the psychotic designer away from him. Niles tried to listen to his headset while Xia kept screaming. He turned to Xia and said, "As I warned before the show, you ran out of closing music. Now there's nothing." He turned to the remaining models. "Girls, just keep on going. Do the finale and pretend there's music. Go! Go!"

There was model chaos, chattering and asking each other, "How do we walk without music?" The dumb model stereotype proven correct.

"Just walk!" demanded an exasperated Niles, pushing them all on stage. Xia followed them to take his bow, which was probably some limp version of a pirouette.

Niles, Lola, and the rest of the volunteer dressers were left backstage and for a quick moment we all thought the same thing: Niles was right. The show was disastrous.

Xia and the models returned, the girls heading to the clothing racks, while Xia went straight for Niles. The designer was so mad, he may as well have shot laser beams out his eyes.

"How could you do that to me?" he screamed. "You ruined my reputation!"

Niles sighed and looked as though he had seen it all before. "Xia, think back to the start of the show. I warned you about the music and I warned you about the bride. I'm sorry things didn't turn out this time, but nothing goes right your first show. You've got to go through these things to be a perfect designer. I'm sure we've all learned from this experience."

"What have I learned? I learned to never work with you again!" huffed Xia. "That's it. I'm not doing any interviews."

"Xia, it is your choice and it has nothing to do with me. That's all I'm going to say to you because I've got to get another show on in an hour. Since we won't work together again, best wishes in your career." He walked away from Xia and came over to me.

"Are you all right?" I asked.

Niles gave me a weak smile. "Yeah, sure. This stuff happens at least once a season. After fifteen years in the business, I'm used to it. This is nothing." He called Lola over and asked, "Can you make sure we get Xia loaded out as quickly as possible? It's best to get him out of here."

"Sure thing," said Lola, and we directed dressers to gather all the garments and accessories and bagged them together.

Fifteen minutes later, everything was in the loading zone and the new designers were loaded in. Xia was forgotten as the design team Flaunt came backstage.

I loved Flaunt clothes. I owned three of their dresses and had recently purchased my new favourite outfit from them: a gaucho jumpsuit. Who made gauchos anymore? Flaunt. That's who. They were the only ones who could pull it off, a pair of rock 'n' roll gals who made fun, flirty, rock-inspired clothes. I looked forward to working with them.

Niles led them from loading zone to backstage and everyone - from the two designers to the volunteer dressers - was in a fantastic mood. We giggled, hooted, and let out rock screams as though we were at a concert. We arranged five clothing racks backstage and the designers walked around, arranged the clothes in groups by model, and placed name cards and polaroids of each outfit on the hangers. I could tell it would be a million times better than Xia's show, and I wanted to watch a well-executed performance.

The designers had finished organizing their outfits when one rushed past me, eager to get to a new batch of clothes. She stopped and came back to me.

"Those are the best shoes ever!" she exclaimed.

I looked down at my polka-dot, kitten-heeled ankle-length booties. They were pretty cool, If I thought so myself. "Thanks," I said. "I'm Gigi, the volunteer coordinator. We're here to help you out, so if you need anything, just let me know, or ask Lola." I pointed to Lola.

"Nice to meet you. I'm Alex." She called to her partner, who walked to us immediately. "Look at these shoes!" Alex exclaimed.

Her partner looked down, danced around, and sang, "Polka dots! Polka dots! We love polka dots!"

I beamed. I loved that the designers behind my favourite clothes loved my shoes. "Thanks. I think they're pretty swell, too."

Alex turned to her partner and said, "This is Gigi. She's looking after the volunteers."

"Oh, cool," said her partner. "I'm April."

"I'm so happy to meet you," I said. "I love your clothes. I just bought the gaucho jumpsuit."

"The gaucho!" they both shrieked.

"We love the gauchos too!" cried Alex.

"We only made ten of them," said April. "You're a lucky and deserving girl," she teased.

"Definitely," I said. "Best of luck with the show. Just let me know if you need anything."

They looked at each other and April said, "Sure, why don't you allocate dressers to models and clothing groups. They can unpack everything, familiarize themselves with the clothes, and organize shoes on the floor."

"Done." I ran to Lola and delivered the instructions. I wanted her to organize this because I was backstage to help her; I didn't want to take her job.

Moments later, volunteers set up and organized the clothes. Lola discussed the models with Niles and the show's choreographer, Sebastian, who was a gay guy version of Alex and April. Together they were a slick rock 'n' roll package. Sebastian had the coolest sunglasses I'd ever seen and looked as though he'd stepped out of a 1972 David Bowie hotel-room party. Dressers were then introduced to their assigned models, who miraculously, all completed hair and makeup forty minutes before show start. In the two earlier shows, hair and makeup hadn't been finished until fifteen minutes prior to start. I was relieved to finally meet people who were as efficient as I was. Not only that, but they were having a blast, too. Maybe it was possible to meet reasonable people in this industry after all.

The models all talked with their dressers, sharing garment intricacies or concerns with the time between changes. Everyone worked well together, and all the backstage volunteers were in place.

Sebastian made an announcement to the Team. "Okay, everyone, we're going to do a run-through in five minutes. Get dressed in your first outfits!"

I went to Niles and said, "It looks as though everything is under control and you have enough volunteers. Do you mind if I just stay backstage to watch the show?"

"I don't mind at all," he replied. "In fact, more people should watch this one. Alex and April are my favourite designers to work with because they're so organized. They were smart to hire Sebastian as a choreographer. He's great, and can deal with the models. This way, the clothes are Alex and April's only concern. It alleviates show stress from them. If only all designers were this good. It's very rare even to have a dress rehearsal."

"Are you serious?" I thought dress rehearsals were imperative to ensure accurate timing, to familiarize dressers with clothes, and for models to understand the choreography, catwalk, music, and attitude. A show was the primary opportunity to introduce clothes to buyers and media in the best possible way. A bad show - such as Xia's - only made a designer look incompetent.

Niles said, "Yeah, you'd be surprised at how many shows are last-minute. I'd say ninety percent of them don't have rehearsals. Many times designers are still making clothes the night before. Sometimes they change their vision. Other times it's because material arrived late. Usually, in those cases, they ordered the material late anyway. There's really no reason to be so disorganized. I love the Flaunt girls; it's always such a pleasure to work with them. Anyway, feel free to stand beside me during the show to learn how to call it. Right now, though, why don't you go into the runway room to watch how Sebastian and Vivian run rehearsal?"

"That rocks! Thanks Niles!" I kissed his cheek, skipped into the runway room, and noticed gift bags were already on the chairs. There was another rock 'n' roll girl working with the volunteers, giving them seating lists. I recognized her from when Alex and April walked in. She must have been their PR lady. Josh L. stood against the wall, looking miffed that he had been overtaken by the rock-girl, but she seemed way more organized than he was.

Sebastian stepped on the runway, more rock star than anyone I had seen in real life. He shouted, "Okay, Vivian! We can start the rehearsal. Ready?"

I looked to the tech booth and saw a middle-aged woman with short, cropped, violet hair. She had the most exquisite pair of cat's-eye glasses. So that was Vivian. After a day and a half of running around, I finally laid eyes on her. She always seemed to be everywhere yet nowhere at the same time. I wondered which of us ran around the venue more.

The lights dimmed and Sebastian jumped off the runway. The first few chords of Revolt's "*Mutiny Ship*" banged through the room. Revolt was Toronto's hottest band ever and was dominating worldwide indie charts. I wasn't surprised the catchy song was Flaunt's runway soundrack; it suited the clothes.

The first model walked out, pure rock 'n' roll attitude. When she posed at the end of the runway, she had the punkest stance and held up her middle finger. It was a better "Fuck You" statement than when Emilio Estevez said it in *Repo Man*. I loved it. Each following model was two parts rock, one part punk, and every part girly. It was a nice combination, which meant it would be a great show. Sebastian stayed at the front of the runway, yelling directions to the girls, advising them on poses. Everyone had a blast. That, to me, was a real fashion show.

Rehearsal ended and everyone was ready. I checked in with Gregor and Chantelle, who reported all was in order and they were ready to let people into the runway room. Chantelle was especially impressed, because it was the first show for which she'd received a complete guest list and seating plan. Niles gave the go-ahead, so we opened the runway room doors and guests spilled in. In contrast to earlier that day, these guests were the coolest of cool. Everyone had fabulous style; I could tell each person had a good story to tell. That was what I considered a fashionable crowd. As much as I loved to people-watch, I decided to go backstage with Niles to pay more attention to what a caller did during a show. Besides, all volunteers in the runway room worked smoothly under the direction of the Flaunt PR girl.

Veronikkah was backstage to give little gift bags to Alex and April. I thought it was a nice gesture for her to give designers a bit of appreciation.

Niles yelled to everyone, "Five minutes till showtime!"

Veronikkah left Alex and April to work their show, and there was an excitement backstage not felt with Xia. The Flaunt girls had such fun; they danced around, sang, and made everyone comfortable.

I stood by Niles, who spoke to Vivian in his headset. From hearing his part of the conversation, it sounded as though Vivian was looking forward to the show too.

Niles nodded and yelled, "Okay, everyone, line up! Alex! April! Come here with Sebastian and me. We're going to start!"

Niles and Sebastian were at the door. Alex and April went through the model lineup, adjusted fastenings and accessories, made skirts shorter and pulled fishnet kneehighs higher. The models were unbearably hip.

"Here we go!" said Niles as the lights dimmed and we heard Revolt. It was such a cool start it cancelled out the cheesy Collections Week theme.

Niles gave technical updates to Sebastian, who ensured the girls walked at the right time. He even had a stop watch to ensuring each entrance and pose matched sound and light cues. Alex and April monitored each girl, and the dressers executed the changes with lightning speed. There was not one change too difficult or too quick. It was only my second fashion show backstage, but I could tell it was a perfect machine.

When it was over, we packed everything up in fifteen minutes. Alex and April monitored clothes and accessories with a checklist to make sure everything was returned.

I rolled a rack to the loading area with Alex, who said, "Your volunteers were fantastic! The best group of dressers we've ever had! You guys should come to our after-party tonight." She handed me a few flyers.

I was thrilled. I'd never expected an invitation to a designer party. How cool. "I'm not sure if we can make it because we didn't get out of here until after two o'clock in the morning last night, but we'll try. Thanks."

"No problem," she said. "Thank you. Bring as many people as you want."

"Cool. Oh, and I loved your show!"

"Well, we love to have fun," she said, wheeling the latest season of Flaunt clothes out of the venue on a rack.

I went backstage to give the volunteers the exciting news about the party; I knew they'd love to go. When I got there, the next show had loaded in, so it was chaotic, but I noticed a gift bag left in the middle of the mess. I figured either Alex or April had forgotten theirs, so I grabbed it and ran after them, but they were busy with television interviews. Maybe it was Xia's bag. In any case, I decided to give it back to Veronikkah so she could decide what to do with it.

For the first time in a while, my walkie-talkie buzzed.

<<Gregor to Gigi.>>

<<Go for Gigi.>>

<<Can you come here for a minute?>>

<<I'll be there in about five minutes, Gregor. I just have to drop something off in Veronikkah's office.>>

<<Okay.>>

I ran up a set of stairs leading to the office. My polka-dot booties weren't used to running up stairs, and I tripped, launching my clipboard papers into the air and across the floor, along with the gift bag contents. Scrambling to pick everything up, I noticed a small plastic bag filled with white powder. Was it cocaine?

Never having dealt with someone's misplaced drugs before, I contemplated my options: track down Alex, April, and Xia to see who owned the bag; return the bag to Veronikkah; keep the bag and try coke for the first time; or keep the bag and try selling it to make a bit of money.

The last two options were out. First, I wouldn't know what to do with the drug; I've only seen people use it on TV and would likely overdose or something, so that was a bad idea. The idea of selling it was even worse. I'd be a horrible drug dealer and end up selling the stuff to an undercover cop. Since I didn't know Alex, April, or Xia's contact information, I figured it was best just to re-stuff the bag and give it to Veronikkah.

I walked down the hallway to the Collections Week office and almost knocked when I noticed the door open a crack. I saw the Bolivian Reservoir Dogs and heard agitated voices inside. It seemed tense, so I thought it best to wait.

A male voice said, "You promised money on this deal, but we haven't sold anything yet. And your associate disappeared with our shipment."

Veronikkah laughed nervously. "Oh, that Darryl. He's okay. He just likes to joke around. He's bringing the VIP clients. Not to worry; he'll be back before the big show tonight. Besides, he arranged for pick-ups tomorrow night, anyway."

"You sure we got the numbers?" growled another accented male voice.

"N-n-numbers," stammered Veronikkah. "Why, yes, we have the numbers. We have top-quality clients, the most reliable in Canada. This is going to be the biggest, most successful deal ever. When I do something, I do it right."

"And if it doesn't go right?" asked the growly man.

"Don't even worry about it," replied Veronikkah. "I have it sorted out. The distribution method can be pinned on Francie and the volunteers. I made documents implicating them. They're all too dumb to understand, especially Francie. She even signed the papers because she was too busy talking on the phone to read them."

I moved flat against the wall, hoping she was talking about clothes, but suspecting the conversation was about the little baggie I'd found in the gift bag. Veronikkah was planning to blame us for Canada's biggest coke deal?! What would I do next?

I didn't have time to think because I saw someone peek around the corner on the other side of the wall. Scared to death, I quietly jumped into a strange, defensive karate pose I imagined was quite intimidating, even though I knew nothing about karate. To my surprise, it was Hot Dan.

"What are you doing here?" we both whispered and froze, knowing we knew something was wrong and neither wanted to get caught knowing we knew whatever that something was.

He put his finger to his lips. I was about to walk to him when, horror of horrors, my walkie-talkie beeped. Someone was calling for me, but I ignored it to save both of us. Knowing we were going to be busted for eavesdropping, I finally put my years of movie-watching to good use and did a super-spy roll-dive thing, knocking Hot Dan out of the way, making it look as though I'd just walked around the corner. I prepared to knock on the door when Veronikkah appeared.

"Oh, LuLu," she said. "Come in. Have you met the Bolivian representatives?" She didn't appear to know I'd just overheard her conversation.

Stepping into the room but staying close to the door - in case I needed a quick getaway - I said, "Yeah, we met this morning." I was too nervous to correct her about my name, but asked, "Representatives? I thought you said they were designers."

They looked at each other and laughed. Well, they laughed as much as a group of big, scary men could laugh. It was more a round of smirks and coughs.

But Veronikkah laughed. Actually, it was more of an evil cackle. She said, "Designers? Nah. These guys are the designer escorts. They ensure clothes and other shipments travel safely. The designers arrive tomorrow morning. Anyway, what do you want?"

She made me feel as though I only had two seconds to talk and always wasted her valuable time. To top it off, I was in a room with four potential Bolivian drug czars. I wanted to get away quickly.

Acting as cool as I could, I held up the gift bag and said, "I noticed you gave these bags to the designers before the shows, and this one was left backstage by accident. I thought I'd return it to you so you could make sure the designer gets it back personally."

Veronikkah beamed. "What a sweetie, and with perfect timing. I was just going to tell my colleagues about these bags." She took the bag and held it up for the Bolivians. "Gentlemen, I would like you to look at this. It is our central marketing tool because I inserted samples of our goods for each designer."

Gak! The conversation really had been about the baggie of white powder because the only other sample in the bag was a perfume tester. The four men were definitely not perfume salesmen.

"As you know, designers are trendsetters. What they do, everyone else will follow. By the time this week is finished, we'll have plenty of orders. We'll be fine, you'll see."

The Bolivians nodded sceptically. They didn't want to say anything while I was there.

Lucky for me, Veronikkah assumed I didn't know the gift bag's illicit contents, so I acted blissfully ignorant of the entire situation.

When she realized I was still in the room, she said, "Oh, LuLu dear, thanks for bringing this to me. Now, can you do me another favour?"

I nodded; I didn't want to piss off that woman.

"As you can see, this room is a mess. Francie is a dreadful assistant. She only cares about her cell phone. I don't know why I hired that girl. Oh right...her mother is my best friend. Ha! Ha!" She ranted, obviously high again. "You know what, LuLu? You're great. Want to be my assistant? I could fire Francie like that!" She snapped her fingers.

When I'd first started with Collections Week, I would have given anything for Francie's job, but as I sat in the room with the schizophrenic Veronikkah and her Bolivian buddies, I wasn't so sure. From what I had seen of Veronikkah over the last few days, she was a nightmarish employer. On top of that, she was a convicted drug dealer, who was very likely re-entering her former profession and planning to frame her assistant. Would I really want to work for someone who would fire me on a drug-induced whim? Based on my limited Veronikkah experience, I figured it was best to distract her.

I laughed off her previous comment and asked, "You were talking about a messy room?"

"Oh yes," she replied. "I would like volunteers to clean it. Can you get that done?"

She wanted volunteers to clean her mess? I thought she asked too much of the volunteers, since her mess was a personal responsibility, but maybe it was normal for the fashion industry, so I promised to get it done. I left the room as quickly as I could.

Hot Dan was gone.

What would I do next? I couldn't plan any action because all I wanted to do was get away from Veronikkah and her Bolivians. Confused and lost, I ran away from the room, fearing Ms. Hendricks.

SPY AND DECEIVE.

My mind was spinning with confusion, fear, and shock as I entered the designer gallery. Gregor saw me and ran right over.

"Gigi, honey, are you okay? You look pale. Well, not that you don't always look pale, but you're whiter than usual." That was a fashion queen's way of showing concern.

"I'll be allright, I've just been a busy running around today and haven't had anything to eat. Maybe I should sit down."

He helped me to one of the Corbusier chairs and brought me bottled water. As I sat there, I tried to figure out what I was going to do with my new knowledge, but I was lost.

I regained some composure and remembered why I had been on my way to the designer gallery in the first place. "So, Gregor...You wanted to see me?" I asked.

"Girl, this Gallery is the centre of downtown dullsville. Nobody wants to spend time in here. My volunteers keep disappearing into the runway room. They only want to watch the fashion shows. What should I do?"

"To be honest, I can see why nobody's here. Volunteers are sitting in the booths making sure people don't steal things, emitting boredom. Why don't you see if you can get music in here? Make it a lounge area where people can schmooze. Get your volunteers into the front entrance and encourage guests to spend time in the designer gallery. Pull them into your area and make it fun. But don't forget to make announcements about showtimes. Then try talking to Patsy the event planner. She should have some good ideas."

Gregor sighed. "It's a good start, but do I have to talk to Camel Toe lady? Her bad style freaks me out. And what about the music? Will Veronikkah go for it?"

By then I'd figured out how Veronikkah worked, so I said, "If Veronikkah says anything, make her think it was her brilliant idea. If she thinks something smart was her idea, she'll be in a good mood. As for Patsy, it's her job to create ideas. She should make the Gallery interesting."

"Okay, done." Then Gregor's face crumpled. "But, uhhh...sweetie..."

"What, Gregor? Don't be afraid to tell me things."

"After watching people work yesterday and today, I don't know what Veronikkah and Francie actually do. I only see them stalking the media or yelling at volunteers. And last night they went out to a party while we stayed late. Then who was first to the venue both days? We were. And now there's Patsy. I've only seen her follow Veronikkah and Francie."

Gregor was right. Francie and Patsy only cared about press coverage. Veronikkah wanted the limelight, of course, but I knew she had other interests. How was I supposed to answer him?

"Gregor, I know what you're saying. I'm as frustrated as you are because I've never worked like this. But we agreed to help and that's what we're going to do. We'll do the best job we can because we love fashion. Together, you, Lola, Chantelle, and I are going to make this the most successful Collections Week ever."

Wow. I was good at pep talks, even if I questioned my own commitment to the cause. I decided it was best not to say anything to any volunteers until I knew more behind-the-scene details. Until that week, I'd thought "behind-the-scenes" meant backstage, but there was so much more.

Gregor smiled. "Okay, I'll do my best, but it's hard to do all this work for bitchy people who don't appreciate us."

I gave him a hug and said, "Just be patient. I'm sure they appreciate our work, but they're stressed. They have a million things to do and tons of people to please. It's hard to make everyone happy, but they're doing their best."

Gregor smiled and went to talk to a volunteer about spicing up the designer gallery.

Alone, I sat in my chair wondering why I defended those people. For one reason, my parents taught me to never quit. That always stuck with me. They also taught me to stay positive; it was not in my nature to see the bad in people (unless it was a bad outfit, of course. I'd learned that lesson on my own). Even at that point, I thought Veronikkah and Francie probably had really good reasons for behaving the way they did. Finally, no matter how frustrating, volunteering at Collections week was a great experience for me. I was learning how to run a fashion show and meeting so many people. If I performed well, I figured I would be able to get some sort of job from someone I met that week.

<<Chantelle to Gigi.>>

The walkie-talkie pulled me out of my thoughts. <<Go for Gigi.>>

<<People are asking about offsite shows. Where are they? I don't know anything about them and don't know what to say.>>

<<Offsite shows? I thought everything was here.>> I said.

<<No, apparently the next two shows are offsite and then the final one tonight is here at nine o'clock.>>

<<Ummm...just a second. Let's ask Lola. Gigi to Lola. Do you know the show schedule?>>

Lola came on the walkie-talkies and said, <<As far as we know, the next show is at nine o'clock.>>

<<Thanks, Lola. Okay, Chantelle, we'll try to get directions for your guests. Has anyone seen Francie, Patsy, or Josh L.? They'll know.>>

<<Francie's backstage, talking to a camera crew,>> said Lola. <<Do you want me to ask her?>>

<<Yes,>> I said, <<and make sure to report the address and directions to Chantelle. Everyone else, it might be a good time for your volunteers to break before the night's big show. My guess is it will probably be as chaotic as last night because it's the famous lingerie show.>>

<<Fine,>> said Lola. <<But now I have a problem. Francie finished her interview and is on her phone. She won't look at me.>>

<<I don't care.>> My frustration intensified. <<Tear the phone away if you have to. It is important for her guests to get to the shows.>>

<<Uhhh...okay...here goes...>>

A minute later, Lola was able to give directions to Chantelle. Then she said to me, <<Gigi, Francie mentioned something about getting volunteers to clean the Collections Week room. She'll unlock the door if you get there in five minutes.>>

Crap! I'd hoped Veronikkah would forget about that task, because I certainly had. I felt horrible asking volunteers to clean up Veronikkah and Francie's mess. Not only that, but I didn't want to expose them to cocaine or Bolivian Reservoir Dogs.

<<Tell Francie I'll be right there.>>

I looked around the designer gallery. Since it wasn't busy, I figured I could steal a couple of Gregor's team. Looking at one girl named Shelli, I remembered she was interested in fashion journalism and had a column in her university newspaper. Reasoning that her experience would provide her with a funny story, I collected her and another girl named Jennifer, a quiet, first year design student, and took them to the office.

Francie and Eva were in the room. As usual, Francie was on the phone while Eva played with the clothes. There was no sign of Veronikkah or the Bolivians.

Eva wore a lime green chiffon dress and asked me, "Isn't this the prettiest dress you've ever seen? I'm going to wear it to the offsite shows."

The dress looked familiar, but I couldn't place where I'd seen it before.

"Yeah, it looks great," I said. It did actually look good on her. "But aren't you staying around to help hair and makeup for the night's shows?"

"No, they're fine. It's all under control." The girl was a liar and clearly only interested in hanging out with Francie. I had to warn Niles he'd be in charge.

Francie finished with the phone and said, "We're going to the offsite shows now, so you guys can clean the room. Gigi, I'll leave the key with you. Give it back to me when I return." She made me feel like pre-glass-slipper Cinderella.

"Are you going to be back to prepare for the night's show?"

She sighed. "Veronikkah must be present at all shows, and I have to be beside her at all times. We talk to the press. That's what we do. Josh L. comes to make sure we say the right things, and Patsy makes sure all the ideas get followed through. So you guys have to stay here to make sure everything is okay."

Wanting to scream at her, I tried my best to keep all my frustration inside because I still wanted to help with the event, no matter how crazy it became.

"But Francie," I pleaded, "we keep getting told things at the last minute or conflicting details. Then we get yelled at for doing something wrong when we were told to do it that way. We're here to help you, but we need your help too. This is your event, and we need guidance."

"We'll talk later. I have to go. In the meantime, just talk to Vivian. She knows what we want. Now clean the room." As she put on her jacket and walked out the door with Eva, she whispered, "Keep an eye on those volunteers so they don't steal anything."

The volunteers looked offended after hearing Francie's comment.

"Sorry about that, guys," I apologized, wanting to vent my frustrations, but knowing better.

"Do we have to do this?" whined Shelli, looking around the room, surveying the mess of clothes, cosmetics, magazines, liquor bottles, and leftover food.

Jennifer looked at me with the same question in her eyes, though she was too shy to actually ask it.

"Unfortunately, we've been asked to do it so we have to. Don't worry, I'll help too." Suddenly I realized it was an excellent chance to dig around and find some answers without being caught. I closed and locked the door so nobody could interrupt. Eyeing the piles of cosmetic samples, I felt subversive and suddenly powerful, ready to take chances, so I promised the girls makeup samples for completing the crappy job. I also tried to talk Shelli into writing about the humiliating experience for her school newspaper along with volunteer abuse. At the same time, I hoped she recognized the mistreatment wasn't my idea.

Their eyes lit up at the mention of free cosmetics and Shelli said, "Yeah, this is a great story idea. A real behind-the-scenes exposé!" They started cleaning.

It wasn't wrong to give them the beauty products, was it? Wasn't it a grosser abuse of power to have poor little volunteers clean the room in the first place? There were close to a thousand lip-glosses, eyeshadows, mascaras, and lipsticks. I doubted Veronikkah and Francie would notice a few missing.

I told the girls to deal with the clothes and bottles, and to let me deal with the papers since most of them involved private Collections Week business. They didn't know I wasn't supposed to read official documents. So they hung clothes while I sorted through miscellaneous papers left on the coffee table. Then I stumbled onto a bunch spilling out of a briefcase, which really meant I saw some questionable things and snooped. But if I worked with a drug dealer, ethics didn't mean much, did they? I was allowed to ensure my volunteers and I weren't involved in anything nasty, wasn't I?

I made sure Shelli and Jennifer didn't look when I took the papers out of the briefcase. It was a mix of financial data, letters, and receipts. I stopped to read a letter:

> Dear Veronikkah:
>
> On behalf of the Collections Week Board of Directors, I am writing to request copies

of all financial documents for the past two seasons.

It recently came to our attention that certain parties have not been paid for their work, and we are concerned not only for Collections Week's reputation, but for our own personal reputations and livelihoods. As you know, the Board is financially responsible for operations, and we must make certain that all transactions are properly handled.

Of particular concern are your trips to Paris and Milan for the haute couture shows. It is important the Board be assured no expenses from these trips were covered by Collections Week funds, since these funds are intended to help Canadian designers stage shows and promote their products, and not to fund personal travel.

Thank you for looking into this matter and understanding our concern. You have until the end of Collections Week to provide us with all necessary documentation.

Richard Locke
Chairperson
Collections Week Board of Directors

I recognized Richard Locke's name as a prominent businessman within the fashion industry. I didn't know too much about him, but knew he was well known in the business of fashion: mergers, acquisitions, partnerships, and so on. From what I knew, he was well respected.

Below his letter was Veronikkah's reply:

Dear Richard:

How dare you accuse me of stealing Collections Week money for my own travels! I am shocked and appalled you could think such a thing! I have never been so hurt in my life. I would never risk the reputation of the Board or deny fabulous design talent the financial opportunity to show their work for personal gain. I am here for them.

Although I can understand the Board's need to see financial records, I have some bad news. All our financial records were on Francie's laptop, which was stolen just before Collections Week. Due to this bad luck, I cannot give financial records to the Board. The police are looking for the laptop, but say it is unlikely we will find the computer. In the meantime, I will do everything I can to provide you with receipts.

Regards,

Veronikkah Hendricks
Director
Collections Week

A bunch of receipts followed that letter with a sticky note stating,

Francie,

Shred these.

- V

The stack of documents appeared to be Veronikkah's collection of receipts for Richard.

There was a credit card slip for the Ritz Paris with Collections Week as the cardholder's name, not Veronikkah Hendricks. I looked through other receipts and noticed the same thing for bills from Parisian restaurants, miscellaneous Milan expenditures, and one for an eight-thousand-dollar Chanel dress. Tens of thousands of dollars were charged to Collections Week.

Veronikkah was lying to the Collections Week Board of Directors! She was not only a drug dealer, but an embezzler too. Things were out of control, and now I was involved. What was I to do?

Looking around, I saw a fax machine in a corner. Did I dare make copies? It wasn't my problem; it was the Board's issue.

Then again, it could be important for someone to have those receipts. Veronikkah had broken the law. It was probably wise to make copies of what I could because Veronikkah could destroy the evidence at any time. It was good Francie was a terrible employee; otherwise the receipts would have been destroyed.

The girls had almost finished cleaning the room, so I was able to copy a few papers, put them in my clipboard, and return them quickly. I wondered why they were here in the first place. Maybe this was the only place where Veronikkah could monitor them. It didn't matter, though. I was sure Richard had copies of the letters, and the credit card company would have records. How did that woman think she wouldn't get caught?

Then I put things together. If I were in her shoes, I'd be desperate because I would know I was about to get caught in a huge scandal. I'd probably try to run away. What better way to do it than to get a bunch of money from a huge drug deal? Shipping cocaine into the country with clothes under the guise of encouraging equal development was a brilliant strategy because she looked like a caring philanthropist.

She was smart, but not smart enough to fool Gigi LaFaux. Not only was she a criminal, she treated volunteers poorly and needed to be taught a lesson. I had to stop her. Taking action was important. If I didn't do anything, her twisted operation would remain the norm in Canada's fashion industry. Young designers would learn to conduct business that way. I envisioned a Canadian fashion apocalypse and wondered how we could avert disaster.

Defend.

I decided to find Hot Dan; I needed to know why he was outside the Collections Week office. While on my mission, I checked on Gregor and Chantelle.

Everything was looking funkier in the designer gallery. Gregor had infused the area with suitable lounge sounds and turned it into a cooler place. Volunteers smiled and giggled. It was a different place.

"This looks great, Gregor!" I patted him on the back. "What did you do?"

"Just what you told me to do," he winked. "But there's a problem. I was just about to call you because a designer is freaking out: a dress is missing!"

"You're kidding!" I gasped.

"No. I wouldn't kid about something as serious as a designer dress. It's a lime green chiffon thing."

Eva popped into my mind. "I know who has it. Francie's friend Eva is wearing it at the offsite shows right now."

"Seriously?"

"I wouldn't joke about dresses either," I said. "Can you explain things to the designer and sort it out?

I have to check on Chantelle, the runway room, and backstage."

"No problem, Gigi. You can count on your Super Trouper." We hugged again and I ran out of the room.

I liked working with Gregor; he was the right mixture of reliability, wit, and catiness.

As I walked to the front entrance, Chantelle smiled. "I'm so glad to see you," she said, pulling me off to the side. "People are showing up saying they're on Darryl's guest list again, but I still don't have one."

That wasn't surprising, since - based on what I'd heard earlier in the day - Darryl was on some killer coke binge. I suspected it was unlikely we would see him at all, especially if he found the Bolivian stash in the car.

"Just do what we did last night," I explained.

She looked worried and asked, "But what about Veronikkah? She'll probably get mad about the papers again."

"Don't worry about it. We explained things to her already, and promised we would have typed pages tomorrow. If she forgets, just radio me." I gave her a hug too, and felt all warm and fuzzy about my team. "Oh, don't forget to try to move all the guests into Gregor's section so you aren't too crowded out here."

"Sure thing."

Walking into the runway room, I checked on the girl I'd left with Josh L.. Everything was fine, but she had some problems since Josh L. wouldn't share the seating lists. He rationalized it by believing he was the only one who should deal with VIPs. I didn't see that logic; it was more important to get everyone seated quickly. Over the two days, it was the biggest complaint I heard while running around. Though it was disheartening to learn I worked at a disorganized event, it was nice to know I wasn't the only one who thought so. I would have talked to Josh L. about the inefficiency, but he was at the offsite shows. The volunteer said he'd left her in charge and she was trying to get the gift bags ready for the last show of the day, the lingerie show. She thought everything was under control, so I reminded her to run backstage and talk to Lola about any problems.

It was my turn to go backstage again, hopefully to talk to Hot Dan about what we'd heard. When I arrived, I found myself among twenty half-naked people. It was an odd scene since one would think twenty half-naked people together in one room would reek of sex, but it felt decidedly different.

As I walked in, one woman grabbed me and said, "Look at my butt! Does it jiggle when I walk?" That meant I had to watch her scantily lingerie-clad bum as she practiced "her walk" in front of me. Jiggle? Who was she kidding? The girl was an anorexic stick insect. I told her there was no way anything could jiggle on her, but she continued asking the same question to everyone around her. The poor girl couldn't have been more than fourteen, and there she was, a lifetime of eating disorders ahead of her.

After assessing the room, I finally found Hot Dan. There he was, back toward me, wearing only boxer-briefs. His body shape burned in my mind from yesterday. Its perfection would never leave my head. I walked closer, wondering if it was appropriate to bring up a serious conversation with an underwear-clad man, but as I got closer, what did I see? Hot Dan curled in a tender embrace with another male model.

Curses! I wasn't ready to see he was fully gay! I wanted my little Hot Dan fantasy to carry on longer. Damn!

I didn't know what to do because I desperately needed to talk to him about Veronikkah and the Bolivians, but I couldn't split up his lover time. I froze for a few seconds in the middle of the half-naked backstage flurry. When I finally made up my mind to leave him with lover-boy, I turned and tripped over a rolling rack in transit. As I ran into the rack, my right foot caught in the bottom bar. Feeling myself fall in slow motion, I grabbed for something, but there was nothing stable to hold. Stupidly, I reached for the top of the rack and knew immediately it was the wrong reaction. I ended up flipping the rack over, crashing it to the floor, along with its clothes and accessories.

Everyone backstage stopped to look at my commotion. For the first time since I'd been backstage, it was silent. After a few long, seconds, everyone laughed at me. I would never recover from the embarassment. To make matters worse, Hot Dan appeared in front of me, offering his hand to help me up. I couldn't look at him, but grabbed his hand.

He pulled me to him and whispered, "We've got to talk."

Since people were watching, I pretended he'd said nothing and executed some self-effacing bows and curtsies, trying to appear proud of my slapstick performance. People continued their business and I was about to reply when my walkie-talkie buzzed.

<<Chantelle to Gigi.>>

I looked at Hot Dan and pointed to my headset. <<Go for Gigi.>>

<<You've got to come out here quick. Darryl's here and he says he's double parked and needs a volunteer to watch the Collections Week car for ten minutes until he sorts things out. What should I do?>>

<<Do you have a spare volunteer?>> I asked.

<<No, we're getting busy out here.>>

<<Then ask Gregor if he has one. I'll be there as soon as I can.>>

<<Thanks, Gigi. Try to get here fast because Darryl's acting weird and has two crazy friends with him.>>

I tried to ignore Gregor and Chantelle buzzing in my ear as I told Hot Dan I'd have to go. He begged me to stay and talk.

"I'm sorry," I apologized. "The show is going to start in less than an hour and I've got to help with a million things. We can't talk now. How about after the show?"

His face wrinkled. "I'm kind of forced to go to the Flaunt after-party," he said. "All the guys are going because it's sponsored by the modelling agency. Are you going? We could talk there."

"I really want to go, but I don't know what time I'll get out of here."

"Send all your volunteers home early and come out. We can't wait about this; we both know it's important."

"You're right," I said. "Okay, I'll try to make it."

"Excellent," he smiled, and squeezed my hand as I tried to leave. Damn those gay-straight men.

Fortify.

"ALL THESE PEOPLE ARE FUCKING CRAZY!" Darryl was standing behind his two friends by the registration desk in a defensive stance. "I never said they could all be on the guest list!"

An alarmed Chantelle tried to deal with the demanding crowd and the very coked-out Darryl. His hands shook, his eyes were red, and he ground his jaw as if he were the gum-chewing Violet Beauregarde from *Charlie and the Chocolate Factory*. Not knowing exactly what to do, but wanting to rescue Chantelle, I approached Darryl's crew.

"What's wrong here? How can I help?"

"THESE PEOPLE ARE FUCKING CRAZY!" Darryl screamed again.

I looked to Darryl's friends to gauge my next move on their reactions. Their pupils were as dilated as Darryl's and their faces indicated nothing in their heads. They were dressed as urban-thug caricatures, complete with baseball caps tipped to the side and oversized everything.

Chantelle cared for the guests while I looked after Darryl. He was not in any state to deal with people, but the lingerie show was his party, so he had to do something. He was right about one thing, though: the crowd was crazy. A quick glance indicated a male-dominated crowd eager to peek at anorexic girls in panties. It was not a fashion crowd.

Cozying up to Darryl, I put an arm around his shoulder, hoping it would calm him. I aimed for his ego and asked, "Darryl, isn't this your party? It's important you represent yourself as calm and collected. If you don't, the crowd will get ugly." They were rowdy already, but we didn't need major confrontations. I continued to explain it would be a fantastic event and he was the centre of everything. As I made progress, Veronikkah entered with her entourage to ruin everything.

"Why is all this chaos in the entrance?" she screamed.

Darryl shrunk away from her screechy voice, so once again I took control.

I yelled back, "We're getting everything organized for tonight, having a little pep talk," There was no need to tell her about Darryl's freak-out.

She rolled her eyes and yelled, "Less talk, more action!" The woman would probably shrivel up and die if she ever said please.

"Will do," I said, turning back to Darryl and his sketchy, paranoid friends. They needed to feel comfortable and enjoy themselves, so I decided to give them a party-type job.

"Hey, guys. Why don't you walk through the crowd with your friends and make them feel good about being here? Calm everyone down so when they get to us, they won't be agitated. We can sign in all the guests as we did yesterday and make everyone feel as though they're on the guest list. They'll feel special, but we'll let VIPs enter first."

"Good plan, sweetpea," said Darryl, patting my ass and smiling. At least my butt made him feel better.

"What about payment?" he asked.

I stepped away - since I knew I'd slap him if I were any closer - and said, "Good question. What about payment?"

"This is a public event. We're sellin' twenty-five dollar tickets. People pay or don't play," he said.

That was different than the previous shows, which were fashion-industry oriented.

"Nobody said anything to us about collecting cash, but we'll do it," I offered. "Do you have a cashbox?"

"We don't deal with that shit. We just get people in. You have the cashbox."

"But I just told you we didn't know about it."

He walked closer to me and I saw his hand go for my butt again, so I tried to end the conversation. The guy was gross; I didn't want to be near him, so I pushed him and his friends into the crowd. A girl in a gold halter and micro-miniskirt - looking as if she'd stepped out of a video - promptly distracted them with her cleavage and they were suddenly the life of the front entrance party.

Meanwhile, we had to complete a job. Chantelle heard everything and set up her crew to record visitors, but asked me about selling tickets. She found envelopes to collect money and though it wasn't the most professional way to do so, it was our best option. We were finally ready to accept guests, but ran into problems with the first customer.

"What do you mean I have to PAY?" yelled another hyper video reject.

"This is a public event. Tickets are twenty-five dollars," replied Chantelle.

"But Darryl said I'm on the guest list," she whined.

"I'm sorry, but our instructions are to charge everyone twenty-five dollars for entrance," Chantelle insisted.

"Listen, bitch," said the irate guest, "I'm on the guest list, see? And I don't need to pay." She moved in close to Chantelle, ready to punch her.

People behind her were also agitated, saying, "Yeah, us too! We're on the guest list. We ain't paying."

A man resembling a professional boxer pushed his way to the front and said, "Who do you think you are, bitches? We're here for a show. Let us in!"

Not knowing how to respond, Chantelle looked at me for guidance.

Darryl was right; these people were nuts and it was scary, especially for the group of fashion design students working at the front entrance. They weren't trained as bouncers, nor did they sign up at Collections

Week to deal with that kind of abuse. A twenty year-old girl couldn't take on a boxer. It was time to do what would quickly earn me a reputation as a wacky girl, bitch, or table-dancer. I climbed up on the registration tables, repeating yesterday's crowd-control regime.

"Good evening, ladies and gentlemen!" I screamed in my best polite, professional, authoritative, yet badass voice. "Sorry for any delays, but we were preparing for your orderly entrance. This is a public event and tickets are on sale here for twenty-five dollars. If you are on the guest list, you will have to consult Darryl, who is standing over by the large schedule. Darryl, please wave your hand."

Darryl shot me a death-look, but I didn't care; I wanted him to pay for the crap he brought upon us. I didn't want my volunteers to get hit by hip-hop gangsta bitches or boxers. It was his party and he had to deal with the angry mob he'd created. When it came to my safety and sanity and that of people I recruited, I had no sympathy for an incompetent drug addict. He had to figure out how to solve the situation. Wasn't he hired to do that anyway?

"Go ahead, Darryl. Wave your hands in the air! It's your party, and wave them like you just don't care!" Hey, I had to turn an evil situation into a fun one. I got to make fun of him and teach him a lesson all at once. "Hey party people, just to be fair, if you're on the guest list, walk over there! Hey-ho, Hey-ho!" I had a great time dancing all over the Reception tables and even if it wasn't the most professional way of dealing with a crowd, people laughed and clapped along with my cheeziness. Even if I was a total loser, I'd eliminated the tensions from the moment before.

The crowd shifted, but there was a problem. Five people approached the registration tables while the other two hundred guests huddled around Darryl. I stayed above everyone so I could assess the situation, sensing another Darryl breakdown.

As predicted, Darryl yelled immediately. "Okay, stop buggin'! You're ALL on the list!"

I couldn't believe it. He sacrificed five thousand dollars because he was sketchy, paranoid, disorganized, and lazy? I jumped off the table to tell Chantelle and her team the news. They had processed the five people and waited for more guests, even though they knew everyone would say they were on the phantom guest list.

"What about the money?" asked Chantelle.

"Just keep it for now. You're in charge of it since I'm always running around," I replied. "I imagine Darryl will pick it up after the show since it's his party."

"Sounds good," smiled Chantelle.

"Great. Now I'll check on the runway room," I said, clawing through the mayhem into the cool, dark runway room entrance.

<<Gregor to Gigi.>>

<<Go for Gigi.>>

<<Have you seen the volunteer I sent to Darryl's car? It's been an hour since I last saw her.>>

<<I haven't seen her, but I'll go find her.>>

<<Thanks.>>

I returned to the front entrance where the mayhem had calmed down. Most guests had gone to the designer gallery to schmooze and sip. I ran around looking for Darryl, but didn't see the guy, so I put out a general APB over the walkie-talkies. Nobody responded, so I announced I would check on the volunteer sent to look after Darryl's car.

Stepping onto the street, I saw the pink Collections Week car on Yonge Street in front of the Carlu, but it was not the same car I'd seen yesterday. Today, it was crunched along the front right fender with dents along the side. I ran to the car and saw a girl crying in the passenger seat. The volunteer had got into an accident! What did I think, sending a volunteer out into a vehicle? Legal battles fought through my head as I knocked on the window. She saw me and rolled it down.

"Are you okay?" I asked.

"I'm scared," she sniffled. She tried talking, but it was hard to understand because of the crying. "I've been here for an hour and the police keep coming, telling me to move the car or they'll tow it." She tried taking a few big breaths, but they turned into hiccups, strands of her blonde hair stuck to her face, and her eyes were red and puffy. "I don't have a driver's license, so I can't drive it. That Darryl guy told me not to move until he came back, or I would get in big trouble." She lost her speaking ability and cried harder than before.

"So you didn't get in an accident? You didn't move the car?" I asked.

She hyperventilated as she tried taking more deep breaths, but managed to spit out, "N...n...no...would...n... not do that!" before breaking down again. "Smashed... before I came...hasn't moved since I got here."

That was a relief, but I saw a police officer walk toward us.

"Ladies, this car must move immediately because it's blocking traffic. This is your last warning. If you don't move in five minutes, I'll tow it."

The volunteer wailed.

I smiled at the officer and explained the situation to him, but he didn't care. He wanted the car gone, and pulled out his radio to contact a tow truck.

"Hey, are the keys still in there?" I asked the girl.

"Yes, b…b…but," she sniffed, getting stuck in mid sentence due to her tears. "It d…doesn't make any d…d… difference." Tears rolled down her cheeks and I feared she would never stop crying.

"It sure does make a difference. I'll park the car."

"You'll...(sniff)...do that?" the girl smiled as though I'd solved the world's problems.

"Sure," I said, hopping into the driver's seat. In the back of my mind, I knew it was a bad idea to drive around with a volunteer, and with me volunteering myself, I had no idea if Collections Week could cover charges if I ended up in an accident. Nonetheless, I thought it best to keep her in the car as a witness in case anything happened.

Luckily, we swung into the parkade and found a stall without any major incident. When we stepped out of the car, I apologized and gave her a hug. I took her back upstairs, got her a sandwich and soda, and dismissed her for the rest of the night. I told her she could watch the evening's fashion show to improve her crappy Collections Week experience.

She looked at me with wide, grateful eyes and hugged me. The previous hour's experience vanished from her memory with the promise of viewing a fashion show.

I led her into the runway room and explained the situation to a stressed Josh L. He was too busy to care, so pointed to a seat and told her to sit down and enjoy the show. The girl was so giddy; it was as though I'd given her a diamond bracelet. Another crisis averted. It was time to find Francie and explain what had happened.

<<This is Gigi,>> I called on my walkie-talkie. <<Has anyone seen Francie?>>

There was no reply.

I was getting frustrated. <<HAS ANYONE SEEN FRANCIE? IT'S URGENT!>> I yelled. Luckily, there weren't any guests around to hear my freak-out.

<<Gigi, it's Gregor. I just saw her get back from the offsite shows. She's heading to the Collections Week office.>>

<<Great, thanks. Is everyone okay?>>

<<All fine here,>> said Gregor.

<<We're almost ready backstage,>> said Lola.

Chantelle tuned in. <<I'm ready to let in guests when Lola gives the word.>>

<<Great. Keep up the good work, guys.>>

I thought about the car situation and decided to check facts before approaching Francie, just to make sure the volunteer hadn't lied to me about the car. I called Gregor and asked, <<Hey Gregor, did you drop off that volunteer at the car downstairs?>>

<<Sure did, candycakes.>>

<<Where are you? We have to talk.>>

<<I'm at the giant lipstick poster.>>

<<Stay there. I'm coming.>>

PROTECT.

Gregor leaned next to the poster, eyeing the party reporter from Toronto's gay weekly magazine.

"What's up?" he asked, tearing himself away from his cruise-y gaze.

"When you dropped off the volunteer at the car, did you notice anything about it?"

"About the car? Apart from the hideous pink paint? Yeah. It was smashed up along the side."

"So the dents were already there when you saw it?"

"Yeah. Darryl gave me the keys, I took the volunteer downstairs, we saw the car, and commented on how tacky it was for Collections Week to have such an appalling car."

"Okay, that's good. I wanted to make sure the volunteer wasn't the one who got in an accident. By the way, she was so upset by being left in the car and dealing with policemen that I dismissed her and let her sit in the runway room to watch the show."

Gregor looked concerned. "Is she okay?"

"Yeah, she'll be all right, but I doubt she'll volunteer for Collections Week again. I didn't realize Darryl wanted her to sit with the car for an hour. I'm new at this volunteer coordinator thing, but I suspect there are some legal issues stopping us from having people drive or sit in vehicles. I'm sorry to have put you in that position, too. Anyway, can you keep this quiet? I have to discuss it with Francie."

"Well, it'll be hard to keep such a juicy secret, but for you, okay."

I thanked him, gave him another big hug, and ran to the Collections Week office, but kept getting stopped on the way. Every fifth person was asking me why the show was late. They assumed I knew everything since I had a headset. I usually replied, "It's a fashion show; they're always late," and kept running toward the office.

I arrived at the door, took a huge breath, and knocked. Thankfully, Francie opened it. Eva was with her.

"What do you want? Make it quick. We have to watch the show."

"We might have to talk alone," I whispered, not wanting to offend Eva.

"Don't worry; Eva knows everything. She's my friend."

I looked at Eva. "I thought you were looking after hair and makeup. Don't they need you backstage? They must be super-busy before the show."

Eva looked at me as though I didn't know anything. "Nah," she sniffed, picking up a glass of wine. "They know what they're doing. They're fine."

"Oh, okay. Sorry, I just thought..." I didn't know what I thought anymore. Those people were the weirdest I'd ever worked with. Were they a bunch of sycophantic partiers or were they just lazy? Or were they simply young and inexperienced? Whatever the case, I couldn't find out more because I was concerned about the car and the volunteer.

"Francie, listen," I began. "I found the car."

"I know. Darryl had it all the time. He was just joking around. Everything's cool," she laughed, trying to push me out the door.

"But wait; there's more," I protested.

She looked at me and sighed as though I was wasting her time.

"The car's all banged up. Someone got in an accident."

Francie's face paled and her eyes bulged out of her head. "What are you talking about?"

"Dents are along the side. Not only that, but Darryl double-parked the car on Yonge Street and requested a volunteer to sit in it for ten minutes while he sorted out some logistics. He left her there for an hour and she almost got towed. She was scared and I think Darryl overstepped his boundaries. I know he's the party promoter, but he can't abuse the volunteers like that."

"She must have been the one who got in the accident!" Francie yelled. "Where is she?"

"No, Francie," I said. "Gregor escorted her to the car, and he said it was banged up before they even got to it. It is Darryl's problem."

"No! Darryl wouldn't do that. If anything happened, he would have told me. I'm sure it was the volunteer's fault."

"Listen, Francie. I have the volunteer's name and number. You can talk to her if you want, but it was probably illegal to have her sitting in a car on Yonge Street for an hour. She could likely sue Collections Week if this gets bigger. It would be best for you to sort this out with Darryl, and please, let me know as soon as you do, because this is important."

By then, Francie looked as though she was wearing those slinky-eye glasses. I worried her eyes would pop out of her head and land on me.

"Francie, will you go talk to Darryl about this?"

"Yes, but promise you won't say anything to anybody about it."

"I won't, but Gregor and the volunteer know. I told them not to say anything."

"Okay, great."

Francie and I rushed out the door, while Eva sauntered behind, apparently not caring about the car damage. As Francie and Eva started down the hallway, I heard the walkie-talkie.

<<Hi guys, it's Chantelle. The guests out front are getting anxious. When can I let people into the runway room?>>

<<Chantelle, it's Lola. We're fine backstage. We'll be ready to go in fifteen minutes. Niles and Vivian say you can let them in.>>

<<Thanks, Lola.>>

Francie was almost around the corner when I called out to her the show would start soon. She waved her hand in acknowledgement and kept running. She would find Darryl and sort things out, leaving me to focus on the actual event.

<<Hi guys, it's Gigi. Do any of you need help? I'm free at the moment.>>

<<I'm fine,>> said Gregor.

<<Backstage is cool,>> said Lola.

Chantelle said she would call me if there were any entry problems, but things were starting well, so I decided to help in the runway room. The fastest way to get there was through a side hallway backstage that nobody seemed to use. My initial reconnaissance tour had come in handy for shortcuts. Since Collections Week people only went to the office, the side hall wasn't a high-traffic area. As I turned the corner, though, I saw two people making out in a doorway. I was about to tell them they couldn't be back there when I realized one part of the couple was Darryl. As I got closer, I saw who he was with: Veronikkah. Not only were their lips locked, but as I walked beside them, I saw Veronikkah holding a compact with four lines of coke cut on the mirror in one hand and a joint in the other. Darryl groped her corseted breasts. I stared right at them as Veronikkah opened her eyes. My shortcut not only helped my feet, but helped uncover some secrets as well.

"Oh, hey Mitzi," she said, pulling herself away from Darryl, placing one boob back into her corset. Her eyelids were heavy and she barely stood up. "Darryl, this girl is the best ever!" She looked down at her compact and over to me. "Hey, Mitzi, wanna line?"

Mitzi? Who was Mitzi? More importantly, who was Veronikkah? How was she in charge of Collections Week? She was an addict and a slut without any morals or ability to remember things.

"Uh…no, but thanks for the offer. Did you guys realize the show starts in ten minutes?"

"Cool. Thanks for telling us," said Darryl, as he went for a line. In other words, he didn't care about the show.

"Um, Darryl, there's some important stuff going on and you're missing your party. Besides, Francie's looking for you." I tried to guilt them into listening to me. How could Darryl and Veronikkah make out when something was happening between Darryl and Francie? It was kind of like he was playing a mother and daughter.

The guilt technique didn't work; Veronikkah snorted back a line and giggled.

"Darryl, listen. You need to talk to Francie. I believe it's about a car."

The car comment jolted Veronikkah awake. "What about a car?" she asked.

"Oh, nothing. We just have a little running joke. I'll go talk to her," said Darryl as he tried to kiss Veronikkah and obviously distract her from the car conversation.

"No, tell me about the car, babycakes," slurred Veronikkah. It was sometimes empowering to see an older woman together with a younger man, but in this case, it was sad to see this lady with a guy half her age (I assumed Darryl was about twenty five), who obviously used her for drugs and as an entry into fashion party promoting. Not only that, but I was appalled that he used both Veronikkah and Francie.

"Don't worry, Veronikkah. Just light up the spliff and we'll go out to the party."

"Right on," smiled Veronikkah, who seemed to be trying to re-live her twenties. She waved the joint and was about to light it.

"Sorry to be a pain," I jumped in, "but I was told there's no smoking back here because the Carlu is a heritage building. They recently restored it for millions of dollars and can't risk smoking in the building."

Veronikkah and Darryl looked at me the way the smokers in Junior High looked at the kids who still played with Cabbage Patch dolls.

"Sweetie, we're the organizers," slurred Veronikkah. "We can do whatever we want."

Darryl laughed at me.

"Okay, fine. Do whatever you want. But those orders were from the owners. If they find you, that's your problem. Right now I'm going to the runway room to make sure all your guests are taken care of."

I walked away, wondering why I cared so much about the event when it was apparent the organizers didn't. I was so mad, I decided to cause a little trouble. "Oh, and Darryl, don't forget to talk to Francie about the dents you put in the car," I said, without looking back. As much as I wanted to hear what happened next, I didn't want to get pulled into the discussion. The way things operated with those people, I suspected they would figure out some way to blame me for the car accident.

Barricade.

The runway room was as mad as the night before. People were everywhere, trying to find seats, fighting with each other, and generally being obnoxious. They had been allowed too much time to drink before the show started, and became a bunch of troublemakers. I waded through the crowd and saw Josh L. in the middle of everything, trying to seat people according to his diagram. Volunteers surrounded him, trying to hear his instructions. Less than a quarter of the people were seated. I estimated it would take two hours to seat people according to Josh L.'s plan and couldn't understand why he didn't copy it for the volunteers. I couldn't chastise him for that, though, so what could I do?

I ran to the volunteers and asked how well they knew the signs and seating arrangements. They said that since they had been putting signs on seats and hanging around the runway room most of the afternoon, they knew the sections pretty well. So I interrupted Josh L. and told him I'd station volunteers along the runway. He could send guests to each of them, and they could direct them to their seats. Before he could protest, I grabbed all the volunteers and told them my plan. I also told them to help anyone who looked lost.

"Let's get everyone seated!" I ordered. In a way it felt like a battle. I laughed to myself about all the strange parallels this event had to a war, starting right back to the military-bunker style urban planning of the Collections Week office. At first glance, fashion and war couldn't be more different, but deep in both trenches, it was about panic, adaptation, defence and survival.

I positioned myself near Josh L., looked over his shoulder at the seating plan, and directed people myself. He shot me a nasty look. I whispered, "Listen. Your system will take hours to seat everyone. Just share your list with me and we'll make the whole thing happen quickly. We have a cranky crowd and need happy guests. Let's work together and get this done."

He sighed the sigh of an aging drag queen and tilted his clipboard in my direction.

Twenty minutes later, everyone was seated. The lights dimmed, and the Collections Week theme song was about to play when I heard my walkie-talkie.

<<Lola to Gigi.>>

<<Go for Gigi,>> I whispered.

<<A model just slapped a volunteer. The show's about to start. What do I do?>>

<<I'll be right there.>>

A minute later, I was backstage, in the middle of a faceoff: a model was yelling at a volunteer. To be honest, it was actually a porn star doing the yelling. When I looked around backstage, I saw more bleach blonde girls with surgery-boobs and fake tans than I saw emaciated waifs. What had happened?

Lola ran to me and begged, "Can you please do something? We're starting and this model is third on!"

"Can't she get pushed back?" I asked.

"No, the designer is adamant about the order. Please help!" She ran back to assist Niles with the model line up.

I stepped between Porn Star and volunteer. "Sorry to interrupt, ladies, but we're starting a show. I don't know what happened, but we don't have time to deal with it right now. Can we let it rest for twenty minutes and solve it after the show?"

"Who the hell are you, bitch?" screamed Porn Star.

"I'm the volunteer coordinator and I understand there could be a disagreement between you and a volunteer. That's where I come in. But there's no time to deal with this now. You have a job to do, and for the designer's sake, can we discuss this after the show?" Porn Star made a face like she was about to spew off a load of profanities. I had to deflect her actions, so I added, "You look so great in that bra and panty set. It makes you look so tanned. And your legs look so long with those Lucite heels!" She was actually a huge skank, but I figured compliments would calm her down.

"Really?" she asked. My plan seemed to work. "I was worried because I'm only 5'5", and being around these tall models makes me self conscious."

"No, seriously. You look great! Now go and strut your stuff, girl!"

Porn Star smiled as I directed her to the lineup while indicating for the volunteer to stay in place. On the way to the line, Porn Star stopped and asked, "How's my walk?"

Why did everyone ask me about walks? Did I look like the walk expert? The headset must have exuded some sort of walk-authority-type vibe. At that point, I couldn't have cared less about her walk, nor did I want to see her ass shake in the silver thong she wore.

"Your walk is perfect!" I exclaimed, hoping I sounded somewhat genuine. "Now walk that walk on the runway. Work it, girlfriend!" I sounded stupid, but it worked.

Porn Star was finally in line, ready to go with one girl ahead of her. Niles and Lola were relieved everything was under control.

I returned to the upset volunteer to find out the scuffle's origins. She said it was chaotic backstage, so Niles and Lola had told volunteers to corral the models in one area near the clothing racks. It turned out the porn star girl really was a porn star; the lingerie designer, Evita MacFarlane, wanted strippers and porn stars to model the collection, accompanied by go-go dancers and model-boy escorts. The volunteer dresser had tried to wrangle the porn star, and found her in a back corner, about to give a blowjob to a go-go boy. The volunteer told her to return to the racks immediately, so Porn Star stood up, said, "Nobody tells me what to do," and slapped her.

I never expected to get involved with porn stars and drug dealers.

After recovering from story-shock, I sent the volunteer into the runway room to watch the show so she wouldn't run into the porn star again. I dressed her models and talked to people backstage to get different versions of the story.

I heard the audience cheer from the other side of the scrim. I wondered what had excited them, but couldn't see the runway. A moment after the screams, Hot Dan returned backstage from the runway, his arm draped around the guy he'd embraced earlier. Both wore boxer-briefs and grinned. I wondered if that was his boyfriend.

"Hey, what happened?" I asked as he ran to his dresser to put on his next outfit: a robe encrusted with Swarovski crystals.

"We had a rather steamy little scene," he said.

Niles called him to the lineup.

"Ooops, gotta go down the runway now with a stripper on my arm," he laughed. "But don't worry, I haven't forgotten about you," he winked, kissed my cheek, and ran to Niles.

Why did he give me such mixed signals? One second he made out with a hot model-boy, next he was giddy because he got to be near a nearly naked girl, and then he kissed my cheek. I couldn't wonder about him any more, though, because one of my models was having a problem undoing her bra.

The rest of the show went okay, but Niles had a tough time organizing the models. Most of them had never done runway modelling before.

When the show wrapped, I heard Niles scream, "ALL RIGHT! NOBODY MOVE! NOBODY'S COMING IN OR OUT ANY MORE! WE'RE MISSING GARMENTS, SHOES, AND ACCESSORIES! GIGI, STAY AT THE SIDE DOOR! LOLA, YOU GET THE BACK DOOR!"

Standing at the entrance between backstage and the runway room, I realized the bodies backstage had tripled. Three hundred people wandered around. They were boyfriends, girlfriends, media, and random partiers. No wonder Niles had lost track of the garments; it was impossible to see the rolling racks.

Niles yelled again, "OKAY, PEOPLE. IF YOU ARE NOT A MODEL, HAIR OR MAKEUP STYLIST, MEDIA, OR VOLUNTEER, YOU MUST LEAVE IMMEDIATELY. WE ARE MISSING ITEMS, SO YOU WILL BE CHECKED AT THE DOORS. PLEASE LEAVE NOW SO WE CAN CLEAN UP!"

Only the ten people immediately around Niles listened to him. The rest of the group carried on partying. Niles was so nice, but he was not an imposing figure. That's when I decided to take charge again. I jumped onto a nearby table (I was starting to enjoy standing on tables) and repeated Niles's announcement, yelling as loud as I could, and looking as mean as possible. By the time I was finished, people were actually looking scared and heading for the exits.

Jumping off the table, I stopped the first people trying to get out and eyed their purses and backpacks.

"Hey, everyone!" I yelled again. "I see you've got full bags in your hands! You have two choices: you can go over to the racks and return anything in your bags that does not belong to you and I will pretend not to see what you're doing. Or you can let me look through your bags and if I find anything, I'll introduce you to my friend Dan, the Security Man!" I gestured over to Dan, who waved at everyone. Half the crowd went back to the rolling racks to return the smuggled goods. Great. I had added thieves to my list of new criminal colleagues.

<<Gigi, it's Chantelle. I need help.>>

<<Can it wait?>> I asked. <<I'm in the middle of making sure people don't steal things from backstage.>>

<<I don't know if it can wait. One guy wants a media bag, but we're running low and we need enough for tomorrow.>>

<<Is he media?>>

<<No, but he's being a real pain about it.>>

<<Keep telling him no, that you don't have the authority to give him one.>>

<<I'll try, but he's being really mean.>>

<<Okay, give it a couple more minutes then contact me again.>>

<<Thanks, Gigi.>>

Twenty more bag checks and five minutes later, Chantelle called again.

<<Gigi, he's now asking to see my supervisor.>>

<<Okay, I'll be right there.>>

I told Dan the Security Man about what was happening and he said he'd be fine checking for stolen goods, so I ran to Chantelle.

When I arrived at the front entrance, I saw a short, slimy, Italian-looking man, who wore a fake Versace top circa 1992, three gold chains, and two fistfuls of gold rings. In short, he was a classic Guido, and he was in Chantelle's face.

"Hello, sir, how can I help you tonight?" I asked, jumping between them, but immediately taking a step back from him and his cloud of cheap cologne.

"All I want is one of them bags for my girl over here," he pointed his chubby, bedazzled fingers over his shoulder to a girl who looked so embarrassed about being with this guy, she was hiding behind her long brown hair.

"Do you have a media pass?" I asked. "I can give you a bag if you have a media pass." I tried moving him away from Chantelle and the bags in hopes he would forget about them.

"Listen, sweetie," he said, leaning into me. "It's my first date an' I wanna impress the lady." His breath smelled of coffee. With the combination of coffee breath and cologne cloud, the guy was lethal.

I could tell the lady had heard, and she wasn't impressed. She wanted to run away as fast as I did.

"If you want to impress her, may I suggest a glass of wine at the bar?" I turned to the general direction of the bar, still hoping he would forget about the media bags.

"No! She really wants a bag." He put his face in front of mine, and I could tell why Chantelle had been so nervous when I'd arrived. On top of the smell, the guy was obsessive.

"Listen, Chantelle said you cannot have a bag if you are not media, and I said you cannot have a bag if you are not media. Those are facts and they aren't going to change. So why don't you grab a drink, mingle, and enjoy your evening?"

"No, you listen, bitch. My girl wants the bag, and I'm not leaving until she gets one."

Why did everyone call me a bitch when I was only doing a job? Not only that, I volunteered my time. People had no respect.

"I'm sorry, sir. I told you the rules and I cannot break them."

"Who are you, anyway?" Guido asked.

"I'm Gigi, the volunteer coordinator."

"Oh, you're just a volunteer? Well, I know Darryl, you stupid whore. We're good buddies. You're nothing. Volunteers are worthless. He can get me a bag."

That explained why he was so obnoxious; he was Darryl's friend.

"I'm sorry, sir, but Darryl has nothing to do with the bags. Nobody can have one without proper media accreditation. Since you don't have that, I cannot give you a bag. Now why don't you get yourself and your date a drink?" I asked, putting my hand on his shoulder, trying to guide him away from the registration desk.

"Get your hand off me! You're trying to assault me! Stop it!"

I noticed Chantelle talking to a security guard nearby who started walking over. Just as I thought things couldn't get worse, my walkie-talkie beeped.

<<Gigi, it's Gregor. Veronikkah wants a meeting with you.>>

I looked at Guido, who was about to punch me. "Sorry, sir," I said, "I have another emergency I need to deal with. Just a moment."

<<Can you tell her I'm busy at the moment?>>

<<She says it's urgent.>>

I turned away from Guido slightly, eyes still on him, for fear of his fist, and whispered, <<I'm dealing with an abusive guest. Tell her I can meet in fifteen minutes.>>

<<Okay.>>

I turned back to Guido and said, "Sorry about that. Where were we? Oh, right. You were telling me I was worthless and trying to assault you. Well, let me ask you this: if I'm nothing, would I be able to get that security guard to throw you out of this party?" I pointed at Chantelle and the security guard, who walked toward us. "What do you think, huh? I spent enough time explaining you cannot have a media bag because they go to members of the media. If you ask me one more time, you will be escorted out of the party, because you are not respecting my colleagues or me, and you are wasting our time. I have other things to deal with at the moment. What will it be? Do you want to take your date over to the party area or do you want to ask me for a bag one last time?"

By that time, Chantelle and the security guard were on either side of me, and the security guard was twice Guido's size.

"Thank you for your time, Miss," said Guido, trying to pull his date to him. She kept her arms crossed and marched in front of him all the way to the bar. She would likely make him buy her so many drinks, and then disappear. So much for impressing a first date.

"Are you all right?" asked Chantelle.

"I guess so," I said, turning to the security guard. "Thanks for coming over."

He smiled. "No problem. It's my job. Next time, call me over earlier. He was an ass."

"Thanks."

Chantelle and I walked back to the registration, and not a second after we arrived, two girls walked up and asked, "Can we have those bags?"

Chantelle and I looked at each other and almost cried.

"Do you have a media pass?" asked Chantelle.

"No, why?" asked one girl who was wearing a canary yellow tube top and super short denim micro-miniskirt.

"The bags are for media only," she said.

"Well, I'm Francie's friend and she said I could have a bag," said Tube Top Girl.

Chantelle looked at me. She was tired of this, as was I. "Look," I said to them with an exasperated sigh. "We just had a huge ordeal with one guy about the bags and we don't want to go through it again. Please, just accept the fact that bags are for media only and go enjoy the party."

"But Francie said I could have a baaaaaag," Tube Top Girl whined.

"If Francie said that, she would have told us," I said. That was a lie because Francie forgot to tell us a lot of things, but the whole night had been filled with people telling us to do special things for them because they knew Francie, Veronikkah, or Darryl. It was annoying and I was sick of it.

"You're the biggest power-tripping slut I ever met!" screamed Tube Top Girl. She stepped forward and spat on my shoes. "I'm reporting you to Francie!"

Nobody had ever spat on me before. Were these the types of people who composed the fashion crowd? Would spitting girls and screaming Guidos forever surround me?

I waved the security guard to come over and said, "Since you did that, you're leaving the party, and guess what? I'm reporting you to Francie. Care to give me your name or are you too embarrassed about your actions?"

"You can't make me leave, bitch!" she exclaimed.

That was my breaking point, and I could tell I would cry soon. There was only so much verbal abuse a girl could take in a day, but before I broke down, I had to finish my job. Why did people insist on calling me a bitch? I thought I was a reasonable person.

"Can't you be a little more creative? You're at least the fifth person to call me a bitch today, and can't you see I'm just doing a job? If you can't respect that, you have to leave."

The security guard arrived and took her away. Chantelle and I ducked into a hidden doorway beside the front entrance area, and I couldn't hold it in any longer. I did something I never do in public, especially in a work situation: I started to cry.

When Chantelle saw me crying, she started too, and she said, "Gigi, today has been so hard. I've only been keeping it together because you've been so strong."

<<Gregor to Gigi. Veronikkah wants to meet with you immediately!>>

I looked at Chantelle through my tears and laughed, "That's exactly the last thing I need right now!"

<<Gregor, I really can't right now. Chantelle and I were verbally abused by two people and need time to recover. I can't meet her no matter how important it is. If we do meet, I'll end up crying, and I don't want to do that in front of her. I need another fifteen minutes.>>

<<Okay. What do I tell her?>>

<<The truth, that her guests are evil.>>

<<Ummm...Okay...>>

<<Just kidding. Just tell her the truth about dealing with a couple irritated guests. If she doesn't understand, let me know.>>

<<Okay.>>

Chantelle and I looked at each other, took two deep breaths and started crying again. It was nice to release all the frustrations that had built up over the last two days. We'd gone through so much; it felt as though we had worked together for years.

GUARD.

There we were, huddled in the corner of the doorway, tears streaming down our faces, hoping nobody would see us, when a volunteer poked her head around the corner. It was Susan, she was in her mid twenties, and she had done any job with a smile.

"I brought you guys something to make you feel better," said Susan, surprising us with glasses of red wine. "The people around here are nasty. You need this."

My heart melted. There was a volunteer looking after me when I was supposed to be looking after her. It was the nicest thing anyone had done for me all day, so I cried some more and we all had a big, sappy group hug.

"I don't understand how some people can be so mean," sniffed Chantelle.

Susan said, "Veronikkah brings in this type of crowd. She treats everyone horribly and it trickles down from there. I've seen her at a few events, and she's always a monster. These past few days have been the worst I've seen her, but at least she's more stupidly stoned than mean."

I was happy to learn another person noticed how high she was and it wasn't just me getting frustrated. I was even happier to have a smart, mature volunteer who brought me wine.

"Where else have you seen her?" I asked.

"Oh, I volunteer for various fashion and music events around the city," said Susan. "I like to keep myself entertained."

"What events?" I asked.

"Stuff like Fashion Cares and North by Northeast. I'm interested in how the different disciplines work because they're so reliant on each other. I'm starting a PR company and it's a good way to meet contacts and help me decide whether I want to focus on music or fashion PR."

"That sounds great!" said Chantelle.

"Right now I'd recommend you stick with music PR," I said, laughing.

At that point, Francie ran over and asked, "Are you all right? What happened?"

Chantelle and I recounted the bag stories and I explained the backstage slapping and theft sagas.

"Are you serious? All that happened?" asked wide-eyed Francie.

"Yeah, it did. I couldn't make this stuff up," I replied. "And honestly, after the last round of verbal abuse, I just couldn't take it anymore."

"No kidding," said Chantelle. "I didn't realize all that other stuff had happened. You must be drained."

I took a big gulp of wine and turned to Francie. "I hope you don't mind me drinking on the job, but I really need this. Plus, this lovely volunteer bought it for me." I pointed at Susan.

"No, I don't mind at all," said Francie, giving me a huge hug. "Gigi, I know we haven't seen each other much over the last two days, but you've been the biggest help. I don't know how we ever functioned without you. You're so organized and responsible that I've been able to focus on helping Veronikkah. I really appreciate it. In past seasons, I wasn't able to do that because I was too busy running around, dealing with emergencies."

"Tell me about it," I said.

"Seriously, Gigi. I know I talk quickly and get right to the point when we talk. In fact, I'm probably rude sometimes, but it's because I have Veronikkah right behind me, breathing down my neck, asking me to do things. You've seen her. She doesn't waste time with hellos or goodbyes. She wants things done fast and it makes me nervous. Not only that, but I'm so busy during the week, that I don't have the time to be nice."

Ahhh...I finally understood Francie; her actions were direct results of Veronikkah's crazy moods. Maybe she wasn't as clueless as I had thought.

Francie continued speaking. "And I want you to know if things get overwhelming again, just tell me. I should be dealing with stuff like this. It's not your responsibility to have people yelling at you. I'm really sorry it happened."

"Me too. Thanks for offering to be there, but I have to be honest with you. It's really hard to find you when you don't have a headset. Do you think you could wear one for emergencies?"

"Well, Veronikkah doesn't want me to wear one because she thinks it will make me look too pedestrian when talking to VIPs, but I'll see what I can do."

"Thanks, Francie," I said. Some of my frustrations lifted away, but I still felt heavy. I hadn't realized how tired I was, but it made sense. I couldn't remember the last time I ate. And I'd had wine. Not a good combination. "Do you have any food?" I asked. "I'm starving."

"Join the club," laughed Francie. "Let's get something to eat in office, and then you can talk to Veronikkah."

The promise of food made the trip to see Veronikkah more palatable, so I left Susan and Chantelle at reception to go behind enemy lines. I wondered what Veronikkah wanted to discuss and if I could trust Francie.

Observe.

Veronikkah was sprawled across the sofa when we arrived, drinking Champagne from a bottle. Camel Toe popped grapes in Veronikkah's mouth in what she apparently thought was a funny way, but really it made her look like a servant. At the same time, Josh L. was giving her a foot massage. Francie whispered something the moment we got in. Eva gave her some chocolate. I felt as though I was in Roman times when an entire civilization got all fat and lazy and had orgies all the time - just before the fall of their empire.

"So, Trixie, why are you here?" asked Veronikkah, making me feel like a slave brought to court.

"Are you talking to me?" I asked.

"Yes, who else would I be talking to?" asked Veronikkah.

"I don't know, but I'm not Trixie." I was fed up with her not remembering me. "I'm Gigi. We've been introduced at least ten times and I'm managing your volunteers. I would think you could remember my name."

Everyone in the room stopped, stupefied I would talk to Veronikkah that way.

"Don't get all huffy," snapped Veronikkah. "I just wanted to know why you wanted to talk to me."

"You're the one who wants to talk to me," I said. "You called me here."

"Oh, uh…" she looked at Francie, who nodded her head in agreement.

"It was about the car," said Francie.

"Right, right," said Veronikkah. "Tell me what happened."

I recounted the story while she drank her bubbly. Every once in a while she closed her eyes, which could have passed for deep thought, but it was more likely she was passing out.

When I stopped talking, she snapped awake, and said, "Fine, fine. Okay, thank you. I just ask that you all keep this quiet."

"Of course," I said.

"Good. I'm glad that's understood. Now then, Francie told me you had a rough evening. Is everything okay?"

"Yes and no. Yes, it's okay because I'm fine now; I can handle a lot. But no because some guests and models were really rude and a lot of the younger volunteers can't handle it. I'm trying to be as polite as I can, but I don't know if I have the authority to remove people if they're obnoxious."

"Sweetie, I noticed your work here, and so has everyone else." Everyone in the room nodded. "You are wonderful; a real asset to Collections Week, and I want you to know you have the power to deal with people however you need to. If they are rude and disrespectful, ask them to leave. You have our support."

She gave me a hug. "Now," she said. "You seem really smart. Can you let me know what things worked today and yesterday? I want to improve things for tomorrow."

Was this the same Veronikkah who did coke in the hallway and tripped in front of an audience? It seemed as though there were two Veronikkahs: the nice, caring, thoughtful one, and the evil twin. I liked the nice one and was willing to help her out, so we all sat in the office discussing how to improve the last two days of Collections Week and how to make the next night's gala the best party the city had ever experienced.

By the time we finished our meeting, most of the guests were gone, but there were still a few people in the designer gallery. Gregor, Lola, and Chantelle were all there, keeping an eye on the clothes.

"Hey sweetie," said Gregor, coming up to hug me. "Sounds like you had a rough night, so I won't tell you about the fistfights that happened while you were in that meeting."

"Fistfights?" I asked.

"Yeah," said Lola. "Darryl's friends are drunken assholes."

"But don't worry about it," said Chantelle. "Security took them away and you had a million things to monitor. You don't need another stress point; we took care of it."

"Thanks guys, you're great," I said.

"No," said Chantelle, "thank you. You held everything together fabulously. You're wonderful."

"Thanks," I said, blushing again.

"I hope you don't mind, but we sent the volunteers home. There wasn't much left to do except sit here and make sure people don't steal things."

"Sure, that's fine. Thanks for making that decision. Now I'm making a decision for you. What do you say we get rid of these last guests and get to the Flaunt party? We deserve it!"

"Damn straight, sister!" screamed Gregor, doing a little disco dance. "Let's go have some fun! I'm in the mood to dance!"

Energize and Prepare.

In the cab, we couldn't wait to share the day's adventure stories. Each episode became more outrageous the closer we got to the Flaunt party.

After recounting Chantelle's dealings with Darryl and his friends, along with the media bag mayhem, Lola discussed her day with demanding models, stressed-out designers, cranky hair and makeup artists, and Evil Eva. The girl had disappeared, leaving the hair and makeup people without direction. Whenever she did show up backstage, she hung around and smoked. Lola managed the area when Eva was gone, but when Eva returned, she told them to start over and do different things, making most shows at least half an hour late. Lola was frustrated, Chantelle was upset, then Gregor recalled his day.

The designers in the gallery complained about how they didn't get what they paid for: the booths were too small, no buyers attended, media didn't offer interviews, and the public touched the garments, damaging a few. Gregor had tried to inform Veronikkah and Francie, but they always dismissed him. At one point, Veronikkah ignored his pleas for assistance and demanded him to send a volunteer out to get ibuprofen and Gatorade (a classic hangover cure). He didn't think it was something he should do, but he did it anyway. What choice did he have? Furthermore, Gregor said Veronikkah had demanded volunteers leave the designer gallery to guard the Collections Week office.

Due to my stealthy spy knowledge of Veronikkah's plan, I worried about volunteers guarding the office. If they were outside the door, could they be charged with aiding a crime if Veronikkah and the Bolivians were caught?

Gregor read my mind because he asked, "Gigi, I'm a bit concerned because when I went in the office to get more magazines, I saw a baggie on the coffee table along with powder residue. It's pretty obvious they're a bunch of cokeheads. Who are these people we're volunteering for? Why should we help them with their partying by making them look good when we do all the work?"

I also wondered how much information to give my team. Should they know about the Bolivian drug connection and embezzlement? Would that jeopardize their safety? Was all my information correct to tell them or would I be a gossip? I decided to confess I had seen some drug use, but stated it was probably common at fashion shows. Until I saw risk to volunteers and ourselves, I decided to stay silent about the other stuff. I didn't want to cause unnecessary panic.

We discussed volunteer treatment and whether or not we should be sent on personal errands. We all figured volunteers were there to learn about fashion show organization, not to be personal assistants to people who abused their power.

By the time we got to the party, we'd calculated the following daily summary:

- Times Veronikkah yelled at volunteers (including us): 12
- Times Francie yelled at volunteers (including us): 5
- Number of volunteers who Veronikkah made cry: 4

- Times drug paraphernalia was spotted in the Collections Week office: 2
- Times people were seen snorting coke: 4 (Lola saw a few backstage)
- People who got slapped: 1
- People who got spat on: 1
- Times I was called a bitch: at least 6
- Times everyone else was called a bitch: 7
- Times we all were told we were incompetent: lost count; could have been at least 10 times each
- Pairs of shoes stolen from the lingerie show: 15
- Necklaces stolen from the lingerie show: 8
- Garments stolen from the lingerie show: 12
- People who tried to sneak backstage without authorization: over 100
- Number of drunken fistfights after the lingerie show: 2

None of us had enough experience to know if that happened at all fashion shows, so I vowed to consult Niles the next morning. If it was unusual, we would have to do something - but what? If it was usual, then at least we could try laughing about it.

With the informal taxi debrief completed, it was time to blow off some of our pent-up frustrations. We flashed our Flaunt party passes and glided into the Drake as if we were the *Sex and the City* girls. Well, the *Sex and the City* girls and guy.

The party was at the hippest hotspot of the moment, and the first bar where I'd felt at home in Toronto. It had been resurrected from its life as a punk bar, all-night rave centre, and eventual flophouse. A couple people had restored historical attributes of its nineteenth century decor and recreated the hotel as a kind of living art piece. At first glance, it was a place of sensible contradictions: computers in the lobby near an old photo booth; old furniture reworked to look new-ish; décor either a starving artist or savvy philanthropist could understand; and a place one could both live and visit. That was just the feeling I got from the lobby and I couldn't wait to run into the lounge.

At one thirty in the morning, the place was jumping. We walked in and ran right into Alex and April, who were celebrating the launch of a successful new season with a couple of Red Stripes, beer with the cutest bottles ever.

"What took you so long?" Alex asked.

"Oh, you know, cleaning up, clearing out drunken partiers…" I said.

"Yeah, we know how it goes," said April. "We've volunteered at a million things, from the Old Clothing Show to Fashion Cares. We never volunteered for Collections Week, though."

Alex jumped in. "It's pretty disorganized. We've never worked with Veronikkah, but we've heard horror stories."

I wanted to tell them I lived the horror, but being new to the industry, I didn't know how much to dish.

They leaned close into me and Alex said, "Something weird happened today and we wondered if you knew anything about it."

April reached into her pocket and pulled out a baggie. "This was in our gift bag, and Veronikkah kept telling us we could get more if we wanted any," she said. "She became kind of manic and obsessive over it. It got kind of scary when those large men surrounded us. Who are they, anyway?"

I didn't know what to do. The Flaunt girls seemed cool, but for all I knew, they were working for Veronikkah. All of a sudden, I lived in a spy novel and felt completely paranoid. Would delusions and hallucinations follow? Maybe they'd already started.

I played dumb and innocent, the best defense when you don't know your enemies. "Gee, girls, I don't know anything about that. I'm really just a volunteer. I know Veronikkah seems out of it some times, but I didn't know that was going on." I'm a horrible liar, but I hoped they bought it.

"Okay, cool," said Alex. Just wanted to see if you knew what was happening because you seemed like the only normal person at Collections Week. Since you don't know anything, we know we're right. That place is filled with a bunch of coke-monsters. We don't do the stuff because it's bad news. We've seen so many lives destroyed because of it and don't want to ruin our company."

They threw out the baggie, dragged me up to the bar, and bought me a beer.

"You deserve this for working with Veronikkah," said Alex. "Good luck with the rest of the week."

"Thanks, guys," I said, taking a sip. "I'm so happy we met. I was starting to think the fashion industry in this city was filled with Veronikkahs and Francies."

"Hardly!" laughed April.

Alex agreed. "Those two embody the worst of the industry. Most people are pretty cool."

Just then, a reporter interrupted us, so I let them chat and searched for my group. Scanning the room, I didn't immediately find my friends, but I did see Hot Dan talking to a bunch of other model-boys. My heart pounded so I took a huge swig of beer and approached the group. Who wouldn't be nervous approaching a group of six red-hot men?

About to tap Hot Dan on the shoulder, I noticed one of the guys had his hand around Hot Dan's waist. Damn! I still wanted him to be straight and available, not gay and taken. Oh well; I had to accept that he was gay and taken. I tapped his shoulder anyway.

"Gigi!" he yelled, giving me a great big hug. "Let me introduce you to the boys."

After a round of introductions, I didn't remember a single name because the guys were so hot; they sucked all intelligence out of my brain. I just stood there, smiling dreamily. I snapped out of it and realized the entire group was standing around smiling dreamily, so I didn't feel so bad.

"Sorry, did I interrupt anything?" I asked.

"No, we were just practicing our catalogue smiles," replied a stunning blond surfer-boy. "Are they believable? Do we look happy?"

"Ahhh...I see," I said. Was he serious? How shallow. How was I supposed to respond without laughing?

The group stared at me as if my answer would solve a world crisis. I had to say something.

"Oh, you're totally believable...so believable that you're almost unbelievable," I said, sipping my drink and pretending to look around the room before I burst into a giggle-fit.

"Wow. You're so deep," marvelled Surfer-Boy. The other models nodded in agreement then stared into space, obviously mystified by my comment.

Hot Dan leaned in. "Don't worry; they're not usually as stupid as that. They have a big day tomorrow, and today's been rather difficult."

"Tell me about it," I said.

"Actually, I do want to tell you about it. Come with me." He dragged me to the dance floor, and surprised me when he actually moved his hips in time to the music. I had hoped he would have one bad trait, but no; he was perfect. Why were the best guys gay?

He suddenly grabbed my neck and back, pulling me near. He was aggressive, and even though I only had hopes of being his gal palqueen, I savoured dancing so close to him.

He pushed my hair back and whispered in my ear, "What were you doing eavesdropping at the office today?"

"I could ask you the same question," I whispered back, resisting the temptation to nibble his earlobe.

Brushing his cheek next to mine, he said, "Gigi, you're the coolest person I've ever met, and even though we've only known each other for two days. I could talk to you forever, but there are some things I just can't tell you right now." His fingers massaged my neck and I dissolved in a puddle of confusion, panic, and lust.

"I don't understand," I said.

"I just want you to be careful. Those are bad people running Collections Week. I don't want anything to happen to you."

Then, without warning, he cupped my face in both his hands and gave me the biggest, sweetest, softest kiss. The people dancing around us melted away; we were the only people in the world. My brain spun and my knees wobbled. I stopped thinking about the day's stress; I stopped wondering if Hot Dan was gay or straight. It was the best kiss. Nothing else mattered at that moment.

Unfortunately, he pulled away and whispered, "I'm sorry, but I've got to go. Just be careful." Then he ran back to the Ken-doll posse.

What happened? It was the best kiss of my life and the guy ran away? Weren't kisses reciprocal? Can one person have a good kiss and the other think it was horrible? Maybe it was my breath. That was it. I tasted of beer. I wouldn't want to kiss me either. Verging on panic, I realized I stood alone on the dancefloor not dancing. I was a total abandoned loser and needed my friends.

Running off the dance floor, I crashed right into Gregor.

"Ooooh, girl! Look at you! What a smoochy-smooch! Talk about kisses of fire! Divulge, babe!" he commanded.

My mind swam through the dancefloor incident in a blur. "I don't really know what happened. I'm confused."

"How can you be confused about that? From my view, it was soooo intense, like a gum commercial."

"Intense...Yeah." It was official: I had lost all powers of speech after the kiss.

"Sweetie, darling, your lipstick's all over your face. Go to the washroom and fix it before you're mistaken for a tramp. Then come back and tell us everything! We're at the bar." Gregor pointed to the bar, where Lola and Chantelle waved and clapped. If only they knew what I felt.

Still stunned, I found the washroom and looked into the mirror. Gregor was right; fuchsia lipstick decorated my face rather than my lips. I hoped Hot Dan was smart enough to wipe off his face before going back to his pals. What did they think when they saw us kiss? Was that why he ran away? Was one of them his boyfriend? Was I so irresistible that I actually achieved the female fantasy of converting a gay guy? I couldn't think about it, though, because I had to focus on fixing my lipstick.

Back in the lounge, I attempted not to look in Hot Dan's direction, so I ended up crashing into Chloe Kirkpatrick and stepped on her feet. The kiss had turned me into a mess.

"Oh...hi, Gigi," she said.

Chloe Kirkpatrick remembered my name! "Hi Chloe. Nice seeing you again. How was your day?"

"It's always nice covering Canadian fashion, but I'm a bit jaded from all these years of reporting."

"I don't think I could ever get jaded; I love fashion so much."

Chloe smiled in an "oh-you're-so-cute-I-want-to-pat-you-on-the-head" sort of way and said, "Trust me. No matter how much you love fashion, some aspects of the industry will end up bothering you. Hey - you must have had a hard day working for Veronikkah. Let me buy you a drink. I'd also like to talk to you because I'm writing an article about volunteering for Collections Week."

"Really? Your readers would find that interesting?" I asked.

"I think so," she said. "I just have to convince my editor of it, so let's chat."

"Sounds good to me. I haven't stopped all day."

"Great."

She bought drinks and we settled into a booth. I looked to Chantelle, Lola, and Gregor, who realized it wasn't a good time to interrupt us, though they were dying to talk about the kiss.

Chloe started by asking, "Does Veronikkah know how organized you are? I've seen you work over the past two days, and you're a valuable asset to Collections Week."

"I don't know," I answered. "She said some nice things to me tonight, but that's only because I got verbally abused by some guests. One even spat on me. This week was the first time I'd met Veronikkah. Before that, I always dealt with Francie."

"How grim. Francie's an absolute ditz and I'm sick of her incompetence. As a journalist, I've had to go through her to get some story information, but it's impossible to work with her. It's her first job out of high school and she doesn't know business etiquette. She's a trust-fund girl; her mom grew up with Veronikkah, and Francie's family contributes tons of money to Collections Week. Veronikkah uses her for her connections." Made sense. Chloe continued. "Wait, did you say someone spat on you?"

I told her the story and she couldn't believe it.

"I have to write about that!" she exclaimed. "In my years of fashion coverage, I've never heard of anyone doing that; it's terrible."

"I don't mind if you write about it at all," I replied. "Some people need to be taught some manners. I thought the fashion crowd was supposed to be elegant and sophisticated."

"Usually they are, sweetie. But Collections Week is different from most events I attend. They don't know their target audience."

"That's what I thought. I wondered where all the artists, musicians, socialites, and other cool fashion-followers were. Instead, we had guests who came to the Carlu rather than going to their usual lame clubland spots."

Chloe laughed. "Yes, it's something many of us have tried to rectify for some time, but it hasn't worked."

We talked for a while, and it was nice to discover another intelligent person interested in fashion. There was a diverse combination of people in the industry, which, of course, is common in any profession. I'd worked with cool urban planners and geeky urban planners; there were assholes, and there were wonderful people. Fashion wasn't that much different, but it had a worse reputation, because the worst people were the loudest.

Finishing our drinks, we noticed the thinning crowd, so I looked at my watch. It was three-thirty and I had to be back at the Carlu for eight. Chloe thanked me for my time and said the article would probably be in her paper's weekend edition.

I found Gregor, Lola, and Chantelle, dancing together, showing no signs of the fatigue I suddenly felt. Two days of running around with only a few hours sleep caught up with me suddenly.

"Eeeek! So what happened?" screeched Gregor.

"Chloe is doing a piece on Collections Week volunteers," I said.

"Seriously?" Lola gasped.

"It appears so."

"Oh, and what about Hot Dan?" asked Chantelle.

The mere mention of the incident sucked me back into the kiss for a moment. "I don't know what happened. Is he still here?"

"No, he left with the model-boys," said Gregor.

Lola made a face. "Bastard! Kisses you then leaves without another word. Why are all the hot ones sexually ambiguous assholes?"

I sighed. "I don't know. That's just the way it is. Anyway, I'm sorry to do this to you, but I'm super-tired.

It's going to be four o'clock by the time I get home, and we've got to be at the Carlu by eight tomorrow morning. I don't know about you, but I need sleep."

I left them wanting to hear more dirt on the kiss, but I said I was too tired to talk about it. A girl shouldn't reveal all her secrets.

ADAPT, PLAN, AND FORM.

At seven o'clock, my alarm blasted Les Sexareenos, my favourite Montreal band. My stereo somehow knew the only way to wake me up was with an early morning 1960s pool party. Or had I actually thought about it before I flopped on my bed the night before?

Thanks to a combination of fright from being late the previous day, adrenaline from the excitement of working at Collections Week, that weird energy from being overtired, and a reed organ in the background, I jumped out of bed and danced around my little apartment. Nothing beat starting the day off with a good dance.

I wiggled and shimmied my way through my morning routine, pretending I was Nancy Sinatra in a pair of fancy boots. I wanjoying it so much, I had to wear my favourite boots - silver John Fluevog knee-highs - and matched them with a black miniskirt and tight black shirt with a peter pan collar. I pulled the "Collections Week, C'est Chic!" T-shirt over the peter pan shirt, and achieved the effect I was aiming for: a waitress look. Since I was treated as a service worker while volunteering for Collections Week, I decided to dress the part. I wondered if Veronikkah and Francie would notice my subversive outfit.

Carrying my 1960s beach-party attitude with me as I half-danced, half-walked to the Carlu, I realized I would be early, so I stopped at the nearest Tim Hortons. What better way to repay Lola, Gregor, and Chantelle for their hard work and tolerance to abuse than with sweet little donut holes?

Since I was in such a giddy mood, I quizzed my Tim Hortons server on her workplace.

"Does Tim Horton own this store?" I asked the grumpy, frumpy girl, who clearly did not want to serve donuts and coffee at seven thirty in the morning.

"Uh, no. He was a hockey player. The store is named after him."

"Is that why there's no apostrophe?"

"Huh? What are you talking about?" she asked.

"Shouldn't it be Tim Horton's with an apostrophe 's'?" I asked.

"Never thought about it. Now how many honey dips do you want?" She didn't care about my question or her place of employment.

Weren't Tim Hortons employees supposed to be cheery because they love their uniforms? At least that's what the commercials said. I figured Tim Hortons employees were the kind of people who knew everything about the company, especially its namesake. Furthermore, Tim Hortons is such a Canadian institution, all employees should know Canadian trivia. They could even take it further and turn all tourist information centres into Tim Hortonses. I decided to write the company with that idea. Plus, I had to write to tell them they needed an apostrophe.

I walked out of Tim Hortons, feeling happily Canadian with a box of 40 Timbits in hand, on my way to celebrate Canadian fashion. The sun shone and I felt like Snow White when all the birds and forest animals danced around her. Rather than cute illustrated bluebirds and charming deer, my birds were dirty pigeons and homeless dudes asking for change while I walked down Yonge

Street, rather than deer hopping around me, but I was celebratory nonetheless.

Lola was already at the Carlu when I arrived. What was in her hand? A giant box of Timbits! I held up my box and we giggled.

"Great minds think alike, eh?" she said.

I smiled and popped a jelly-filled Timbit into my mouth. "You got it."

Gregor and Chantelle arrived at the same time. When we saw each other, we all laughed our heads off. We'd had one collective thought that morning: Timbits.

We stuffed our faces with donut holes while giggling, debriefing the day before, and anticipating what the new day would bring. The first show wasn't scheduled until two o'clock, which meant models, hairstylists, and makeup artists would probably arrive around ten. If this day was going to be anything like the others, though, we knew there would be surprises in store.

Sure enough, our first shock came at eight-thirty. A troupe of makeup artists rolled in, looking tired, but armed with coffee and suitcases filled with makeup.

"Where do we set up for the noon show?" one of them asked.

"Noon show?" I asked back.

"Yeah, it's Madame Hortence's show…last minute addition. She called last night at ten and told me to assemble a makeup team. I was told to speak with Eva."

Madame Hortence was the grande dame of Canadian fashion. She'd been a designer for forty years, and while she had once been a wild child, her clothes were now tired, drapey things aimed at seventy-year-old hippies. Nevertheless, she was Madame Hortence and held prestige in Canadian designer circles. She paved the way for the industry. It was an honour to have her at Collections Week, and I couldn't wait to meet her.

I explained the concept to the makeup team and Lola organized them backstage, ignoring Eva's absence. Chantelle and Gregor prepared their areas and we were ready. They dealt with guests, models, and hairstylists when Veronikkah and Francie arrived around ten-thirty.

"Good morning," I said, smiling. "Timbit?"

"I CAN'T STAND THOSE THINGS!" Veronikkah shrieked, slapping the tiny, sweet confection out of my hand. "Where's the money from yesterday?" she yelled.

"I…I…" I stammered stupidly. I didn't know what she was talking about.

Her eyes blazed. "Well, don't just stand there wasting my time. Where's the money?"

"What money?" I asked.

She rolled her eyes. "The money from the ticket sales, you moron!"

"I didn't deal with ticket sales," I said, hoping she would leave me alone and return five minutes later as the nice, caring Veronikkah I'd seen the night before.

"Didn't your volunteers take ticket money? That's what Francie told me. She said you were in charge of ticket money."

"I guess the volunteers took some of the money, but I don't think there was very much of it. Darryl ended up letting everyone in."

"What?" she asked. "You were supposed to be in charge of the ticket sales!"

"Sorry, I wasn't told that. I only found out five minutes before the event."

Veronikkah turned to Francie. "Is this true?" she asked.

Francie looked scared and said, "No. I told you to look after the money. I trusted you."

Was that true? Did I forget a job I was supposed to do? I never forget things.

"I was really busy yesterday, so unfortunately I could have forgotten your request, Francie. If that's the case, I'm really sorry. But honestly, I wouldn't have forgotten a request as important as looking after money."

Veronikkah turned to me. "What are you going to do about this?" she asked.

Me? What did she want me to do about it? Wasn't it Francie's problem?

"Let me check with Chantelle. She'll know where the money is." I said, adding, "Oh, Madame Hortence's people are all getting set up backstage."

"Madame Hortence!" Veronikkah screamed. "That aging, wrinkled witch! What's she doing here? She's been banned from Collections Week since she spread nasty rumours about me in *Flare*!"

It wasn't a good morning for Veronikkah, so I turned to my walkie-talkie to get the money scoop from Chantelle. When I finished, Francie calmed Veronikkah down, reminding her how Madame Hortence had made a huge donation to Collections Week and they'd agreed she could hold an intimate noon show.

I interrupted their conversation and said, "I was right; Chantelle gave the money to Darryl."

"What money?" asked Veronikkah.

I wondered for the millionth time how someone that clueless could run such an important event, but still did not find an answer.

Francie argued, "Darryl told me he didn't have the money."

"Chantelle and her volunteers tell me they gave one-hundred -and-twenty-five dollars to Darryl at the end of the night."

"One-hundred-and-twenty-five dollars?" Francie gasped. "That's all?"

"Yes. He let everyone in for free, saying they were on the guest list."

"We were supposed to make a couple of thousand dollars from that!" Francie whined, as Veronikkah stared off into space.

"I don't know what to say about that, but I can say we have some problems with Darryl. It's not my place to complain about your colleague's work, but he freaked out in front of the guests yesterday and seems like he's only around to party. You should speak to him to resolve these issues, especially if he's organizing the huge Bolivian showcase tonight." I hoped Veronikkah would listen and figure out some way to get Darryl to complete his work.

"Don't you tell me how he should do his job! You're just a volunteer!" Francie snapped back.

I was shocked she said that, and I didn't want to start the day off with insults; I'd had enough of being the quiet little volunteer. "Francie, I'm trying to help, but if you don't want me around, I can go."

Veronikkah finally clued in to our conversation. "Are you quitting on us? You can't quit! We need you!"

Why didn't I quit? I didn't have to stand for insults and thievery accusations. I grew with empowerment and finally said what I felt. "If you need me - and I think you do - then I have to ask you for more respect. Please don't insult me or treat me any differently because I'm a volunteer. If anything, you should give me more respect because I'm donating my time and doing a damn good job. I took enough abuse from guests yesterday, and getting it from you, along with accusations of not doing my job, will not make us work better as a team."

Veronikkah and Francie stood silent, not knowing how to respond.

Since they were quiet, I kept going. "I have to say I'm sick of being treated like crap by you and your guests. Consider this your first warning. If we can't work better as a team and the volunteers don't get treated better, we'll walk. I'll give you one more chance, but if you make another volunteer cry, I'll give you a second warning. If things get worse, I'll leave, and I'm sure the volunteers will come with me."

Confusion, fear, and contempt plastered their faces. After what seemed like an absurdly long, unpleasant silence, Veronikkah finally spoke.

"Calm down. We're all stressed. Sorry we didn't realize how we've been acting. How can we all work together to make things better?"

I had to take baby steps toward improvement. "We have to strengthen communication. With the money thing, we should have been warned ahead of time what was expected, and we could have planned for money collection. Madame Hortence's show is another example. Why weren't we told about it? It made everyone look stupid when we didn't know about it. We tried to cover as best we could, but it's getting difficult because you don't tell us anything."

"There's not much we can do about that," said Veronikkah. "Last minute changes come with the industry. If you can't handle them, you're in the wrong place, honey."

I felt as though I was talking to a stained Prada hat left over at a sample sale; there was no reaction. On second thought, the hat probably would have paid more attention to me than Veronikkah and Francie did. I realized things wouldn't change.

"I can deal with last minute changes," I explained, "but if you have advance notice, why not tell me? You could have told me about Madame Hortence's show last night."

Veronikkah sighed. "But I never see you; I'm too busy doing interviews and PR."

"Well, these chats do wonders. We should have more meetings so we can catch up and ensure we all know what's happening."

Francie interrupted. "We're too busy to do that! We don't have time for you."

"You're too busy to do something to help you run a smooth event? Then why don't you at least wear a headset so I can consult you on things easily?" I asked.

"Okay, I'll look into it," she said, though I knew she wouldn't.

"That solves that!" smiled Veronikkah. "Now's my time for a *Globe and Mail* interview. Sweetie, can you get a volunteer to bring a coffee to my office?" she asked, walking off as if the entire conversation hadn't happened.

I was wrong; it wasn't like talking to last season's Prada shoe. Talking to Veronikkah was like talking to a big, old rock. Nothing went in or out. I took a deep breath and went to find someone to get Her Majesty a cup of coffee.

MANEUVER.

<<Gigi, it's Lola. Is Madame Hortence around? It's eleven-thirty, half an hour before her show, and all the models are ready, but I haven't seen her.>>

<<Let me see if Francie's on headset. Maybe she'll know.>>

<<Gigi to Francic.>>

No answer.

<<Gigi to Francie.>>

No answer. I'd figured as much, but at least I tried.

I ran to the Collections Week office to find Veronikkah and Francie there with Chloe Kirkpatrick. When did she sneak in? We smiled at each other, but Veronikkah was peeved.

"Sorry to interrupt," I said, "but have you seen Madame Hortence yet? Her show is supposed to start in half an hour."

"Francie, get that old hag on the phone! Deal with it!" shrieked Veronikkah. "Fuck! This is the last thing I need!" She lit a cigarette and fell back into the couch. "Chloe, now, before we were so rudely interrupted…" she said in a syrupy voice while shooting me a death-look,

"I was talking about *my* vision for Collections Week, and how *I* put Canadian fashion on the map…"

Was it my imagination or did I see Chloe roll her eyes? She hated Veronikkah.

"Madame Hortence will get here at noon," said Francie.

I made a face. "Isn't that when her show is supposed to start?" I asked.

"Yes, but she works on her own schedule."

"What will we do with her guests?"

Francie flicked her hand in an "I-don't-care" gesture. "Don't worry about it. She's always late. They'll understand."

I tried to smile through my frustration. I left the office and conveyed the news to my team.

<<But the guests are irritated,>> worried Chantelle.

<<There's not much we can do,>> I said. <<Why don't you walk around and give them Timbits?>>

That last comment spread giggles across the walkie-talkie system.

<<You're joking, right?>> Chantelle asked.

I laughed. <<Of course I'm joking; we're gonna need all the Timbits we can get by the end of the day! Keep them for us!>>

A moment later, Gregor called. <<Hey everyone, Francie told me Madame Hortence's show will be in the designer gallery. Do you have any volunteers to spare to move chairs in here from the runway room?>>

<<It's Lola. I have ten volunteers until the designer arrives.>>

<<It's Chantelle. I have six you can borrow unless the crowd gets rowdy.>>

<<It's Gigi. You can have all the ones in the runway room. They're sitting around waiting for Josh L., so they're yours until he arrives.>>

<<Great,>> said Gregor. <<Send them over.>>

Fifteen minutes later, the designer gallery was set up for an affair reminiscent of 1950s atelier shows. The runway room volunteers were ready with Gregor, so we decided to seat the cranky guests.

At noon, Lola called everyone on the walkie-talkie. <<Has anyone seen Madame Hortence yet?>>

Nobody had.

Five minutes later, Lola called again.

Still, nobody had seen her.

She didn't arrive until twelve-fifteen, and at that time, she showed up backstage, with her assistant in tow, throwing clothes at Niles and Lola. Niles and Vivian had arrived only an hour earlier, also not knowing anything about Madame Hortence's last-minute show.

<<Heads up everyone! Madame Hortence is in the house, and she's going to see that the Runway area is ready.>>

I decided to hang around that area in case Gregor needed my help.

Sure enough, Madame Hortence was not pleased with the seating arrangements. She whispered something in her assistant's ear, prompting him to make the following announcement: "Ladies and gentlemen. Will you please stand up at once? We will not show here, but in the larger room to your right."

The crowd groaned. It would take longer to get the chairs back into the runway room than it had the last time because Lola's volunteers had to stay backstage.

To minimize damage, I ran to Madame Hortence and her assistant, introduced myself, and explained how it could take twenty minutes to re-arrange the chairs.

Madamae Hortence whispered to her assistant, who said, "Madame Hortence doesn't care. She wants the big room."

"We'll have to run it by Francie because she's the one who told us to set up here," I said.

Madame Hortence had a problem with direct communication because she whispered to her assistant again. He said, "If the chairs don't move, we're leaving!"

There was no alternative, so I agreed to the change. By that time Gregor was beside us. "Gregor, do you want to organize this the same as you did for the last chair move?" I asked.

"Of course, sweetie," he said, half singing to me, but half sneering at Madame Hortence.

At twelve-thirty, chairs and guests were in the runway room, ready for Madame Hortence's collection. I was in the designer gallery, congratulating Gregor on a great job of coordination, when I heard Francie yell, "Gigi, where are all the guests? WHERE ARE THEY?"

She ran to me as I explained, "Madame Hortence wanted to show in the runway room, so we had to move everything back."

"She can't do that! The lighting's different! The sound is different! She has to come back in here! What were you thinking?"

"I had to make a quick decision, Francie. You weren't around, and you weren't on headset. What would you have done in my position?"

"I don't care! This is MY event; you do what I say. You're moving the chairs back!"

"You can't be serious!" exclaimed Gregor.

I agreed with him. "Francie, think about what you're doing. The guests moved once already and they're settled now. On top of that, the volunteers have moved the chairs twice already. Madame Hortence will leave!"

"Oh, she won't leave. Just do it. I'll go talk to her while you move the chairs."

Gregor and I froze in amazement.

"MOVE!" Francie screamed at us.

Once again, we mobilized volunteers via walkie-talkies and tried to get grumbling guests to oblige.

At one o'clock, chairs and guests were back in the designer gallery and the show was ready to begin. Music filled the designer gallery and Madame Hortence's assistant stepped out to make an announcement.

"Ladies and gentlemen. Since you are Madame Hortence's best clients, she thanks you for attending today's show. Unfortunately, she wants you to know that due to the disorganization of Collections Week - Veronikkah Hendricks and Francie Scrimshank in particular - she will not show today. She apologizes for the inconvenience, but promises an intimate boutique show next week, where today's show tickets will be honoured. If you keep them, you can redeem them for twenty percent off any purchase. Once again, thank you for coming, and thank you for understanding the circumstances of today's events and reasons for postponing the show."

That was an interesting development, and while it was unfavourable for Collections Week, I hoped Veronikkah and Francie had learned a lesson.

Gregor and I looked at each other, not knowing whether to laugh at the absurdity of the situation or cry because we had to move the chairs back into the runway room. We chose to laugh because crying was too easy. Repeating the process, I heard volunteers complain; they weren't happy about moving chairs and I couldn't blame them. They wanted to help backstage, not rearrange chairs. I tried to tell them something uplifting about how it was a learning experience in the many aspects of planning fashion shows when I ran into Chloe Kirkpatrick.

"Hey Gigi," she smiled. "Tired?"

"Tired of moving chairs? For sure."

Chloe laughed. "That was the funniest thing I've seen in a long time. Veronikkah is so disorganized."

"I'm starting to realize that," I said. "I still don't know what happened."

She leaned in and whispered, "Let me tell you a secret. It's too good to resist. I don't normally gossip, because nobody would tell me anything. Then I wouldn't have any stories to print, but I want to warn you about Veronikkah because she's dangerous."

My mind flashed back to Hot Dan's warning the previous night. That was two danger warnings, Bolivian drug dealers, fistfights, and sex-trade workers. Things were adding up to a disconcerting sum.

"Anyway, the secret is Madame Hortence staged this to discredit Veronikkah; she didn't intend to show her collection. Veronikkah has been so power-hungry that she's ruining the reputation of Collections Week and Canadian fashion in general. Some of us think it's time she smartened up."

Juicy stuff, but I didn't want to get involved in any of it. I wanted to be a quiet volunteer and learn how to organize a fashion show. I'd certainly learned there was more to it than hard work and good clothes. Industry politics apparently played a big role too. I wanted to ask Chloe a million questions and share everything I saw, but I didn't know if I should. Was she a good person? Would she screw me over for a story? Or what if she was actually Veronikkah's friend and Veronikkah was spying on me? Paranoid delusions wormed through my brain.

What was I thinking? It was a fashion show, not a war. What could really go wrong? So I asked Chloe why Veronikkah was so dangerous.

"Well," Chloe began, "she only looks out for herself. She'll make other people look bad to make herself look good. Take this morning for instance. She'll likely call in a few favours from her magazine friends and she'll try to pan Hortence to them."

"That's understandable, isn't it?" I asked. "I mean, Madame Hortence made her look terrible."

"The thing is, Veronikkah deserved it. Not only that, but journalists despise Veronikkah, no matter how many favours she is owed. She has been mean to every fashion journalist in the country. She's backstabbed and manipulated too many people, so none of us will put up with her bullshit. That's why so many of us are here today; we knew Hortence was going to do this."

"Seriously? That's awful," I said.

Chloe thought for a moment. "I guess it is when you don't really know Veronikkah," she said. "But I've known her for twenty years, and she's the devil."

I couldn't believe anyone was that bad, no matter how spacey or drug-addicted they were, so I asked, "What did she do that was so wrong?"

"She destroyed many careers by claiming work as her own," said Chloe, "including mine."

"What happened?" I asked.

"We went to Ryerson and became best friends in the program. When we graduated, we went to be Mods in London. When we got there, she partied, but I landed some good design jobs. Then things changed, and as we both shifted into punk, I helped Vivienne Westwood and Malcom MacLaren with the Sex Pistols and the Sex shop. When Vivienne took off, Veronikkah begged me to get her a job with Vivienne, so I did. One day I arrived at work to find she'd stolen all my ideas for a huge presentation, leaving me with nothing to show and a bad reputation. Word spread that I'd stolen the designs from her, and nobody wanted to hire a thief. I returned to Canada, but I lost the desire to design. My heart wasn't in it, but I still loved clothes, and somehow I managed to land writing jobs because of my expert knowledge of European trends."

"Oh, that's so sad," I said, "but at least it led to a good career in journalism."

She sighed. "I guess so, but Veronikkah was meaner than that."

"How could anyone have been meaner than that?"

"She stole my boyfriend at the time. He was the lead singer of the coolest band in London, Sweet Evil."

"Sweet Evil?" I squealed. "You dated Screaming Jared?"

Chloe made a dreamy face. "God, Jared was so hot," she said with a smile. "He was the hippest guy ever."

Chloe Kirkpatrick suddenly became my idol. Screaming Jared was a million times cooler than all the Sex Pistols combined.

Her smile faded. "Well, he was the grooviest guy until Veronikkah got her hands on him. One night after a concert, she gave him heroin and a blowjob, and that was that. He never played again. The two of them only cared about getting high."

I was a sucker for a good sob story and sniffed, "Oh, that's so sad."

She continued, "That's not all. One day he disappeared. Veronikkah had lost her job with Vivienne by that point, since her whole life was spent locked up in her apartment with a needle and vial. She was under investigation for his disappearance and possible death, but there was never enough evidence to convict her. She was ruined in London and couldn't get into any other countries, so she came back to Canada."

"Is that all true? She was behind his disappearance? How come I never heard about it? I know everything about music and fashion!" I exclaimed.

"Well, it was tabloid news in Britain, but when she came back to Canada, she changed her name and vanished for a few years, but then dabbled in dealing drugs. Her family is pretty rich and powerful, with links to the media, so her dad tried to cover up the story. Trust me, it's true. Her name was Millicent McFadden. Look it up, but it may take some effort to find anything."

"No way!" I screamed, but tried to be quiet at the same time. "She's a McFadden, as in the McFadden Beer

McFaddens who brew Rocky Mountain Ale? She was the groupie behind Screaming Jared's disappearance? That's such a huge rock 'n' roll mystery! I can't believe it!" I was such a music and fashion geek, how could I not have known? Rocky Mountain Ale was the oldest brewing company in Canada, and the family was well known and powerful throughout the country, owning everything from newspapers and publications to department stores. I couldn't believe Veronikkah Hendricks was a McFadden!

INVESTIGATE.

Chloe looked around and suddenly I remembered she was telling me the story in confidence. I worried I'd blown it for her by talking too loud since I was so amazed at the news.

"Why are you telling me this if it's such a big secret?" I asked. "We only met a few days ago."

"I'm a journalist; I can read people. You're a good person and you'll go far, but I don't want Veronikkah to do to you what she did to me. She can be a smooth talker, so don't fall for it."

That's when we spotted Veronikkah across the room with the Bolivian Reservoir Dogs.

Chloe pretended she were just passing by, worried Veronikkah would see us talking. "If she sees you with me, she'll make your life miserable," said Chloe. "Just be careful. Call me if you need anything."

Left alone to process all the information, I wondered what to do with it. Nevertheless, I didn't have to think for long because Veronikkah and Francie appeared beside me.

"You're the best little volunteer we've ever had," purred Veronikkah. "You did such a good job this morning."

"Thanks," I said, wondering if she actually noticed the work we all did for her or if she was too occupied with interviews, schmoozing, and getting high.

"Now, since you're new, I want to warn you about the press, my dear." Her voice took on a slithery tone, and she reminded me of Madame Medusa, the villainness in the cartoon *The Rescuers*. Both had red hair and wore low-cut dresses revealing saggy breasts. She must have seen me talking to Chloe.

Francie cut in. "Volunteers can't talk to the press!"

Veronikkah shoved her aside, demonstrating the contempt she held for her uncouth assistant. "It's not as though volunteers are forbidden to talk to journalists," Veronikkah hissed in my ear, "it's more about saying the right things to journalists."

She paused, trying to find the right words to say next. "I know that you see things during the event, things that might not reflect nicely on Collections Week in the press. This is a national event; we're trying to raise consciousness and prestige of Canadian designers together. We're all on the same side. But to be consistent, I am the official Collections Week spokesperson. All interviews go through me. Do I make myself clear?"

Clear? She told me not to talk to journalists, knowing she couldn't specifically tell me not to talk to journalists. My head spun wondering what I'd gotten myself into, now censorship had been added to Veronikkah's list of shady activities. I was sick of all the weirdness and didn't want to be part of questionable deals going on behind the curtains. Veronikkah wouldn't be happy to learn I'd chatted with Chloe last night.

"Yeah, I understand," I said. "Just so you know, some journalists asked for interviews on pieces about the volunteer experience," trying to cover my new friendship with Chloe. "I didn't think it would be a problem."

Veronikkah gritted her teeth. "No, no problem. Just make sure future interviews go through me. Speaking of interviews, I've got to go speak with *Elle Canada*." She pushed me aside, but she stopped when Francie followed her. "Francie, you stay here and direct Lulu on the dog show." She was gone instantly.

I couldn't believe she called me Lulu again. Wait..."Did she say dog show?" I asked Francie.

"Yeah. It's another last minute addition," she said. "Veronikkah's friend owns a boutique that sells designer puppy clothes and accessories. They decided it would be fun to add a puppy fashion show to this afternoon's events."

"What? Are you serious?" I didn't know what to do. I'd hated dogs ever since one bit me when I was nine and selling Girl Scout cookies door-to-door. Maybe I hated horses more because I was bucked off one when I was ten, but I really hated dogs. Apart from my dog-phobia, there were so many things wrong with the dog show idea, and after that morning's last minute show-turned-fiasco, the dog fashion show news set me off.

"Dog show!" I screamed. "I didn't volunteer to help with a dog show, and neither did anyone else!"

Francie jumped back, scared of me for a moment, but regained her composure and said, "Veronikkah wants it, so it has to get done." Something in her demeanour hinted she thought it was a terrible idea too, but wasn't allowed to say so since she was Veronikkah's lackey.

"I can't do it, Francie. Remember that warning I told you about this morning? This is warning number two. One more thing like this, and I have to leave."

"I don't understand. What's so bad about it?" Francie asked. "If Veronikkah wants it done, it has to be good."

"How can you not see how bad this idea is? Having a dog show alongside a fashion show is an insult to designers, models, and the entire Canadian fashion industry, especially if we're trying to promote it. Can't you just see the headlines in the paper? '*Canadian Collections Week Goes to the Dogs!*' Everyone will have the same headline!"

"But that's what Veronikkah wants: to put Collections Week on the map," whined Francie. "She says any press is good."

"I really don't think the event needs negative press about a dog show; it needs positive press about our great designers," I said.

"Well, I'll talk to Veronikkah about it, but in the meantime, you have to do this because you're just a volunteer."

I was frustrated, so I said, "Fine. You feel that way, but I feel that because I'm *just* a volunteer, I don't have to do it. I won't do it for a couple reasons: first, I'm afraid of dogs; second, I think it's degrading to everyone involved; and third, it's not what I volunteered to do when I agreed to help with Collections Week. What I will do, though, is collect volunteers who are willing to work on this project and I will give them to you and you can be in charge of them."

Francie looked at me, trying to gauge if I was serious.

"I am serious," I said, reading her mind. "And I'm serious about the second warning. If something this outrageous happens again, I will have to resign."

"I just don't understand why this is such a big deal," said Francie.

The girl would never understand morals. I tried to explain it by saying, "I'm volunteering to learn about the fashion industry, not about how to dress dogs. If that *is* part of the industry, it's the part that is the most ridiculous. Even though I'm volunteering, I am doing a job, and I don't want my work or name attached to something I don't believe in."

She stared at me, not knowing how to reply, so I continued.

"As I said, I'll help you get people who don't feel as strongly as I do, and I'll send them to you. Where will you be and when will it start?"

"I'll be in the office and the show will start at four," she said.

"Fine. I'll send people to you in fifteen minutes."

"Thanks," she said, and walked toward the office.

<<Gigi to all volunteers.>> I didn't know quite how to start, so I jumped right in. <<We have another schedule change. There will be a dog fashion show at four o'clock, and Francie needs people to help with it. Do you have interested volunteers?>>

<<Did you say *dog* fashion show?>> asked Gregor.

Lola laughed on the walkie-talkie. <<She's kidding, you loser! Who would ever think of anything that stupid?>>

<<Ummm...I'm not kidding, you guys,>> I said. <<It's Veronikkah's idea. She thinks it'll get good publicity.>>

<<You're such a kidder. You are kidding, aren't you, sweetie?>> asked Gregor.

<<No, I'm not,>> I said. <<I'm serious. Francie wants some volunteers. Can you ask your teams if anyone is interested in this project?>>

<<You're really serious?>> asked Lola.

<<Yes, I am.>>

<<Okay, I'll ask,>> she said.

<<Me too,>> said Gregor.

<<I love puppies, but isn't this weird?>> asked Chantelle.

<<It's Veronikkah's idea,>> I said, <<so we have to do it. Let me know if you find anyone to help.>>

<<Okay.>>

Five minutes passed and Lola called saying none of her volunteers wanted to do the dog show, which was what I expected. I secretly hoped nobody would help, just to illustrate the stupidity of Veronikkah's idea. If nobody volunteered, Veronikkah and Francie would be stuck doing everything. Chantelle didn't have any volunteers, either, but Gregor found one.

<<I have one girl who wants to help out,>> he said. <<Her dream is to own a puppy boutique.>>

I thought that girl was probably a real loser, but said, <<Great. I'll take her over to the office.>>

We found Veronikkah and Francie sprawled across the office couches with a half-finished bottle of Champagne between them.

"I've got one volunteer for you. Her name is Piper, and she loves dogs."

"Only one?" asked Veronikkah. "We need more than one."

Though I sensed a confrontation, it was time to stand up to the crazy lady, so I said, "I'm sure Francie gave you my thoughts on the dog show idea." I paused to see Veronikkah look at Francie, clearly not having any clue, but I continued. "I tried to recruit volunteers for the dog show, but everyone agreed they were here to volunteer for fashion shows."

"But you're all here to work for ME," Veronikkah gasped, her shock turning to rage.

"Yes, but we agree that a dog show is not a fashion show. Every volunteer has been asked to help, but most do not want to do it. But you're lucky to have Piper here to help, because she wants to own a puppy boutique."

Veronikkah acknowledged Piper, but started to rant. "What the FUCK are you talking about? You have to do what you're asked!"

It was becoming too much, so I blurted, "Consider this your second warning. If you place any more unreasonable demands on me, I'm leaving."

"What are you talking about? Aren't you enjoying the experience? You're too sensitive. Last-minute things always come up at fashion shows," said Veronikkah.

"Yes, I'm having an interesting experience and learning a lot. And yes, I'm sure last minute things always come up, but I'm not going to do anything that compromises my respect or dignity. Nor will I make other people participate in tasks I would not do myself. Please understand that we're people, we're all equal, and we're here to help you out, as long as it doesn't interfere with our sanity or safety. Now I'm going to leave you with Piper and she can help you with your dog show."

I left before I could hear anything else. How could I talk to Veronikkah Hendricks like that? Would I get away with it? My hands shook and there were butterflies in my stomach as I walked away.

Veronikkah followed me down the hall and said, "Gigi, can I talk to you for a minute?"

Uh-oh. I was toast. She would rip me apart and I'd be banished from the Toronto fashion scene forever. I stopped so she could catch up and thought, "Well, being an urban planner wasn't so bad. I guess I don't really have to switch careers."

"Gigi," she began, "I appreciate your honesty. People are scared to tell me what they think, especially Francie. She's of no use to me, but you can be. You've got guts. I'm going to fire her after this season. Would you like to be my assistant?"

I couldn't believe she got my name right or that she was serious about the assistant position. I had to think fast for a reply. Flattery was the way to avoid the question since I didn't want to offend an embezzling, psychotic cokehead by saying there was no way I'd ever work for her.

"Why, thanks, Veronikkah. That would be a great honour," I lied, "but I really moved to Toronto to start a clothing company. I'd like to work for myself." Hey, that sounded good.

"You're a designer?" she asked. "You simply MUST show with us next season!"

"Thanks. I'll think about it," I lied again. No matter how badly I wanted to start a clothing company, I would never do business with Veronikkah Hendricks.

We stood for a few moments not knowing what to do. It was awkward for me, but it was embarrassing for Veronikkah because she seemed to have forgotten why she was talking to me in the first place.

"Well, I guess I should go get my hair and makeup done," she sang. "Toodles!"

"Okay, have fun," I said. I did not want to remind her she needed to organize the dog show for fear of her wrath and also because I wanted it to fail. It was mean of me, but they needed to see I was right.

PATROL.

The Carlu was a mess. Francie and Piper had frantically - yet feebly - set up for the dog show in the designer gallery while the rest of us ran the afternoon shows. When guests exited the runway room, Francie yelled at everyone to stay for the dog show, but nobody paid attention to her since her voice was too high to carry in the designer gallery. As most people left, Francie brought out a portable stereo and played Reel 2 Real's "*Move It!*", creating a scenario reminiscent of a 1994 high school fashion show fundraiser.

Some people gathered to see what Francie was doing, so there was a small cluster blocking the path where the first model was supposed to walk with her dog in a matching outfit. She began, but by the time people realized what was happening, she was mixed up among them. The dog got excited and nipped at people's heels. Eventually everyone realized it was a show and cleared a walkway. At that point, guests were more concerned with getting out of the dog's way than they were with examining the pink plaid jacket it wore.

Gregor appeared beside me and sneered, "Can you believe this? It's a fashion disaster of Titanic proportions."

"Shhh...We're volunteers, remember? We have to pretend this is a good thing," I said, stifling a giggle.

Next up were a model and dog wearing matching raincoats and hats, but the rain hat blocked the dog's eyes, so he sat there, refusing to move. The model was forced to drag the pathetic pooch along the carpet.

Gregor and I looked at each other, but had to turn away because we almost burst into laughter.

The nadir of the show came when one dog entered in a knit sweater that said "Doggy Style." He got too far on his leash and humped a journalist's leg. At least he got into character. It couldn't have been choreographed better.

As the last outfit was shown, I noticed Chloe Kirkpatrick beside me. "Ohhh..." she moaned. "Say it's not so."

I looked to the makeshift runway and saw a model and dog in matching pink tutus. It was the worst of fashion extremes: doggy evening wear, accompanied by snickering journalists. I was right; the show delivered a Collections Week death sentence.

Chloe leaned in and asked, "What's the story behind this? I didn't see it listed on the program."

"One of Veronikkah's friends owns a doggy boutique and added this at the last minute. They thought it was a good idea," I said, trying to hide my disgust, but realizing the complete absurdity of the situation.

We both looked at each other and giggled. Soon there was no way to stop. Gregor, Chloe, and I all exploded into unrecoverable laughter, complete with tears. There was no way to hide it, which became infectious. Instantly, everybody in the crowd either held their stomach from laughing so hard or dabbed their eyes from crying. The model couldn't even keep it together, it was that absurd. She tried to strike a pose, but kept snickering. I couldn't blame her; it was more hilarious than *Best in Show*.

In the corner, Veronikkah and Francie frantically evaluated their mistake. Neither was pleased, and I noticed Veronikkah's wrath was about to erupt. They walked our way.

"Chloe, Veronikkah saw us and she's pissed," I said. "Run! Gregor, you too! Go somewhere and occupy your volunteers. I'll take care of this."

They bolted while I tried to act busy rearranging some magazines at a nearby display, pretending I didn't see them.

Veronikkah looked at me with fire in her eyes and said, "You knew this would happen, you little witch! You did this on purpose to make us look bad!"

"How could you think such a thing?" I asked. "It was your idea. It's just common sense that if you put animals in a show, they might not cooperate."

Veronikkah pondered my words and said, "I guess you're right, but why were you talking to the press? I told you not to talk to the press."

"I wasn't talking to the press."

"Little liar!" she spat and bared her teeth at me. "You were with Chloe Kirkpatrick. That bitch is out to get me at all costs. You're forbidden to speak with her!"

There was no doubt about it; Veronikkah was a scary psychopath. I had to be careful.

"Why is Chloe out to get you?" I asked.

"She's a whiny girl with an old grudge. So what if I stole her little boyfriend? She should get over it. And she thinks I stole her job from Vivienne Westwood. So what if I did? This is a tough business and only the strong survive."

Not only was Veronikkah a scary psychopath, she was heartless as well. At least she confirmed Chloe's story. I had to think of some way to escape from her before she put a bounty on my head or decided to make me her assistant. I didn't know which option was worse.

At that moment, the Bolivian Reservoir Dogs joined our party. They exchanged glances and nonverbal communication with Veronikkah, who said, "Is everything ready for tonight's Bolivian designer showcase?"

Francie looked at me. It was apparently my job to organize the showcase.

"I'll check Backstage and let you know what's happening. Is there anything in particular you need?" I asked.

Veronikkah looked at them, then at me, and said, "Oh, you know, the usual. When things are ready, let me know. We'll be in the office."

My job description blurred. Was I the volunteer coordinator or did I run the entire event? It was hard to tell, and I was happy to get the experience (even with the psychotic episodes), so I just went with it.

<<Gigi to Lola and Niles.>>

<<Go ahead,>> said Lola.

<<How are things looking for the Bolivian show?>>

<<Not good.>>

<<What do you mean?>>

<<Well, we have most of the models, but no art direction, since there's nobody from the Bolivian delegation here. But right now we're focusing on the other shows. We have one more to go before we start on the Bolivian one.>>

<<Okay, I'll try to get some guidance for you so we don't get behind.>>

<<Thanks, Gigi.>>

I ran to the office, knocked on the door and held my breath; I had no idea what I would see when the door opened. It was possible there would be a drug frenzy, maybe some crazy orgy, or even a dead body. Going to the office had become a source of simultaneous fear and amusement.

That time, Francie opened the door to reveal a rather mundane scene: Veronikkah tapped at a laptop while the Reservoir Dogs stood around her. It seemed relatively normal, but then I thought back to the papers I'd seen earlier. Veronikkah had a laptop, but told the Board it had been stolen. She still had the financial records! She was a big, evil liar!

"What do you want?" she barked.

"I want what we all want: a nice home, car, a million dollars," I joked.

She didn't find it funny. She was too busy for jokes.

"Okay," I said, "Backstage needs hair and makeup direction. They also require clothes. Any thoughts on how they can get those things?"

"Isn't Eva downstairs? She should have everything. She was going to pick up the Bolivian designers and bring their clothes."

"Let me just check to see if anyone's seen Eva," I said.

<<Hi everyone. It's Gigi. Has anyone seen Eva?>>

<<Not me,>> said Chantelle.

<<She's backstage,>> said Lola.

<<What's she doing?>> I asked.

<<Hanging around with the makeup artists, smoking and chatting. Hey - are they allowed to smoke in here?>>

<<Smoking isn't allowed anywhere in this building! Tell them to stop or we'll get kicked out. Anyway, Francie says Eva is supposed to provide the Bolivian show art direction and pick up the Bolivian designers. Can you remind her of that and let me know how it goes?>>

A minute later, Lola walkied me back and said, <<Eva said it was too early to get the Bolivian designers, but it was pretty obvious she'd forgotten she was supposed to do it. She left hair and makeup with the direction to start on models with an eighties glam look.>>

<<Thanks,>> I said, and relayed the information to everyone in the Collections Week office.

"Great. It all sounds under control. Thank you," said Veronikkah. "See that you don't bother us again."

Francie pushed me out the office and slammed the door. Frustrated, I decided to check in on backstage.

The scene wasn't much different than for previous shows. The main difference was that models stood around staring at each other, while makeup artists and hairstylists chatted and tried to sneak cigarette puffs. They hid their smokes as soon as I walked by because they knew I would bust them for smoking in a heritage building. They got sick of my nagging, but kept trying to trick me. Just as I spotted a makeup girl who hadn't been warned of my cigarette wrath, I felt a hand slip around my waist and knew it was Hot Dan.

INTERROGATE.

"Why'd you run away last night?" I asked, turning around to face him.

His face flushed and he looked down, flustered. "Yeah...uhhh...I didn't mean to...uhhh...It's just that things are, you know, complicated."

Complicated? Sure he was hot and sure he was a great kisser, but there wasn't anything complicated about it, so I said, "A kiss isn't complicated. What are you trying to do, turn it into a soap opera?"

He looked into my eyes with his deep blue ones, and I slipped into another world. With eyes that powerful, no wonder he was a model.

Searching for the right words, he stammered, "Uhhh... in this case, ummm...well, it is kind of complicated. For me it is a soap opera."

Struggling against the pull of his eyes, I finally looked away and regained some inner strength. "Why is it complicated? I don't think I've done anything complicated."

"Ummm..." he paused.

"What is it? Do you have a girlfriend? A boyfriend? What is it that's so complicated?" Normally I wasn't confrontational about girl-boy stuff, but it was turning into a game I didn't want to play. I'd had enough boy-girl games in my twenties.

"No, no, it's nothing like that. Actually, really, uhhh...maybe it's not that complicated."

"What are you talking about? I don't understand."

"There's just something I want to tell you, but I can't right now."

"Listen, Dan, I like you. You're cool. But I don't like secrets, especially after kissing someone. If you're interested in me, I don't want to start something with secrets."

I couldn't tell what he was thinking, but he said, "Okay, it will probably be okay if I tell you, but you have to promise not to tell anyone. It's serious."

What could he possibly tell me that was so serious? I looked at him, unsure, but said, "I promise." He was serious, but I felt I was back in junior high with all this secretive talk.

"You're sure I can trust you?"

I looked at him, exasperated. He got the message.

"Okay," he started. "I'm kind of a different person than who you think I am…"

He got cut off when I heard Lola yell, "Gigi! The designers are here! Can you help?"

I looked at Dan, and damn, those eyes got me again. They reached right into my body and hugged my heart.

"It's okay," he said. "Go. We'll talk later and I'll explain everything. Trust me."

I had no idea what he was talking about and started wondering about him. Maybe he was a transvestite. Worse yet, maybe he was a eunuch. Was he a serial killer? No, he was probably in the mob. Yes, that was it. He was a crime lord. Considering this week's track record of drugs and embezzlement, the next logical step would be mobsters. Nevertheless, Hot Dan was hot, and he squeezed my hand as I walked away from him towards Lola.

"What's up with you two?" Lola asked when Hot Dan couldn't hear us.

"I have no clue. There's obviously chemistry, and he was the one who kissed me last night, but now he's all skittish and mysterious. I don't get it."

"Boys," sighed Lola.

"You're telling me. But we don't have time to discuss it now; that's meant for hours sharing chocolate cake. How can I help?"

Lola nodded in the direction of hair and makeup. "There's no sign of Eva, so Niles needs you to keep hair and makeup on schedule. The designers gave instructions to the artists, and you need to push them to be quick. When models are done, send them to us; we'll get them fitted and ready for the show."

That sounded easy enough, so I went over and saw a few artists chatting. Walking up to the little clique, I asked, "Hey guys, do you need some models?"

"Who are you?" snapped one girl.

"I'm the volunteer coordinator."

"Where's Eva? We get directions from her, so until she comes around, we're on a break."

Didn't they want to finish hair and makeup? That way they'd get to leave earlier. And what was with the attitude? I responded with, "I'm only doing what was asked by the backstage production crew. They're in a hurry to get models through hair and makeup so they can get fitted."

"Oh, okay," sighed the girl. "Get us some models, then."

I found a few girls, sent them to the clique, and made announcements to everyone, reminding them they were on a deadline. I was being annoying, but we needed to get it done.

After half the models were ready, Eva ran up, pushed me from behind, and demanded, "What do you think you're doing, bitch?"

Shocked by such a confrontation, I said, "I'm just trying to facilitate hair and makeup."

"That's my job, you stupid whore!" she said, shoving me again.

I was about to shove her back and quit, but that would only mean I'd leave all the volunteers with these abusive lunatics. I couldn't just leave; I had to take a stand

and stop these people. A plan of attack started forming in my mind: we'd need a grand gesture. Something really big...like a walkout...all of us quitting en masse...There were too many revolutionary ideas swirling in my mind, so I just stood my ground and said, "We couldn't find you, but needed to start working."

"Did you even look for me, you piece of trash, or are you trying to steal my job?" She stepped closer, fist clenched, ready to hit me. Her pupils were dilated and her hands shook. She must have been doing coke somewhere with the gang.

"No, no, I don't want your job," I said, stepping out of her reach in case she swung. "In fact, I'm too busy to do this because I have to make sure all the volunteers are happy. You came at the perfect time."

"Perfect time, my ass. If you want the job so bad, just take it!" She stomped off.

"But I don't want your job," I called after her, but she ignored me.

After a few more models finished hair and makeup and were happily getting fitted, Francie stormed up to me and asked, "Why did you take Eva's job?"

I should have predicted the confrontation. "I didn't take Eva's job," I explained. "We couldn't find her when it was time to get the models through hair and makeup, so we started. I don't think I need to explain to you we're on a deadline."

"Well, she's all upset, and she's our best worker."

Her best worker? Eva was her best friend, not her best worker.

"Francie," I pleaded, "I'm not trying to take her job. I told her that. I'm too busy with other stuff, but someone needed to do this while she was gone. She should be working here so I can look after the volunteers."

"And you'd better look after the volunteers!" Francie snapped.

It was the stupidest conversation I'd ever had. "I will get back to the volunteers, as soon as Eva comes back to do her job."

"Okay, I'll get her then."

"Fine."

"Fine." Francie stormed away.

I couldn't believe that conversation had actually happened, but I didn't have time to marvel over it because Eva shoved past me and spat orders at everyone. She stopped at the clique, whispered something, looked in my direction, and they all laughed. She was the reincarnation of my kindergarten bully, though I knew I was right. I would never understand why those people acted so childish, so I walked away without saying anything to Eva.

I did, however, check in with Niles and Lola, who, as it turned out, had also been visited by Francie. She yelled at them for going ahead without Eva. Niles tried to explain things to her, but she wouldn't listen. We all had the same pointless conversations.

"Is it always like this?" I asked Niles.

"No. This year is by far the craziest. I don't know why."

At that point, one Bolivian designer wailed, tore at her swimsuit collection, throwing bikinis everywhere.

"THIS I CANNOT DO!" she screamed.

Niles, Lola, and I looked at each other, not knowing how to react.

"I'll go and talk her down," I sighed, wondering how I ended up doing all this work when I was merely supposed to look after the volunteers.

"What's wrong?" I asked the crazed Bolivian designer.

"My clothes...terrible...wrong...a failure. I cannot put swimsuits on runway! Oh! I am sick!" She doubled over, as though she would vomit all over her bikinis.

"Then get away from the clothes!" I half-joked. "Come with me; I'll take you to the washroom to get some water." I pulled her away from the clothes and motioned for Niles and Lola to fit the models while we were gone.

We passed where the flats of water for volunteers should have been, but they were empty. Why couldn't I get it together to make sure there was water for volunteers? It seemed to go so quickly, so I decided to get a drink for the designer.

"No, stay!" she begged.

I had no choice but to stay with the depressed designer. While she leaned over a toilet, I sat down on a chaise lounge. I realized it was the first time I'd stopped moving in ten hours. It was a big mistake because only by sitting did I realize how tired I was. I could have stayed there and slept for a week without noticing any flushing toilets. I never expected fashion to be so tiring. Caught in my fatigue, I barely registered that Depressed Designer was babbling on about her entire life in half-English. But when she started talking about ending things with a bottle of pills, I had to intervene.

"What are you talking about?" I asked, amazed she would discuss suicide with a total stranger.

"I live in dead country, have dead husband, and have dead dream about clothing designer. Nothing works," she said, half to the toilet, half to me.

Inwardly cursing her for disturbing my rest, I sat up and looked over to make sure she didn't actually have any pills. She didn't, so I mustered my best positive attitude and began to talk.

"Nothing works for you? How can you say that? You're showing your clothes in North America; that's something great. How many of your colleagues have done that?"

"This is first time."

"Exactly, and look at you. You're the first. I'm sure you're an inspiration to people back home."

She moved away from the toilet, curled up in the stall doorway, smiled, but suddenly remembered she was supposed to be sad. She slumped against the door.

I had to continue trying to cheer her up. "And have you really looked at your clothes? Your swimsuits are amazing!"

Something twinkled in her eye as she looked up at me. "You think?" she asked. "Really?"

"Oh yeah," I lied. Truthfully, I didn't like her creations because they were tiny bits of sparkly fabric that hid only the important body bits. They would only look good on size two models. Admittedly, though, they were pretty nice for what they were and it was great someone from a Southern country could show her stuff at Collections Week. Depressed Designer still looked a bit sad, so I kept talking. "Think about the hard work you put into this, and all the people who are supporting you."

She smiled a bit.

I was on a roll; nothing would stop the pep talk. "And what about your country? You're here to put Bolivian fashion on the map. When everyone sees your work, they won't stop talking about it."

"You think?" she asked.

"For sure. It's not like anything we usually see in Canada. It's fresh! It's new!" I felt like an insincere journalist, but I wanted to do anything to make this woman feel good.

My pep must have worked because she got up, walked over, and hugged me.

"Good Canadian friend," she said. "Thank you."

That dilemma was solved, so I shuffled her out the door so we could get backstage. Unfortunately, her eyes became pools and she cried again.

"Why so nice to me?"

"What are you talking about? You deserve to be treated nicely."

"No one like that. Not like fashion people. Not Miss Veronikkah. No. She only wants...um...how do you say... coca..."

"Coca? As in cocaine?" I asked.

She nodded. It certainly wasn't news to me, but it was good to hear someone else's opinion.

"She thinks all Bolivian people take coca. She try to make me take today. Not for me. I ran."

"Really?" I asked. "You actually ran away from her?" The thought of Depressed Designer running away from Veronikkah was slightly amusing.

"Yes and those men. Bad men. All Bolivians know. Drug men. Why they here?"

"I thought they organized this trip for you. We were told they were your representatives."

She snorted. "No representatives! Bad men! Not us! I think friends of Miss Veronikkah."

"Yes, I think so too," I agreed. Everything I discovered pointed to Veronikkah and a ring of Bolivian drug lords. What was I supposed to do? Was it my obligation to call the police? Or was it something that happened at all fashion shows? I wanted to ignore it because it didn't affect me directly, and I was scared to get involved with Bolivian drug lords. But what if there was a bust? Was

I an accomplice? How would it affect other volunteers? Would the girls who helped clean the office be implicated too? It was a whole new culture for me and I needed guidance. To catch Veronikkah and teach her a lesson, I needed to find trustworthy people with the same goal. Though I'd only just met Niles, I knew I could trust him.

We arrived backstage and Depressed Designer saw the models wearing her swimsuits.

"Look at your clothes!" I squealed. "They look fantastic!"

She smiled and said, "Better now. Thank you."

"You're welcome. Do you think you'll be okay?"

"Yes, yes. Okay."

"Great. Have a wonderful show and let me know if you have any problems."

She gave me a hug then focused her attention on the models.

Niles and Lola peeked out through a forest of models in various states of undress, so I ran to them and said, "Everything's fine. She's all right now. She just got nervous."

"You're wonderful, Gigi," said Lola.

"Well, yes, I know," I winked.

Lola turned to button up a sparkly pink evening gown that looked like a *Strictly Ballroom* outfit, so I whispered to Niles, "I know you're busy, but I have to tell you something about Veronikkah."

"What is it?" he asked.

"That Bolivian designer said those Bolivian men are drug lords. I think Veronikkah's doing some business behind the scenes. Maybe I'm crazy, but Collections Week might be some elaborate front for some other venture. I'm scared."

"Are you serious?" he asked, his face contorted with a frown and unbelieving eyes.

"I wish I was joking. I don't know what to do."

"Are you sure? How do you know?"

I looked around to make sure nobody could hear us and checked the walkie-talkies to make sure they were off; I didn't want that news to be broadcast. "Well, the Bolivian designer cemented my theory of the suit-guys not being fashionistas. Veronikkah's giving out samples in some exclusive gift bags to get people hooked. Since you told me about her past, and since she's so clearly been using this whole week, everything's adding up to a huge cocaine deal; she doesn't care about Canadian fashion at all."

Niles didn't know what to say, so he stood still for a moment. Finally, he said, "I knew Veronikkah was using, but I had no clue about the rest. Vivian doesn't know either. Are you really sure about this?"

Leaning in, I whispered, "I found a bag of cocaine in one of the gift bags. When I returned it to Veronikkah, she told the drug lord guys all the bags had 'product samples' of cocaine for designers. They're aiming for the fashion and party crowd. I overheard her telling them."

"Oh, this is serious," said Niles.

"Not only that, but she mentioned something about pick-ups tonight. I think there are going to be some major sales, and if they're caught, she'll pin it on Francie and the volunteers. What do you think we should do? Do we call the police?"

"No...no...not yet. This could cause the downfall of Canadian fashion. This is huge. Let me talk to Vivian and I'll get back to you."

Niles ran to the runway room, while I stayed backstage to help Lola. As I pinned together a model's pantsuit, I saw Hot Dan across the room. Our eyes locked; we both wanted to talk. Unfortunately, we were both dealing with fittings. Even more unfortunate was when Francie appeared out of nowhere and said, "Gigi, we have an important project for your volunteers. Come with me."

I gazed back at Hot Dan with a long, lingering, pining look, and told Lola I'd have to leave. She knew what she was doing; after three days, she was a pro.

Francie led me to the office, where Veronikkah sat with the Reservoir Dogs. "Ah, darling," she purred. "I have an important job for you and your volunteers. Do you see these gift bags?" She pointed to the wall in a *Price is Right* gesture.

I looked at the wall and nodded, fearful of what was ahead.

"These are VIP bags. I want you and your volunteers to distribute them. Francie has our VIP list and will make sure everything gets to the right people."

My worst fear came true: I was being asked to help move the cocaine for Veronikkah and her Bolivian buddies. She obviously didn't know I'd figured out her operation, so I played along. If she thought I was stupid, I'd give her stupid until I thought of something better. "Oh, I thought all the gift bags were the same. What's so special about these ones?" I asked innocently, digging for more information.

"They've got some extra cosmetics and things. There's actually this really special powder in there." Everyone around the room exchanged eye contact and knowing glances.

She seriously thought I wouldn't understand the powder reference. Veronikkah apparently thought I was really stupid, but it was a mistake to underestimate me.

"Oh, okay," I said, playing along. "I'll take one down to the volunteers to show, then I'll send a few to collect the bags." I scooped up a bag and ran out of the room before anyone could say anything. I wanted to check the bags to confirm my suspicions, so I ran down the hallway to an empty room off the backstage area. Rummaging through the bag, I found perfume samples, mascara, eye shadow, some coupons, and a red velvet box tied with a sparkly white bow. If that red box contained what I thought it did, I had a major problem. Making sure nobody lurked nearby, I untied the bow, opened the box, and sure enough, it was filled with a bag of white powder. I didn't know much about cocaine, but I figured an M&M sized bag of the stuff was probably a lot.

My walkie buzzed and I was so edgy, I jumped and banged my elbow on the wall. Not only was I freaking out about being used as a coke dealer, I had to answer a walkie call and tend to my excruciatingly painful funny bone injury. It wasn't funny.

<<Yeah, Gigi here,>> I moaned into my headset.

<<It's Niles. Can you meet Vivian and me at the production booth?>>

<<I'll be there in a minute.>> I couldn't wait to get there because it was a serious situation. If I'd

had any doubts before, they were gone. Collections Week volunteers were about to participate in a giant coke deal.

Vivian and Niles were both worried when I arrived at the sound and light booth.

"Niles told me everything. Is it true?" Vivian asked.

Feeling spy-like, I looked around to ensure nobody was near and whispered, "It's totally true, but now it's worse." I pulled them close to explain the coke delivery setup.

"You've got to be kidding!" exclaimed Vivian.

I sneakily showed her the contents of the velvet box.

"I guess you're not kidding," said Niles.

"I had no idea this was happening," said Vivian.

"Can you help me?" I pleaded. "I don't know what to do." As fashion veterans with previous Veronikkah experience, I needed their advice.

We looked at each other, slightly panicked, somewhat confused, and quite scared.

A smile spread slowly across Vivian's face. "I know what to do."

UNIFY AND ATTACK.

In my years of working on urban planning projects, I learned a good leader is intelligent, trustworthy, compassionate, courageous, and - at times - stern. I hoped my team and I embodied those traits to the other volunteers because I would need everybody's support to manage our counter-attack.

<<Gigi to Lola, Gregor, and Chantelle. We're having a meeting at the Corbusier sofas in five minutes.>>

<<But we have guests here,>> said Chantelle.

<<And backstage is crazy,>> said Lola.

<<It doesn't matter,>> I said. <<Just get there as soon as possible. This meeting is top priority, and it's an emergency.>>

Five minutes later, three worried volunteers huddled together on the sofa. I started the meeting by asking them about their days. They all said they were having fun and learning a lot. Slowly and surely, the truth emerged.

"To be honest," started Gregor, "I've been grumpy ever since the chair episode. It really pissed me off."

"Yeah, we're totally taken for granted," agreed Lola. "You know what I had to do today? I had to hem Veronikkah's skirt. She threw it in my face and told me to fix it. When I gave it back to her, she never even said thank you."

"Ohmigod!" cried Chantelle. "She asked me to run out and get her antihistamines! I sent someone else to do it because I didn't want to leave my section, but she yelled at me for not going myself. I didn't want to bother you about it, Gigi, because you were so busy. Later in the day, she also asked one of my volunteers to go across the city to get her a cake from Dufflet. It took her two hours because she took transit. She's a student and couldn't afford a taxi. When she returned, Veronikkah told the girl she was too late and threw the cake in the garbage."

I hadn't been in Toronto long, but long enough to know Dufflet Bakery made the city's most exquisite cakes. The Caramel Dacquoise was particularly amazing, with alternating layers of meringue, whipped cream, and caramel sauce. How could anyone throw out a Dufflet cake? I went into a state of semi-consciousness just thinking of the Dacquoise, but Gregor snapped me out of my dessert dream.

"Yeah, Veronikkah's been unbearable today. She asked some of my volunteers to clean up dog poo," he sneered. "Everyone hates her."

"I knew that dog show was an awful idea," I said.

Chantelle looked at me and asked, "Do we have to do this stuff, Gigi? Are we supposed to do things like run personal errands for Veronikkah? I'll do them because I volunteered, but most of the volunteers signed up to work a fashion show, not to run personal errands for Veronikkah."

"It's not only Veronikkah," said Lola, "but it's Francie and Eva, too. They keep sending volunteers out to get wine and cigarettes for them and the makeup people. Then they sit around drinking and talking. That's why shows are late."

"Why are we helping these people?" asked Gregor. "We've all been used and abused. There's nothing we can do."

Chantelle and Lola nodded their heads in agreement, so I said there was something we could do. I explained everything: the drug dealing, embezzlement, and Veronikkah's past. With wide eyes and a dose of disappointment and disillusionment, we agreed something needed to be done and that we were the ones to do it.

Commence.

Everyone returned to their sections and reported our strategy to their volunteers. I was worried because I didn't know if they would act with us or not, but it could only work with a unified group. Veronikkah's illegal activities were still a secret to most volunteers, so I didn't know if they would believe us.

I ran into the runway room and talked to my volunteers. They stood around me, amazed when I presented the gift bag contents they were supposed to distribute.

"I can't believe it," said one shocked girl.

"What do we do?" asked another.

I explained the plan, worried they'd be too scared to follow through with us. They looked at me nervously, but one girl smiled and said, "It's about time we showed Veronikkah Hendricks she can't treat us like dirt."

"Yeah," agreed another girl. "She made me scrape gum off her shoe yesterday and called me a worthless slut."

Soon, all the volunteers were sharing stories about Veronikkah's wickedness and how they wanted retribution. To be successful, we had to appear as though everything was normal, so we headed toward the Collection Week office to transport the illegal gifts to the runway room.

As we set off, Chantelle walkied and said, <<Everything's ready backstage. All the volunteers are going to make this happen.>>

Lola joined in, saying, <<I didn't have to convince anybody; they all knew something illegal was happening. We're ready backstage.>>

<<Us too,>> said Gregor. <<They hate the witch and want to bring her down. This is our Waterloo. Wa-wa-wa-wa-Waterloo!>> He broke into song.

<<I was defeated, you won the war,>> I sang back, surpising Gregor with my ABBA knowledge.

<<Knowing my fate is to be with you!>> Gregor finished.

<<See? We are a great team!>> I exclaimed. <<A group that sings together stings together. Now, just to let you know, runway room volunteers are heading up to get the gift bags now and I'm going with them. Niles and Vivian, did you get that?>>

<<Got it,>> said Niles.

<<I'm with you,>> said Vivian. <<Let's do this.>>

I felt like a general heading toward the Collections Week office with my team of soldiers. Before I knocked, I reminded them to act normally. Veronikkah answered and looked at us blankly. She forgot why we were there.

"We're here to pick up the VIP gift bags, Ms. Hendricks," I said.

Her face softened as she said, "Please, you can call me Veronikkah, Lulu my dear. But you…" she pointed at the other volunteers and said, "You must all call me Ms. Hendricks. I like that...Ms. Hendricks."

As I shuffled all the volunteers in to collect the bags and leave as quickly as possible, I looked at the coffee table and noticed a little pile of white powder, a razor blade, and a little gold tube. Apparently the higher they got, the sloppier they became. I figured it would be easy to thwart her plan, but remembered I could not underestimate the enemy.

We got in and out of the office in five minutes, none of the volunteers making eye contact with the Bolivian Reservoir Dogs. Good thing that was normal behaviour around those scary men. They were frightening, so nobody wanted to acknowledge their existence.

As we carried out the last bags, Veronikkah called after us, "Be careful, now, all you little people. We don't want any accidents with our precious gifts, do we? They're for our VIPs, you know. Francie will meet you down there to make sure they go to the right people. This is very important. Don't let me down, little ones."

She was the most insensitive person I'd ever met. I fumed as I led my brigade down the hallway on our way back to the runway room. I turned a corner and crashed into Hot Dan. We hit each other head-on, producing gift bag casualties. Cosmetics and velvet boxes littered the floor. It was a terrible time to run into him.

"Let me help clean this up," he said, looking ultra-hot with his makeup and rock-star hair. Then he leaned in close and whispered, "I need to talk to you."

He made my stomach jump. I couldn't talk to the hottest guy on earth and try to nonchalantly bring down a huge drug deal at the same time.

"Now's not the best time," I said, gesturing to the volunteers.

He stared at me and whispered, "Tell them to go ahead." It was an order.

Looking at the volunteers, I said, "It's okay, guys. Take all the bags to Vivian in the runway room. She's waiting for them and you know what to do after that. We'll look after this mess."

I watched them run toward the runway room, when Hot Dan said, "This looks pretty fancy. What's in here? I'll bet nobody will mind if I peek."

I looked back, in time to see him peeling back a sparkly white bow from one of the velvet boxes.

"No! Don't do that!" I practically screamed as I dove into him.

My combat move backfired, as the box flew open and sent the cocaine bag flying across the hall.

"Catch it!" I ordered.

It was his turn to dive, catching it before a coke explosion happened in the hallway. He looked at the bag, at me, and then asked, "What's going on?"

"Let's just get this cleaned up before anyone passes us."

"I'll only help if you tell me."

I was stuck. The situation made me look like a drug dealer and I didn't know what would happen, so as we restuffed the bags, I quickly told Hot Dan the story about how the volunteers were being used to facilitate a huge coke deal. As I told him, I panicked, afraid someone would hear or that somehow he was involved with everything.

"So what are you doing about this? You aren't going to distribute this, are you? You could get caught for trafficking," he said.

"No, no. We're bringing the bags downstairs so we can keep them as evidence. We have a plan with the producers, Vivian and Niles, so we're taking everything to them."

"You aren't involved with this, then?"

"No way! What kind of person do you think I am?"

He smiled, winked, and said, "A good person, but I also thought you could be very, very bad."

Why did he do that to me? I was in a potentially life- and career-threatening predicament, and he was making sexual innuendos?

"Listen, bub," I'd never said "bub" before, but it was a fun word to use and made me feel tough like Wolverine, "I don't have time for you while this is happening. I'm freaking out and I can't deal with your little games. And hey, while I'm sharing a story, why don't you tell me one of yours? Why do you always lurk around? You show up at strange times, usually relating to Veronikkah and her drugs. What's up? Are you working with her? Oh no! You are, aren't you? The first hot guy I like in two years turns out to be a drug dealer! You're going to take me to her, aren't you? You're going to tell her everything, and then the Bolivians will drown me in Lake Ontario. Oh, my life's over..." I was slightly hysterical; the pressure and gravity of the situation had finally got me.

He looked at me, smiled, and asked, "You think I'm hot?"

"What?" That actually came out of my mouth? How embarrassing. I wasn't supposed to tell him how hot he was. I had to recover, but there was no way, so I had to leave. "I don't know...Not anymore...You're a drug dealer, anyway! That's not hot! Get out of my way!" I pushed past him and ran toward the runway room. I had to get to Vivian and Niles.

PREPARE.

Huffing and puffing, I arrived at Vivian's production booth and threw down the gift bags.

"Is everything in place?" I asked.

"Shhh…" she said, motioning over to Francie and Josh L.

I'd forgotten about him. "What about Josh L.? Does he know about all this? Is he involved?"

Vivian shook her head. "No. We've been friends forever, longer than he's known Veronikkah. He thought something was up, but didn't know what it was. Now he knows the plan and will help. Everyone is on our side except Francie, Eva, and that useless event planner, Patsy. It's best not to tell them because they're loyal and stupid, especially Francie. Even though Veronikkah wants to pin the whole thing on her, she'll still tell because she'll do anything to maintain her posistion. She's too young for such a job; she's not bad, just dumb."

It was always rewarding to hear someone else support my suspicions.

"Great!" I said. "What about the Board?"

"Since I'm a Board member, I held a quick meeting while you were gone. We were trying to overthrow her anyway, since she's stealing money from us. What kind of person steals money from a non-profit organization? Unfortunately, we didn't have any proof because she lost all the financial documents. Personally, I don't think she kept the financials on purpose."

I smiled at my cleverness for knowing those receipts would be useful.

"Not to worry," I said, patting my clipboard. "Guess who has copies of them?"

"You? How? You're amazing, Gigi!"

"Long story. I'll have to tell you later," I was anxious to finish with all Veronikkah's crap once and for all. "Wait a second...So we've got most people on board. What about the media? Did you arrange for coverage?"

Vivian winked at me. "Not to worry. Everyone hates her. Journalists only wrote positive things about her in the past for the good of Canadian fashion."

"Wow." I marvelled at how we pulled together a fashion army comprised of Veronikkah's previous supporters, based on a simple strategy: if you treat people well, they'll follow, but if you treat them poorly, you're the enemy. Our odds for success were good enough to proceed with the plan.

"So we're ready to go?" I asked.

She nodded. "Ready as we'll ever be."

I couldn't believe it. There I was, just a girl from Calgary without any fashion experience, poised to topple one of Canada's top fashion personalities. I had never been more frightened, especially when Francie approached me.

"What are you doing standing around?"

"I'm not standing around; I'm organizing the VIP gift bags." I tried not to look nervous.

Francie looked back and forth between Vivian and me. "What are we waiting for? Aren't we ready to start the show? Where are the guests?"

I detected a twist of disgust on Vivian's face as she walkied Niles on backstage status. She winked at me, then said to Francie, "Backstage is ready to go. Are you ready?"

"YES! How many times do I have to tell you? Now where are the volunteers?"

I called everyone over to Francie, and they positioned themselves behind her, ready to greet guests and deliver the illicit gift bags.

While Francie ordered the volunteers around, Veronikkah appeared on the runway and the Bolivian Reservoir Dogs gathered around her feet. "VIVIAN!" she hollered. "Get me a microphone! This is an important night! I need to address the crowd before the show starts!"

Vivian rolled her eyes and whispered, "We never discussed a speech." She found a microphone and ran it to Veronikkah.

Veronikkah grabbed the mic and screeched, "TEST, TEST!"

The microphone reacted to her harshness with violent feedback. Everyone in the runway room stopped, screamed, and covered their ears.

Veronikkah kept screaming into the mic, "VIVIAN! WHAT ARE YOU DOING TO ME? YOU'RE GOING TO RUIN ME! FIX THIS MICROPHONE NOW!"

The microphone feedback kept reverberating as if we were in an electronic grand canyon. We were all paralyzed.

Suddenly, Vivian's calm voice floated over the music. "Veronikkah, please move the microphone away from your mouth a bit and speak more softly."

"I'LL DO WHAT I WANT!" she yelled, accompanied by more horrible, screeching feedback, "AND I WANT YOU TO FIX THIS FUCKING MICROPHONE! FIX IT NOW!"

"All you have to do is speak softly," said Vivian.

"OH, FUCK THIS!" yelled Veronikkah. She threw the microphone at Vivian's booth, missing it by a lot - fashion people are not known for their pitching skills - and she yelled, "FIX THE MICROPHONE, BITCH!" Veronikkah looked around and saw us all gaping at her huge meltdown. "WHAT ARE ALL YOU LITTLE RETARDS STARING AT? MY MICROPHONE DOESN'T WORK! DON'T YOU KNOW WHO I AM? I'M VERONIKKAH HENDRICKS, QUEEN OF COLLECTIONS WEEK. EVERYTHING IS SUPPOSED TO WORK FOR ME. THIS EVENT IS ALL ABOUT ME. IF SOMETHING DOESN'T WORK, IT'S YOUR FAULT, YOU LITTLE SHITS! CHRIST, I CAN'T WORK LIKE THIS…" She walked down the runway to backstage, twisting and turning, looking behind her shoulders. Her imaginary demons were back, obviously plaguing her.

We all stood around, wondering how to react, eventually turning to Francie for some indication. She was just as dumbfounded as the rest of us, no help at all, embarrassed and afraid. I noticed the fear in her face when she chased after her boss.

<<Guys, it’s Lola. Veronikkah’s backstage, and she’s snorting coke out of a little vial thing she took off her charm bracelet. She’s doing it in front of everyone. What should we do?”

<<Just keep going as planned,>> I directed. <<It’s actually good she’s doing that because now we have evidence against her.>>

<<But she looks crazed. She might hurt someone.>>

I thought for a second and said, <<Try to distract her for a bit. Flatter her; that always works. Francie will probably be there in a second.>>

<<Oh, here she comes,>> said Lola.

<<Great. Keep us posted.>>

I scanned the runway room, where all eyes looked to me for guidance.

"Everything will be okay," I said. "Francie’s looking after her and the backstage crew will let us know when to proceed."

<<Gigi,>> whispered Lola over her walkie-talkie.

<<Yes?>>

<<Veronikkah’s going crazy! She’s trying on clothes off the racks, but ripping seams because she’s too big. Francie can’t stop her.>>

<<Tell her she’s brilliant! Do anything to calm her down!>>

<<I can’t do it, Gigi. We’re all scared. She’s on a rampage, throwing things all over the place.>>

<<Okay, I’m on my way.>>

I yelled to everyone in the runway room that I’d return quickly. On my way backstage, I tried to figure out what I’d say to calm the peaking crazy woman.

Backstage was manic: Veronikkah stood in her underwear in the centre of everything, making a mess by trying on clothes then tossing them everywhere; Francie was beside her, desperately pleading with her to get dressed; Bolivian designers tried to guard their clothes from the madwoman; volunteers picked up garments Veronikkah threw; Lola, Niles, and the models stood back stunned; and the Bolivian Reservoir Dogs kept to the side like threatening statues.

Not knowing exactly what to do, I had to make Veronikkah feel like a star, so I ran into the middle of things and announced, "Ladies and gentlemen! Look at our star of the night. Isn't Ms. Hendricks gorgeous?"

Veronikkah turned around, looked at me, smiled, then dug into her coke vial for a sniff.

"Veronikkah, Francie has the perfect outfit for you to wear, don't you Francie?" I motioned to Francie to get Veronikkah's clothes back on her. As Francie shuffled the garments back on to Veronikkah, I kept trying to make Veronikkah feel important by calling over hair and makeup people to give her touch-ups. Soon enough, Veronikkah felt like a princess and was distracted enough for Niles and Lola to recover all the clothes and get backstage operational again.

"Is everything cool?" I whispered to Francie.

"Oh yes, Veronikkah's great. I think we're ready to go," she whispered back.

"Wonderful. I think everyone's ready then. Why don't we get to the runway room so you can deal with your VIP bags?"

Francie nodded and we left Niles and Lola with Veronikkah and the rest of the backstage craziness. Veronikkah seemed fine, so Niles and Lola took control.

As Francie and I walked back to the runway room, she began shaking and crying. "I can't take this anymore!" she wailed. "Veronikkah is a crazy woman! She makes me feel like shit, and I never know how to handle it. How can you deal with her? You're so calm. How can someone treat others so horribly? What a wench."

I was stunned; all I could say was, "I thought you liked her."

"Like her? How can anyone like her? She's evil. She's high all the time and I have to cover for her. She never tells me what's going on and then yells at me for not knowing. Are all fashion people like this? If they are,

I don't want to be in this business. It's terrible." She cried harder and buried her face in my shoulder.

It was quite a change in Francie, and I felt sorry for her. Though I was shocked she'd confided in me, I didn't know what to do, so I awkwardly patted her on the head and said, "Everything will be okay, we just have to get through tonight and tomorrow. Tomorrow night is the closing gala, isn't it?"

"Get through tonight? Get through tomorrow?" she wailed. "How can I even get through this night? My boyfriend was missing, but then I caught him in a back hallway with my boss! Not only that, but the Bolivian dudes scare the shit out of me. I don't know who they are or what they're doing here. How am I going to get through this night? I can't make it to tomorrow." She leaned back against the wall and slid down, ending on the floor in the fetal position. "I thought this was going to be such a cool job," she wailed. "Instead of getting into the glamorous world of fashion, I ended up in this torturous Hell. That woman is so evil; she makes me do the most horrible things. Do you know that I have to flush the toilet when she's finished in the bathroom?"

I looked at her incredulously.

"Do you know I had to wish her mom a happy birthday on her behalf because she was too high to talk?"

I shook my head.

"How can anyone be so mean?" she asked.

"To be honest, I've been thinking that same thing since I started working with you guys," I said.

Francie looked into my eyes and I saw her make a startling realization. "Oh my god. I'm turning into her. I've been horrible to you, haven't I?"

I nodded and started to make up some excuse for her, saying, "It's okay, Francie...I'd do the same thing if I had to deal with her all the time."

She cut me off and said, "No, Gigi, you wouldn't. You've been amazing this whole week, and we've been awful, haven't we? I stopped being a normal person and got caught up in what I thought was high fashion. But it's just Veronikkah's world, isn't it?"

I nodded again.

"How could I have been so stupid? How could I treat people like that?"

"It's easy to get caught in other people's fantasies, isn't it?" I extended my hand out to Francie's and pulled her up.

We hugged for a while and she repeated, "I'm so sorry, I'm so sorry."

"Everything will be okay, but we've got to get this show going," I said, remembering the opportunity to take down Veronikkah Hendricks. "You need to get those VIP bags to your guests."

"I don't even know what the big deal is about those bags. Veronikkah says they have some special powder sample in them, but they're going out to most of Darryl's friends. They're not VIPs; they're mostly club owners and weird guys. I thought the media and celebrities would get them, but Veronikkah's very particular about this list and she's been super weird about it."

So Francie had no clue about the drug deal and really was too stupid to understand the powder reference. I thought she knew everything that was happening, but in reality, she was simply a young, naïve girl who learned how to behave on her first job from an evil, conniving boss-zilla. Though we'd shared a bonding moment, I thought it best not to tell her we were about to ruin Veronikkah's big plan. Francie may have hated Veronikkah at that moment, but I figured her loyalty would still lie with her boss.

We returned to the runway room and directed everyone to prepare for guests. <<Niles, Lola,>> I walkied. <<How's it looking?>>

<<We're all ready, but Veronikkah's asking for you. We've been trying to distract her, but it's not working. She wants you here.>>

<<Why?>> I asked.

<<All she'll say is she wants you for a special surprise, and she won't start the show without you.>>

A surprise? In Veronikkah's world, a surprise meant many things, none good. Why did she need me? <<I'll discuss things with Vivian,>> I said.

Vivian and I agreed it would be best to appease Veronikkah, so I delivered orders on the walkie-talkie. <<Niles, Lola… tell Veronikkah I'll be there in a minute. Everyone else, go ahead as discussed. You'll know the cue when you see it. Gregor and Chantelle, are you ready?>>

Gregor answered affirmatively and Chantelle said, <<Gigi, you won't believe this: Darryl's been out here with me all night, and he actually has a guest list. He's been very strict with it, calling it the VIP list and mentioning the gift bags. Gigi, I think he's in on it. What should I do?>>

<<Good going, Chantelle. You're right; he and Veronikkah are having an affair too. Just make sure you keep an eye on him. Can you do that?>>

<<Sure thing.>>

<<And communicate everything to Vivian. Vivian did you get all that?>>

<<I did, Gigi, now get to Veronikkah and make her happy. We'll take care of everything out front.>>

<<All right. Good luck, everyone! Let's go!>>

It was time to tackle Veronikkah Hendricks. Music blared in the runway room while a light show began. The place felt like a mega-club, but one filled with apprehension and excitement. Volunteers roamed the runway room skittishly when Chantelle opened the main doors and guests poured in. Francie, Josh L., and the volunteers seated guests frantically, but distributed the illicit gift bags carefully.

Everything was smooth in the runway room, so I turned on my walkie-talkie and announced, <<Okay, everyone, I'm going backstage.>>

<<We've got your back, baby,>> said Niles. <<Come on over.>>

Backstage, Lola babysat Veronikkah, sitting with her and stroking her hand, while Niles organized the show. Veronikkah saw me and screamed, "Lulu! I love you! I want you to come on stage with me tonight to introduce the show!"

"What?" I asked. In the other breath I caught Niles and whispered, "She can't go in front of people like this; she's a mess."

"Think about it, Gigi," whispered Niles. "It's perfect for her to go into the public like this. That way everyone will see how awful she is, and she'll definitely lose her job. Right now, the Board is in charge of her employment. But if she embarrasses them in public, they'll have the perfect excuse to fire her. So many of us have wanted to get rid of her for years. She's only doing Collections Week for personal glory, not for the love of Canadian fashion. This is going to be a great night because it'll be a new start."

Veronikkah reached over, grabbed my arm, and pulled me into her lap. "Lulu, I want to take a volunteer out with me on the runway, to show how much we love our little helpers, and you're my favourite volunteer. Everyone will love that! Everyone will love me! You love me, don't you?" she asked, and tried to kiss me.

I wriggled away from her collagen-enhanced, flaky red-lipsticked lips and thought hard. She wanted me to go on the runway with her before the fashion show? That was a great opportunity for the volunteers to make their move. Niles was right; it would be perfect.

"What do you want me to do?" I asked.

Veronikkah smiled as she wobbled around in her chair. "Sweetie, I want you to walk out with me and I'll say something nice about volunteers. Then I'll pass the mic to you and you can say something nice about me! How does that sound?"

It was a perfect way to kick-start our planned act of civil disobedience and Veronikkah would finally recognize our importance. I told her I had to fix my makeup and ran around the corner to communicate the news to my team. <<Hey guys, it's Gigi. I have great news. I'm going on the runway with Veronikkah. It will be the perfect time to strike. Can you prepare your volunteers?>>

<<Of course,>> said Chantelle.

Gregor said, <<We're all ready.>>

<<We're with you,>> encouraged Lola.

<<All right. Let's get this going!>> The plan would work better than I imagined. <<Chantelle, how are the guests coming along?>>

<<Everything's smooth. I'd say everyone will be seated in five minutes.>>

<<Five minutes is ideal,>> said Vivian. <<I'm ready.>>

Five minutes later I was beside Veronikkah, ready to make my mark on the Canadian fashion scene. I hoped everything would work as planned.

STRIKE.

The lights dimmed and that annoying "Collections Week, C'est Chic!" music exploded from the loudspeaker. Vivian announced, "Ladies and gentlemen, welcome to the Collections Week Special Bolivian Designer Showcase! Please welcome Collections Week director, Veronikkah Hendricks!"

Veronikkah was finally dressed and ready for the stage. She wore a camouflage-print ball gown embellished with sequins and safety pins, with layers of black tulle fencing her in to her outfit. She grabbed my hand. Taking a deep breath, I looked around. Niles and Lola were supportive, the volunteers looked excited and nervous, all the models practiced their walks and poses, and there was Hot Dan. He was trying on different shoes to match his camouflage flight suit; with it unbuttoned down to his navel, he looked hotter than ever. I had to check my mouth to see if I drooled, and at that exact moment, he looked over at me. Those eyes killed me, and he winked. I didn't care if he was a drug dealer; Hot Dan made me melt, and I was happy he was there to distract me from my impending Collections Week attack.

Veronikkah tugged me down the white runway because all the lights were momentarily blinding; I couldn't see where I walked, except for a long, shiny sheet of white. When my eyes adjusted, I saw a packed house. Rows of people sat shoulder to shoulder, and I was above them. It felt powerful to walk the runway, even if I was wearing a lame "Collections Week, C'est Chic!" volunteer shirt. It would have been nicer to strut down the runway in a fabulous designer outfit, but it was neat nonetheless. Looking in the front row, I didn't see any recognizable press; they were all in the second row, which was unusual. The front row must have been Veronikkah's VIPs. We walked toward the photographers at the end of the runway, and I noticed a wall of volunteers behind them, near Vivian's booth, ready to strike. Chantelle and Gregor waved, I waved back, then all the volunteers returned my wave. It was so sweet and I felt a moment of happiness and pride, mixed with a bit of fear for what I would do next. We stopped at the end of the runway and adopted a series of cheesy poses.

Veronikkah froze in what she thought was her best supermodel move, turned on the mic and screamed, "ARE YOU HAVING FUN?" Luckily there was no feedback this time, and the front rows screamed wildly. Everyone behind them remained silent. The fashion community was pissed at Veronikkah Hendricks.

"Guys and gals," continued Veronikkah, "thanks for coming tonight. We have the best-kept secret in world fashion on display. Bolivia's top designers are here to show us what's hot and sexy for next season. I'm sure you'll love them, and you'll see Bolivia making international headlines soon." There was a bit of clapping from the front row, but Veronikkah kept talking. "Before we treat you to those wonderful designs, though, I want to take a moment to introduce you to someone very special. This is Lulu, our head volunteer."

Lulu? Why was it so difficult for her to get my name right? And head volunteer? It made me sound so childish. Oh well. Part of me didn't want her to remember my name anymore because after tonight, she would never want to see me again.

"Lulu and her group of little people have been working very hard to make sure Collections Week runs smoothly. Let's give them a round of applause for their hard work." There was some clapping, and I was touched she actually acknowledged us, but that didn't excuse her previous actions.

Veronikkah glowed from the attention, begging for more applause. She stood at the front of the runway, smiling, obviously proud of Collections Week. She was hypnotized by the applause and adoration, so I pounced.

Hugging Veronikkah as though she were my best friend, I snatched the microphone out of her hand. She had a moment to register my action, but it was too late; I was talking before she had a chance to retrieve the mic from the lowly volunteer.

"Let's hear it for Veronikkah!" I yelled into the mic to lukewarm crowd response. Well, her front-row cohorts cheered, but most guests were silent. She'd scammed them all one way or other, so they would be thrilled to hear what was coming.

Veronikkah didn't know how to react, so she stood still, smiling a confused, crooked smile that revealed her love for attention.

"On behalf of all the volunteers, I want to thank Ms. Hendricks for directing this fabulous event. And you know, Collections Week wouldn't be anything without its special guests. Tonight, we have many VIPs with us, and I'd like to thank every one of them for making our experience wonderful. Ladies and gentlemen, please recognize our VIPs!"

The audience was confused, but Veronikkah beamed, then clapped and jumped around. It was great PR for her clients.

"That's not enough appreciation for these special people," I practically screamed into the mic. "All VIPs, stand up and take a bow! This night is all about you!"

Veronikkah kept cheering, oblivious to what would happen next, so I kept talking.

"Ladies and gentlemen, I'd like you to recognize Veronikkah's generosity. She's so kind, she gave very special gift bags to all her VIPs. VIPs, show us those gifts!"

A few of them waved the bags around, while others froze. They sensed something was up. The hall fell silent, except for Veronikkah cheering herself. She still thought everything was in her favour, so I preyed on her vanity and made my move.

"I want you all to know the volunteers have a few special gifts of our own. First, we all quit!" There was a cheer from the volunteers standing in back of the hall and some sounds of shock from everyone else. Veronikkah froze in confusion. "We've been abused by Collections Week staff and guests, and we're not going to take it anymore! See if you can run an event without volunteers. Good luck with the rest of the shows!" Gandhi would have been proud of our civil disobedience.

"We can't! You can't quit!" pleaded Veronikkah. "Whatever we did, we'll fix it. I'll have you know I do volunteer work! I know what it's like to be a thankless volunteer. When I'm walking down the street, I tell people when they wear bad outfits. It's my civic duty; I do good!"

I rolled my eyes at her. "It's too late. We gave you warnings. It's over. You can't treat people so badly. Oh, and by the way, we have a second gift for you and your VIPs," I said, hoping Vivian had completed her portion of our operation. "Boys, will you bring out the surprise?"

Members of the Toronto Police Department appeared from behind the crowd, surrounding Veronikkah's VIPs. Some tried to run, while others tried to hide their gift bags. One bag flew on to the runway and landed at my feet, so I picked it up, ready to show everyone why police had invaded Collections Week.

The whole time, Veronikkah stood in open-mouthed astonishment. When she saw me fishing for evidence, she jostled herself out of her confusion and yelled, "What are you doing, you little bitch? You'll ruin everything!"

She lunged at me as I opened the cocaine-filled box. She knocked my hand, sending white powder everywhere, and with the momentum she gained, she flew past me and rolled off the runway onto the floor. Flashes exploded everywhere; the photographers snapped juicy photos of the Collections Week director flailing in fury.

The crowd still didn't know what had happened, so I offered a quick explanation. "Ladies and gentlemen. What you saw was evidence that Collections Week is not the celebration of Canadian fashion Veronikkah Hendricks claims it to be. Instead, Collections Week is a front for her execution of Canada's biggest cocaine deal."

A collective gasp rose from the crowd, along with chattering, more flashbulbs, and Veronikkah's protests.

"Little liar!" she shouted. "You're making up that shit! I'm as shocked as you are about that powder. I'll bet you put it in the bags you witch! No, wait! It was Francie who did it! Yes! Yes! It was Francie!" She was so angry she was disoriented, spinning in every direction.

Not many people could hear her amid the general confusion in the venue, so I kept explaining into the mic.

"Bolivian designer showcase?" I laughed. "Tonight has nothing to do with fashion. Veronikkah has Bolivian partners who want to increase their coke distribution. Tonight's VIPs are not journalists, buyers, sponsors, or involved with fashion in any way. They're drug dealers! Not only that, but Veronikkah stole money from the Collections Week organization to go on vacations and buy couture gowns. I have receipts as proof."

At this news, the journalists in the crowd surged forward to get the story, while several people in the back rows tried to leave, but were stopped by police.

"I'm sorry, but nobody can leave yet," I announced. "The police are now in charge and will question everyone, starting with Veronikkah." I looked down to where she'd fallen off the runway, but she was gone. "Where is Veronikkah Hendricks? She escaped!"

Everyone looked around, but nobody knew where she went.

"Everybody stay here while the police conduct their investigation. And if you see Veronikkah, turn her into the authorities."

When I finished talking, the police had people lined up in different groups, handcuffing VIPs and anyone found with drugs. They corralled everyone into the main hall, even the models and designers from backstage. An officer got up on the runway and I gave him the mic so he could organize the chaos and provide direction to his colleagues and the crowd.

I hopped off the runway and ran to the volunteers, but Eva intercepted me.

"Wow!" she exclaimed. "I knew it all the time. Veronikkah and Francie are such stupid twits. All along I knew that you were the smartest person around."

"I thought they were your friends. How can you say that about your friends?" I asked.

Eva snorted. "Friends? There are no friends in this business. You and I would make a good team. We can take over Collections Week now Veronikkah and Francie are out of the way."

I gasped. "Is that the kind of person you think I am? You've got the wrong idea, baby. Please excuse me while I talk with my friends." I walked away from her and over to the volunteers.

"We did it!" yelled Vivian and Niles, giving me a huge hug. Everyone cheered and some volunteers sang, "Ding Dong the Witch is Dead!"

"Hold up," I said. "Veronikkah is still missing, as are the Bolivians, so we aren't clear yet."

"Don't the police have her?" asked Vivian.

"I don't think so. We can't let her get away. Do you have any idea where she might be?"

"How about her office?" asked Lola.

"Good thought," I answered. "Let's go check.

We left the other volunteers and ran to the door leading out of the hall, but were blocked by two burly police officers.

"Where are you going girls?" asked the taller one, who was probably moonlighting from a pro wrestling gig; he was a giant. "We can't let anyone out of the hall until everyone has been questioned."

"We think we know where Veronikkah might be," I said. "We've got to find her; she can't get away."

The wrestler-officer's sidekick towered over us and said, "You can't go by yourselves. Rico here will escort you."

Rico? Wrestler-officer's name was Rico? It suited him perfectly: he resembled the 80s one-hit wonder rapper, Rico Suave, only he was twice as big. Lola and I grabbed wrestler-officer Rico, shouted, "Let's go!" and ran out the door.

As we ran down the hall, I realized I didn't have my clipboard - the clipboard with Veronikkah's incriminating e-mails and receipts. Where was it? I mentally flipped through my day, remembering I'd set the clipboard down backstage moments before Veronikkah had pulled me on the runway.

"I have to go backstage," I said, stopping, turning in the opposite direction.

"You have to stay with us!" bellowed wrestler-officer Rico.

"I'll just be a second...I need my clipboard; it's got important papers about Veronikkah. I'll meet you back at the door we came from." I ran away from them before the policeman could argue with me.

Turning into the backstage area, I spotted my clipboard on a shoebox beside the curtains. As I ducked behind the curtain to pick it up, I heard voices on the other side.

"You little snoop!" screeched a woman. "How did you get my laptop? The bust was your fault!" It was Veronikkah. "You ruined me! I was about to escape this country. You think I liked working here? No! I deserve to sit on a beach drinking margaritas for the rest of my life. Now you've destroyed my plan!"

"Don't you think it was time someone found you out anyway?" asked a male voice.

"Don't be smart with me, you little worm. How did you get my laptop? Who do you work for?"

"I work for myself, and if you think I'm telling you more, you're wrong."

"I have ways of making you talk," sneered Veronikkah in a James Bond villain voice.

"Try me," spat back the man, but who was he? Did I dare peek out and risk getting caught?

Holding my breath, I peeked around the curtain and saw Veronikkah surrounded by her Bolivian Reservoir Dogs.

"Hold him, boys," ordered Veronikkah to her minions, as she pulled out a lipstick tube.

The Bolivians scuffled around, and I finally saw who Veronikkah had threatened: Hot Dan. He held a laptop.

He looked at the lipstick and laughed. "What are you going to do? Give me a makeover? Ohhhh...I'm scared."

"Bah ha ha," cackled crazy Veronikkah. "I'm going to do much worse to you, little boy." She lifted the lipstick, made some clicking motions, and revealed a knife. The woman had a lipstick switchblade! It would have been a cool little gadget if she hadn't intended to carve up Hot Dan's gorgeous face with it.

Hot Dan - what a man - didn't even flinch when she moved close to him and sneered, "Little boy, you'll never model again once I'm finished with your pretty face." And in true villain fashion, she said, "I'll give you one last chance to tell me who ratted."

Hot Dan struggled against the Bolivians, but gave up and stared at Veronikkah. How she didn't melt from those eyes, I'll never know, but in a flash, she swiped the lipstick switchblade across his handsome face.

"Noooo!" I yelled, cursing the Gods for allowing damage to such a beautiful face.

The next few seconds blurred in my memory. I remember thinking I needed to save Hot Dan from becoming a Jack-o'-lantern, so I looked around for something to throw at Veronikkah. I found a pair of stilettos in the shoebox beneath my clipboard, so I grabbed them and threw the shoes as hard as I could in Veronikkah's direction.

My timing was perfect, or incredibly horrible, depending on one's perspective.

I yelled, hurling the shoes into the air as hard as possible. Everyone in the little group turned to see who had yelled when WHAP!

Veronikkah got a stiletto right in the eye.

"Fuck! My eye!" she screamed, spurting blood and falling to the floor.

SCHTUNK! The other stiletto miraculously landed on a Bolivian's nose. He sunk to his knees, onto his stomach, and when his head went down, the heel lodged further into his head.

"Ohmigod! Ewww!" I screamed. "Ahhh! I killed him!" Gandhi would not have been proud that I'd let a peaceful act of defiance advance to the stage of death, and I couldn't believe I might be a murderer.

The other Bolivians glared at me and pulled out pistols, bent on revenge, forgetting about Hot Dan.

"AAAAAAHHHHHHH!" I screamed, ducking behind the curtain, hoping it was magically bulletproof. After running around the Carlu the previous three days, I knew there was nowhere to hide. "Sorry, sorry! I didn't mean to hurt anyone!" I really was sorry, but I didn't think they believed me.

Frantically, I searched for potential weapons, wishing for the same good luck I'd had seconds before. I dumped out some gift bags, found a few makeup and perfume samples, and jumped out from the curtain, striking a stupid fashion-ninja pose.

Hot Dan beat one Bolivian's face into a bloody pulp, Veronikkah writhed on the floor, and the remaining Bolivians ran at me.

"Dan, help me!" I called. "Get their guns!"

This confused the Bolivians; they didn't know where to look, so I flung the cosmetic samples at them, ninja-throwing star-style. TZING! TZING!

"Take that!" I yelled, hitting the first guy in the neck, knocking the wind out of him. I couldn't believe my aim, so I threw all the makeshift weapons I had, trying to get the gun out of his hand.

Hot Dan shoved the last Bolivian from behind, sending him to the ground and his gun flying. I ran to the fallen thug and dumped perfume in his eye, hoping to temporarily blind him.

"*Puta madre*!" he screamed in agony. I figured the perfume had worked, so I poured it on the other guy's eyes to keep them incapacitated. The act received a rousing "Puta madre" chorus.

Hot Dan and I were the only ones left standing, both in shock.

"Holy shit! You rock!" he pulled me to him. "You are seriously the coolest girl I ever met," he said, staring into my eyes and touching my cheek. I wanted to stare right back, but his poor, slashed face was gross and bleeding. I pulled back, ripped off my dumb T-shirt, used it to dab the blood, and tried to determine whether the butterflies in my tummy were from first aid queasiness or love.

Would he ever kiss me again? It was his chance to make a move and my chance to determine his gay-straightness once and for all.

In the corner of my eye, I saw movement from Veronikkah's direction. I turned my head and saw her crawling across the floor, trying to escape. That woman was really out to ruin my life. Why did she have to interrupt my kiss with Hot Dan? I pulled away from him, jumped over a few Bolivians, and shoved Veronikkah with my Fluevog boot so she ended up on her back.

Resting my foot on her stomach so she couldn't move, I asked, "Where do you think you're going?"

She looked at me pitifully with one eye, fumbling with the stiletto in the other eye and said, "Lulu, please let me go. I've been nothing but nice to you. I even offered you a job."

"Nice?" I asked. "You call yelling at volunteers nice? You call unreasonable demands nice? What about covering for your drugged-out stupors? To top it off, you can't even remember my name! I don't call that nice!" I shocked myself with my anger; I had never been truly enraged in my life until that point. All my repressed emotions emerged that night.

"Listen, Lulu. If you let me go, I'll give you some of the cut. Sixty for me, forty for you."

I didn't budge. For once in my life I discarded the compassionate, caring Gigi. Evil Gigi wanted to hear her grovel.

"I'll make you my Collections Week co-partner," she bargained.

"What are you talking about?" I asked. "Everything's over. You blew it. You lost everyone because you only thought about yourself and crammed the event with stupid ideas. To top it off, you were untrustworthy and cowardly; you backstabbed your faithful - albeit slightly stupid - assistant and tried to blame a giant drug deal on your volunteers...nice people who work for you for free! You think that's nice? You haven't been nice since I met you. You're over! This is for treating people poorly," I opened one of the perfume samples and poured it into her eyes. It must have killed her stiletto-infused wound, but I didn't care and I couldn't believe my nerve.

"You little witch!" she cried. "You'll never get away with this!"

"No, I think you're mistaken. You'll never get away with what you've done," I said. "And now I want you to think about how you treated people this week. You might want to improve your behaviour because you don't want to make enemies in jail."

"How did you find all this out anyway? You're just a little, teensy-weensy nothing."

I had to laugh (it was a maniacal laugh at that and I felt as though our roles had reversed. Had I turned into the villain?). "Since that's the way you thought of me, I can thank you for practically telling me your secrets. By pulling me close to you as a reliable - but lowly - volunteer, you revealed everything. You didn't do your homework, Ms. Hendricks. If you checked on who worked for you, you would have known I was smarter than your previous volunteers."

"You bitch!" she hollered.

"It's not bitch; it's Gigi LaFaux, and nobody messes with Gigi. You'll never forget my name again, will you? I'm trying to help you, Veronikkah. Can't you see that? Calling someone a bitch gets you in trouble. If you aren't nice, people desert you. Right now, I'm calling the police and it's the nicest thing I can do for you and for Canadian fashion."

I turned on my walkie-talkie. <<Is anyone there? It's Gigi. I've got Veronikkah backstage, so send the police!>>

<<Got ya, Gigi,>> said Gregor. <<They're on their way.>>

Backstage was filled with police in two seconds, and I saw the carnage from their perspective.

"What have I done?" I asked myself, falling backwards, right into Hot Dan's arms. "I've never hurt anyone in my life, let alone blinded someone! Am I evil now? Will I be another Veronikkah?"

He squeezed me tight and said, "You're not evil. You did what you needed to do. Everything will be all right."

His arms around me made everything better. I looked up into his slashed face (which was still handsome - nothing could ruin it) and those blue eyes sucked me in. Everything faded away. Bliss lasted only a moment until I remembered something Veronikkah mentioned.

"Hey," I said, pulling away from him. "Why did you have Veronikkah's laptop? She wanted to know who you work for, and so do I. Are you a dealer too? Should I knock you out with a clog? You've got to be honest with me."

"Please don't hit him with a shoe; you're deadly. He works for me."

It was Chloe Kirkpatrick, showing her press badge to police.

"What?" I asked, stunned.

Chloe explained, "We knew about the drugs and embezzlement, but had no proof. Board members had told me about the missing laptop with the financials, but when I interviewed Veronikkah, I noticed she still had it in her office. It was our job to get it and rescue Canadian fashion from her."

Hot Dan looked at me and said, "It was my mission to get the evidence. I'm not a model. I'm a journalist. Chloe and I have followed Veronikkah's operation for a year."

"You're kidding me," I laughed. "Well, if that's true, I guess the gash on your cheek won't affect your modelling career."

"Not in the least," he said, trying to smile, but realizing his wound hurt. "Now I guess I'll have a big scar."

"No more pretty boy," I sighed.

"I hope you like guys with scars," he said coyly.

What was his deal? He was ready to kiss me, but would he turn gay ten minutes later? He still confused me.

"Tough boys...mmm...yes, I love the tough ones. Do you?"

"What? Do I like guys?" he asked and laughed. "The modelling and everything that went with it was a façade. I was undercover, you crazy girl!"

Chloe appeared between us. Curses! Were Dan and I ever going to kiss again?

"Christian, you're bleeding," she said, stating the obvious, and making me realize how extra hot and tough he looked with blood trickling down his face. "Are you okay?"

"Just a second!" I exclaimed. "Christian? Did she say Christian?"

He looked at me, full of guilt, and explained, "My name's not Dan; I was undercover for this story. My real name is Christian VanDorn."

I couldn't believe it! Hot Dan was wunderkind journalist Christian VanDorn! His articles had been awarded with every kind of literary prize imaginable, but for journalistic integrity he made a point of never being photographed. I loved his writing, but never dreamed he was that...well, dreamy.

"You're Christian VanDorn?" I squealed, then blushed after sounding too giddy. "I always read your articles. You're a fantastic writer."

He smiled. "And you're a fantastic woman. You're smart, stylish, and into great music. Oh, and you kick ass too...all the things I look for in a girl. I can't believe you exist."

He cupped my face as though he were a 50s movie star and pulled me to his lips. With that kiss, there was no question anymore. Hot Christian was definitely straight.

"Oh I exist, baby," I said, kissing him again and again and again.

REWARD.

"Ha ha! I'll never forget Veronikkah's expression when you held up that coke baggie on the runway!" laughed Chloe. "A toast to Gigi, the most fabulous girl!"

A month after Collections Week, life was perfect. I was dining with Chloe and Christian at a swanky supper club on Queen Street. Christian and I had been dating since the shakedown night, and I had been offered a ton of fashion jobs and recently accepted one at a major company. I was so excited: I was finally going to be a designer!

I smiled to Chloe, then gave Christian a kiss and understood why I moved to Toronto in the first place: I'd taken a quote to heart. Goethe wrote, "Whatever you can do, or dream you can, begin it. Boldness has genius, power, and magic in it." What began as a dream had ended with magic.

Printed in the United States
By Bookmasters